CASSA'

Also by Lilian Roberts Finlay

Always in My Mind
A Bona Fide Husband
Stella
Forever in the Past
Cassa

Lilian Roberts Finlay

CASSA'S CHOICE

A Mount Eagle Original Paperback

First published in 2001 by
Mount Eagle Publications
Dingle, Co. Kerry, Ireland

10 9 8 7 6 5 4 3 2 1

Copyright © Lilian Roberts Finlay 2001

The author has asserted her moral rights.

ISBN 1 902011 15 5

Cover design: id communications, Tralee
Typesetting by Red Barn Publishing, Skeagh, Skibbereen
Printed by The Guernsey Press, Channel Islands

The heart's heart whose immured plot
Hath keys yourself keep not,
The keys are at the cincture hung of God,
Its gates are trepidant to His nod,
By Him its floors are trod.

CHAPTER ONE

As reluctantly as if it were unclean, Dermot Tyson picked up the American letter. The spikey aggressive writing was unmistakable, the date easily decipherable: 5 June 1984. A week ago. She would have driven her Pontiac through Californian sunshine to post this letter, her hair as glossily golden as ever, her eyes as brilliantly blue, her lips like cut strawberries. Why a letter? She who was already wealthy had sunk her avaricious fangs into all his resources when she put her spikey signature on the judicial separation order. Her furious screaming anger resonated in his mind. She had demanded a Mexican divorce with a three-weeks' residence. The thought of another hour in her company had settled his mind on the separation, no matter what the cost.

He threw the letter back on the desk. He had lost nothing; money came easily. He had kept his cherished daughters and he had bought out the house. That had irked her; the house was her mother's wedding gift to her darling Nicole. Already the house was worth twice what he had given in the settlement. Their home was essential to the contented happiness of his daughters, who were growing into girlhood there with all their schoolfriends near about. For a while they had written little letters to their mother, but it had become a pretence and an effort. The same elderly housekeeper filled a comfortable familiar presence in their lives.

Read the damned thing or shred it. He despised his own curiosity as he opened the letter.

You thought I was back for more money, didn't you? Well, I'm not. This is about Cassa. I have always felt a responsibility for her because she's such a fool. My mother knew that, and she had her Rules. I know you always jeered. Two Gilbey cousins, Janet and Rey, took a holiday on the Shannon in a cruise boat. The weather was ghastly and they had to put into a town. The woman in the hotel told them a sad story about a woman from Dublin who had married a local gent whose brother had been killed in an earthquake and the woman had a stillborn baby. It was all the talk of the place, and Janet found out that it was Cassa. She went to the house and she said that Cassa looked like death and scarcely had a word to say. Janet couldn't remember the exact address or the married name. I will ring and sympathise if you will let me have the number. That's not much to ask.

Nicole

Dermot tore the letter into bits, and then into smaller bits. Sympathy was not in Nicole's nature, never had been, and certainly not for Cassa. The letter had distressed him: the tragic news, the reference to her sister as "a woman from Dublin" and the hurried informality. The lack of style of the writing was quite out of keeping with the high social tone of her actual person.

Dermot walked across the office looking up at the portrait of Elvira as one would look to the beloved for understanding. Here was his Cassa; she had given it to him as her special gift. No words were exchanged, a gift is sufficient exchange, and Dermot had accepted a hidden promise. She had entered into the proper silence of a proper married woman. Until the separation he, too, was married and always conscious of his eminent standing in his native Dublin. He knew where Cassa resided. Not long after Nicole's abrupt departure, the wedding invitation had come; she married a John Gowan. He knew a baby would be proudly expected. He had watched in his Saturday *Irish Times* for the birth announcement; he would share in Cassa's joy if only distantly and silently. Now he felt for her the shattering sorrow of a baby's death. Looking into Elvira's glimmering brown eyes, the tilted black lashes so exactly like Cassa's, he murmured his consoling words.

Would he be able to tell this sad news to Orla and Sandra? The girls were always waiting for Cassa's return.

"Daddy, when do you think we will see Auntie Cassa again? We only used to see her in the paper shop on Saturdays, but I still miss her."

"She was so lonely after the dogs died, wasn't she?"

"It was mysterious the way she disappeared: she never said goodbye, and we were her friends." Sandra who was twelve sounded very sad.

"I don't suppose she went on a sabbatical to America the way Mamma did?" Orla didn't sound nearly so sad about her mother. Dermot assumed that the girls expected their mother to show up any day now. Time enough to tell them about the separation, and about Cassa's marriage, and about the baby.

He wondered sympathetically if the baby had been a boy. In Elvira's world of a hundred years ago, nothing was kept secret; she would have known the depth of Cassa's unhappiness. Was there a reason for the death of a baby? Not for the first time, he wished there could be a form of telepathy between the beautiful ancestral portrait and his lost Cassa. She had belonged to him since she was a little girl crying in his arms outside Donnybrook church. His drive from his home in Stillorgan to his office in Harcourt Street brought him by that church every day, morning and evening. The memory of that first encounter had grown ever stronger. He would never give up the hope that someday their lives would mesh again. Perhaps this was the time to remind her of her friend in Dublin who had been close to her when her father died so suddenly, of that night when she had responded to their intimacy. And the night she had run away rather than go to London with Nicole. He knew she had tried to warn him then. But she had needed him when she pressed her softly parted lips against his throat, murmuring "wonderful plans". A future they had neither of them envisaged was threatening, and now it had foundered. Now perhaps she would turn to him as before. Perhaps more than ever. Now Dermot felt poignantly the depth of his identification with his dearest Cassa.

Only Cassa's loneliness could have driven her into marriage with a countryman whom she would have known for so short a time – loneliness and her abiding fear of her sister. Since the auction of Firenze, she knew that Nicole had gone to America, but she would not know yet about the judicial separation. Yes, there would never be a more immediate time to reopen for Cassa the world he had offered her on that intense night, her last night in Firenze. Slowly a plan began to form in his mind.

CHAPTER TWO

To use her own constant words, Melia Tracey was feeling her years. Climbing these two sets of stairs really got to her. It was the left knee was twingey. She had her two nieces to help her, and they made even more work as she guided them and instructed them, telling them to keep their voices down.

They had all been looking forward to the baby. To mention the very word "baby" now was a disaster, bringing forth floods of tears all round. Except from the mistress herself. It was the best part of a year now, and she had never talked it out – not with Melia anyway. Maybe with John, but by the stressed look of him, Melia doubted it. A quiet chap, and Melia knew him since he was twenty, he had always left the banter to his missus before. . . well, before that happened; and it was made all the harder because of that cursed earthquake. With the tray at an angle of inviting interest, Melia pushed open the bedroom door.

"Isn't that the grand sunny mornin', ma'am! Just what we should expect in the month of June, although nowadays we seem to be deprived of the regular run of the seasons. Last night wasn't it lashin' rain." The weather was always the safe way to introduce the breakfast these days. A sad smile was all the answer you got. How much longer could this go on? Melia wondered should she – what was that word– oh yes, remonstrate. Mrs Cassa used to be a great one to take advice. Well, noting the silence, better say no more. Leave it to John himself. The two of them used to have their breakfast in bed, snuggled up and laughing. That day was over. But only for the present, Melia hoped, as she settled the tray down on the bedside table.

"Thank you, Melia. You are very kind."

For once, Melia Tracey was at a loss for her usual patter: the pale face, the downcast eyes, the frozen politeness. Making a servant-like bob that she knew had long gone out of fashion, she hurried from the room. On the landing she wiped her eyes. The will of God was a strange thing, but you had to accept it. What else could you do?

In her flurry to depart, Melia had not mentioned the envelope on the tray. Cassa now studied it, reflecting that a letter from Father Frank was the only one she had ever received in this house. Long since . . . but she dare not think of that. This envelope bore a Dublin postmark, Baile Átha Cliath, and the handwriting on the notes was like careful print. They were from her nieces, Nicole's children. Cassa read them letter with a sense of timid pleasure, an almost joyful sense of being remembered from a distant place.

Dear Auntie Cassa,
Daddy told us the sad thing about your baby. Sandra and me think it is the saddest thing we ever heard of, the baby going back to the angels before you had time to know him. We both were wishing you were near us like you used to be so we could give you a big hug and kiss. I am sure Mamma would be very sad for you too but she is not here at the present.
   Love from Orla

Dear Auntie Cassa,
We miss you very much and we were crying and Daddy was too. I wish you would come for a holiday. We could talk about all the things we talked before you went away. Please think of coming.
   Lots and lots of love from Sandra

Cassa tucked the little notes back into the envelope and put it under her pillow. To be reunited with a part of her own past was satisfying, like being drawn back into a time of youth before decisions were forced on her, that time when her elders took the blame for life's mismanagement. Orla and Sandra were into their teens now. That had been her own happiest time, before the long years of her mother's illness. Into their teens, and she had never seen their babyhood. Cassa turned her head into the pillow, forcing down the image of Orla as a baby, or any baby. Against her will, there came back the remembered sight of little Sandra buying comics in the village and into focus the handsome face of Sandra's daddy, he who had wept with the girls when he told them the story about Cassa. She pictured the three of them. The absence of Nicole was a relief: Nicole, who had never wept, not even when their father died.

The good-natured letter under her pillow softened the outlines of the world around her. Dermot had wept for Cassa's loss? It was even possible to admit the memory of his kiss in the garden, that last night in her old home – darling, dearest Firenze. There was no one here to talk with her about Firenze, no one who knew that old life. Now she began to understand that she needed those memories to flood into her imagination to shore up the sorrow of all that had gone wrong in her marriage.

Dermot's kiss. Maybe he had kissed and been kissed a thousand times, was what Melia Tracey said of everyone about everything: "Sure, they're experts at it." But it had been Cassa's first kiss of adult passion. The memory persisted because John had never kissed her in that way. Within Dermot's kiss, desire had erupted like a volcano. She had wanted to tear at his shirt, to feel his shoulders, to hear his heart closely beating as on his wedding day when he had danced with her, she in her filmy bridesmaid's dress, out on the lawn in Firenze. Cassa remembered his heart beating in rhythm to the dance music. What was that old tune? Something about three o'clock in the morning – a waltz? Her mother had ordained the music: only old-fashioned sentimental songs. She had not thought of her mother, Sadora, for ages. Would Sadora as a mother have been here to assuage the cataclysm of tears? She'd have been here had the tears been Nicole's tears, but Cassa had been expected to be strong and brave and well-behaved, as in Sadora's Rules.

Best to please Melia by taking the breakfast and stave off all the cheerful aphorisms about the weather and the days getting longer and God shutting one door to open another. Cassa managed a cup of tea. The temptation was inviting to draw up the sheet, to pretend sleep and go on thinking of impossible kisses. Thinking and dreaming of the past were new. Cassa touched the letter under her pillow gratefully. She had been remembered by two little nieces, and Dermot had shed his own tears in sympathy. While she dressed, Cassa found it easier and more acceptable to dwell on Dermot's sympathy than on her own sad loss.

It was disloyal to wish herself far away from Melia's voice, very disloyal. Melia was, in another of her own pet sayings, the best in the world. Cassa took her time as she dressed, going slowly to fill the hours until lunchtime when John would be home for an hour. He had learned not to berate her for laziness, not that he would use the word, but it was a relief when he had started to accept the fact that she had lost interest. In Cassa's mind, it was enough to blame herself for . . . for . . . all that had gone wrong. She shied away from the idea of discussing herself with a doctor or, more horrible, with a psychiatrist. John's friend, Dr Eoin Magner, had talked about the benefits of analysis.

"Actually, Cassa, the problem could go further back: the shock of the earthquake in Peru perhaps. I think now that something to soothe the nerves at that time. . .? I have been thinking that the high blood pressure may have started up then; there was no sign at all in your early pregnancy. Stress, Cassa, stress can get out of control if it is not dealt with early on."

Cassa gazed at Eoin's kindly face. He is blaming himself,

she thought. To help him I should allow my lack of effort to be attributed to some single factor. How little he knows about the ironic abyss of despair in a woman who has everything, all the money in the world, surrounded by worthy souls who carry all her burdens, indebted for life to the man she calls husband "to love, honour and obey". Honour and obey were easy. How lightly had she taken the duty of love? In this bedroom, standing at this window, the ardour of love had followed every vessel up the broad river, seeking the reedy channels of Carnadoe still echoing to the music of Mozart, her eyes every moment responsive to the sapphire gleam in Frank's dark blue gaze. At this window, reaching out and catching up on a passion which had no affinity with the unknown life within her body.

Cassa could not dwell on that thought. "Of course, Eoin, you are right, and I will do everything you suggest. Only perhaps you will give me a little more time, please?"

That was six months ago.

She always made sure not to be standing at the window when John came in at lunchtime. Today she was in the dining-room to greet him.

June was the beginning of the busiest time of the tourist season for him. There were hundreds of cabin cruisers engaged on the river, hundreds more to be booked in the coming months. He was a formidable organiser, employing a very large staff. Cassa supposed he came home every day expecting a miracle: a fully recovered wife with a warm embrace, lovely smiles brimming with interest in his concerns. The lack of energy, the wan look, the limp form had become a disappointment. Today he noticed a change, but he had learned to be cautious.

"How are you today, Cassa?"

"Don't mind about me, John. Just tell me all about the office, and Joan, and your new man, and what you are doing this afternoon."

Yes, he thought, a definite change. Just then, Melia brought in the tray and made all her inevitable comments about the weather and the dishes she had prepared. The room was filled with the aroma of food and stray remarks. . . and then a little silence fell as Cassa took up her knife and fork to prove she had a good appetite. John would like to see her "doing justice to the meal". Melia's phrases had become their shared language, and they used always to exchange a complicit grin; John missed that.

"Directly after lunch," John told her, "I am making the usual trip to Sligo. I thought I could put it off, but next week looks a bit crowded. I was hoping you would feel equal to coming along today, but as it happens I have to take the new chap with me. He's a dull dog, heavy going, and his fiancée is coming. She is from Enniscrone and wants to visit her father in the hospital – he's a very old man, Tom says."

"Next time, John."

"That would be wonderful, darling. I'll look forward to that." Another little silence. This was how their social intercourse had become.

Cassa made a big effort. "I was very surprised to get a letter from Dublin today, from my nieces, Nicole's girls. I can see you are surprised, too."

"Of course, I am. I know you felt that they had forgotten you. Is it a nice letter?"

"Oh, it's very sweet! They both wrote and expressed their sympathy."

"Oh? Did they write at the time? Is this another letter?"

"No, this is the only one. They mustn't have known."

John had not fathomed the reasons why he and Cassa, by this time, were unable to talk about the death of their baby, the perfect tiny son whose eyes had never opened to the world. These fraught silences were becoming mighty wearisome. He was suddenly glad he was going to Sligo, seventy miles away. Maybe he would stay overnight. It was becoming clear that he would not be missed in the big double bed. Neither missed nor needed. Clear and clearer, but no word was ever said. Their lunch was being eaten in a peaceful room empty of all sound. Should he suggest the radio? Why had he so cravenly acquiesced in this silence?

He looked across at his wife, delicately beautiful; he realised that for once she was starting a conversation.

"And Sandra even asked me to come for a holiday. Sandra is the younger girl, she's very pretty. . . I must've told you, John?"

If she had talked about her nieces, it was in the earlier days when talk between them was free and easy.

John chewed carefully, and then he swallowed. "A holiday?"

"Seemingly Nicole is away. Maybe they are lonely."

John stood up; his instinct was not to hear out the rest of this talk, to let it be passed over lightly as so many of his suggestions about little holidays had been passed over. Was it only yesterday he had brought up the subject of arranging a break? "Sorry, dearest, I just realised the time. When I get back, perhaps you would show me the letters."

And with a bit of luck, my dear, perhaps you'll have forgotten.

Cassa held up her head for his kiss, a fatherly kiss on her forehead. A kiss that was no more than a gesture. Their kisses at lunchtime had once been the prelude to long afternoon *siestas*. Not lately, they hadn't. John hurried out to his car. He passed the window with a cheerful wave in case she was watching out for him like before. Maybe she was and maybe she wasn't.

The prospect of the long boring drive with the new works manager and his ghastly woman stretched ahead. He had not yet met the woman, but all works managers' wives or fiancées were the same: she'd be trying to entertain the top boss with a tourist account of every hedgerow they passed.

And she would get it all wrong. He had known every mile of the road from Monaghan to Carrick-on-Shannon and on to Sligo, and most of the people who lived on it, since he was eight years old travelling up and down with his Uncle Tim who had willed him the Sligo place. Those were great times when he was a carefree kid, especially when Frank came along. Frank's name brought Cassa back into his mind. Better to think about business, about introducing the new guy to the Sligo depot. Tom Frame was this fellow's name and his womans name was. . .? Miss would do fine; all this first-name business nowadays left you with too many names to remember.

They were waiting for him in the main office. The first thing John noticed was that this Miss was amazingly pretty, and young compared to balding Tom Frame's late thirties. Her dark hair was drawn back from her face into a thick ponytail, and her eyes and her teeth were smiling most attractively.

"Oh, no, thank you," she laughed softly to the opening front passenger door of John's Bentley; "in a car like this, I should much prefer to sit in the back and luxuriate."

His friends knew that when you wanted to please John Gowan, you commented knowingly on his Bentley. Despite all misgivings, the afternoon had got off well. "There are some tapes in the seat pocket, Miss, if you get tired of the view."

"I'll have a look and see if I know them," she called back.

Tom Frame took out a notebook and balanced a ledger on his lap. "If you don't mind," he said, "there's a few figures I want to bear in mind. Hazel always puts on music when she's driving. She says I'm tone-deaf." He had a deprecating sort of half-smile.

Hazel leaned forward to give a tape to John. "Pay no heed to Tom," she said, smiling. "He only likes brass bands, or the Artane Boys. Here's one I found in your collection, an old musical, a favourite of my dad's: *The Desert Song*. He and my mum used to sing some of the songs at our Christmas party and sometimes on Sunday nights when we were young. My mum died four years ago, and I'm hoping to visit him today . . . I'm hoping he'll be a bit better."

John was drawn to her open, friendly manner, and he, too, liked old musicals. Cassa was, as Melia remarked not unapprovingly, "strictly classical". In Melia's kitchen, her young helpers were "into modern". John dragged his mind back to the road and found himself humming along with "the lonely desert breeze". Every so often he caught a glimpse of Hazel's face in the rear-view mirror; sometimes she returned his look, and the words of the song, "in some woman's smile" caught her and suited her.

In Sligo, Tom Frame was getting off at the Cabin Cruisers Depot, and John offered to drive Hazel to the General Hospital. Apparently, her older sister lived in the town, and the engaged couple would be staying with her for the weekend; she and Maura would go up to the hospital together, she told John. At some part of *The Desert Song*, John Gowan had decided to stay overnight; telephone excuses would be easy to convey through Melia.

"Why don't we meet here at the hotel for dinner?" John's invitation seemed very welcome to them. "Would your sister come, too? I think this place has a good reputation; will I book a table for seven-thirty?"

Tom nodded sagely. "Best place in the town since the Greville Arms closed – not for want of custom either; it was family rivalry about money."

Happens everywhere, thought John, then deliberately shut out the idea. He had a purpose in coming to Sligo, so he took the road out by the racecourse and cut across by the tip of Lough Gill. The lake was shining in the sunlight. The wooded islands so inspirational to poets and writers were dearly familiar to him, the more so because of Uncle Tim.

The Colgagh road was rough, and there were few enough habitations on it. The land here was Uncle Tim's bequest: "Hold on to it, boy. It'll improve with time." The ancient stone house was still able to battle the northern blizzards from the Atlantic. Since his marriage to Cassa, he had not come back, and there was a certain guilt in that. No one had ever been as good to him as his Uncle Tim. Those were the best days, when he was spirited away from his mother's iron fist. He was a carefree boy for a few weeks in every season. It could only happen when Deirdre had a holiday from school; Frank never had a holiday. Ah, Frank scarcely knew Uncle Tim.

"Stand here, up on that crag, boy, and you'll see Ben Bulben. He wrote a lot about that oul' flat mountain."

Uncle Tim always referred to the poet Yeats as "he"... probably with a capital H. "He's buried out there, too, y'know. A local lad, of course." A local lad – it was said so often that John was unlikely to forget. "A local lad with great feet on him, he'd walk this stony road from Cashelgarran to Drumcliff to Sligo town. This is the oldest road in the whole of Ireland. The megalithic people lived here."

"When was that, Uncle Tim?"

"It was long before your time, boy. Your mother's people are buried in this ground thousands of years. Thousands!"

"Is it older than the big drumlin we have in our own fields, Uncle Tim?"

"Older by far, boy. Monstrous old." But Frank always told them that their drumlin was on their mound before Christ was crucified. Johnny used to stare at Uncle Tim and wonder.

These fields were marked off with stones as if it had been cultivated a long time ago, and there were many fields stretching to the edge of sight. Beautiful in weather like today, but out here there would be other weather come October. Nevertheless, John paced out the area around the old house, and in his mind there was an architect he knew.

Houses, long low houses built to brave the winters and rejoice in the summers. The Leitrim border was six miles to the east, and two roads converged on Colgagh. Lately there had been talk of greater tourism to come into the country, and talk of this area as Yeats' Country.

John had once told Cassa that he was a commercial sort of bloke. He was most at ease when he was caught up in complicated calculations of a planning nature. The last year had drained his mental energy. Getting into the Bentley did not turn his thoughts towards his home and his wife. He observed this, but only barely. Into his vision came the hotel and the dinner, and the fresh delightful face of the new works manager's Hazel.

CHAPTER THREE

Letters were exchanged between Cassa and her nieces. With reluctance on John's part, and some apprehension on Cassa's part, the holiday was finally arranged for the beginning of July. When the journey was discussed, John offered to drive her down to Dublin and out to Stillorgan. To his surprise, Cassa demurred in her gentle fashion.

"To really get back on my feet, I should like to hire a car in Dublin and retrace that little bit of the expedition on my home ground all on my own. I'd like that; I don't drive often enough up here. You and your fabulous Bentley!"

Because he truly needed to see his wife restored to the serene and even-tempered person she had been before the tragic birth, and in spite of his inner resentment, John gave in to whatever plans Cassa proposed. He would be permitted to drive her south on the last day of June. He would be entrusted with the car hire, and he would be allowed to buy their lunch in the Gresham and to wave goodbye as she took off on the first lap down O'Connell Street. John was not too happy with this whole idea.

"Will you satisfy me then by driving around a bit in Carrick between now and the end of June? At least I'll be sure you still remember to pull up at traffic lights. The Council is putting some in the main street," John was teasing her, "in your honour, of course!"

"The Bentley, did you say?" she teased back.

This drew a burst of laughter, and Cassa joined in. The atmosphere in the household had become shades lighter, although they both knew there seemed to be a long way yet ahead to overcome the chastening restraint of their tragedy. When John suggested their second car for practice, she was firm in her refusal. A local hired car would be just fine. She did not say that their second car was the Rover driven by

Frank two years ago. John wished he could blow aside that barricade, but silence had become precious to her, her protection from further hurt. John held his fire but escaped when he could. He asked no questions as to who was below in Dublin; he had to presume she would stay in her sister's palatial villa in Stillorgan with the nieces. The housekeeper? The tyrannical Tyson (for so Frank had described him)? As for her sister, Nicole, "Mamma is not here at present," he had read in the child's letter.

Accompanying her practice drive on the last few days in Carrick, he drew out all the stops of encouragement. "I hadn't known you had driven so much in Dublin, Cassa – you're a real professional." Her slightly raised eyebrows let him know he was being patronising, so he back-pedalled as he did so often these last days. "Oh, I am stupid. I was forgetting that you drove yourself into work every day. Sorry, my dearest, and that was an accident-prone road, you told me."

"And as you remarked yourself, dear John, my father's old car was very heavy. This little Ford Princess is a joy to drive." Cassa in this airy mood was a joy herself. He should have suggested a trip to Dublin months ago, although her home there was gone into other hands. She had mentioned Firenze frequently when they were first married, but never now. He wondered if she would go to see her old home. Wasn't it across a few fields from her sister's place?

"Cassa, you will let me have a note of your safe arrival, a phone number?"

"Of course I will, darling. Luckily, I don't have to worry about you because I'll know Melia is looking after you."

He was on the point of indignation, of blurting out, "That's not quite the same thing!" but he let it go and said instead, "I'll ring you every morning, dearest Cassa, and I'll hope you are sleeping better." He had not said, there was no point in saying, that he had woken up to see her lonely figure holding aside the casement-window. He was able to guess at her thoughts, and being able to guess didn't lessen his growing acrimony at not being included in her dreams. His brother Frank was rarely far from his own thoughts; he had been there since they were kids. His brother had reigned there, king of all decisions, arbiter of the choice which had brought Cassa into their lives.

"Take the next left, Cassa. There's a few miles of the new main road coming up; let's see you speeding."

She laughed softly. "All of fifty miles an hour?" The quality of a light heart had been absent from her laughter for a long time: that holiday letter from her nieces had certainly made a big change in her disposition. What was down in Dublin to attract her now when they had ignored her for so long?

"You're a real flyer, Cassa." It had never been in John's mind to question Cassa. She was perfect, and she was recovering. When they drew in at the garage, he gave her a big hug. "Best of luck, dearest girl." Maybe, he thought, a question or two tomorrow on the Dublin road – in the seclusion of the Bentley?

"The last thing you can depend on is the weather," Melia remarked on the doorstep. The Bentley was well able for any sort of weather, and it was as smooth as ever in the thunderstorm that accompanied them out of Carrick all the way to Mullingar. After Maynooth, the thunder eased into a steady downpour of heavy rain. If John had hoped for an intimate conversation, the noisy weather defeated him. All Cassa exchanged with him was the odd contented smile. He did not want her to be contented leaving him on his own. He wanted her to say something, some affectionate words that only a woman would know how to put together in a situation like this.

As they passed the airport, with Dublin city looming through the rain, John Gowan knew that Cassa was already on the other side of the fence, as if there were a difficult necessity to drum up the emotions of love. He was not a man given to fanciful imagination, yet in some dim way it seemed that two years ago he had taken a captive princess and now he was returning a hostage. But she was his, wasn't she? In law and in the eyes of God, Cassa belonged to him.

CHAPTER FOUR

In her last letter to Orla and Sandra, Cassa had told them it would probably be about six or seven o'clock in the evening when she would arrive at their house but they were not to be disappointed if she were to arrive a bit late. She was looking forward enormously to seeing them, and sent best love from Auntie Cassa.

All went according to plan. Cassa heard the six o'clock Angelus bells in Stillorgan when she was very slowly driving through the gates of her sister's house. Orla and Sandra were waiting on the veranda, and they rushed down the drive and ran alongside the car as she pulled in. They had grown and changed, but only a little, and Cassa responded with a full heart to the hugging and loving and kissing. This family warmth had been an element missing out of her life for years. Pausing neither to estimate nor to analyse it, she hugged them and kissed the top of their heads as they drew her into the house. Then when they released her, their father Dermot was standing there, his arms held out in welcome. It took no effort, it was wonderfully ordinary, to be lifted into his arms and to stay there in his embrace until he chose to set her down again. Perhaps his kiss lasted only seconds, but for Cassa there was an eternity of restoration in it. For just a moment she was in the garden of Firenze again as the lights of his car disappeared down the avenue. Strangely, a small jutting precipice on the rock face of her emotions had settled back in line; with Dermot she could surely be at ease now.

Dermot had planned this reunion carefully. He was at once the gracious host concerned for Cassa's safe arrival and the pleasant daddy directing Orla in the taking of Cassa's things into the hall. Sandra had obviously been instructed to indicate the cloakroom to their auntie should she wish to wash after her drive from the city. Cassa had not forgotten that he was a handsome man, but she was not prepared for his actual effect on her. It was impossible to stop glancing at his height, his well-set shoulders, his olive-skinned features, the perfection of his mouth when he smiled and the cut of his clothes. She had become accustomed to the countrymen met in John's convivial company, who were jokingly scornful of the changes in fashionable Dublin – to amuse her, the Dubliner, no doubt. But that had been months and months ago, not recently.

A settled-looking woman in her sixties came out into the hall.

"Cassa, let me introduce Mrs Flynn, our housekeeper. Mrs Flynn, this is our guest for tea, my sister-in-law, Mrs Gowan.

"Mrs Flynn has set some tea for us in the lounge," Dermot said, taking her hand to direct her in. "I know this house is strange to you, but I'll give you a tour after tea." Cassa's hand in his felt safe. She would like a guided tour: she had thought of Nicole's wonderful house often when she was working in the hospital.

"Isn't it funny," Sandra asked her daddy, "that Auntie Cassa was never in our house and we were in hers only once for the funeral?" Orla gave her younger sister a little push and a "ssh!" Cassa remembered that when she and Nicole were children, she was the one who had to be shushed. Being back on such familiar ground was pleasantly relaxing, but, as she had tried to do all her life, she pushed aside the image of Nicole: the house would be enough. It was reassuringly evident that Nicole was not in residence.

"You have a very beautiful house, Sandra. Mine was old and worn-out." Dermot detected a small note of bravery in Cassa's soft voice, on the watch for chinks in the façade of Cassa's married life. To capitalise diplomatically was second nature to Tyson.

"We have a swimming pool, Auntie Cassa," said Orla. "Tomorrow maybe you'll come in with us?"

"I hope you brought your togs. We asked Daddy to remind you," said Sandra.

Cassa looked smilingly at their faces and nodded in agreement; acceptance on her part would suit Dermot, she was quick to comprehend. He also was smiling.

"Maybe you two could think of something to do while I tell Cassa of our plans for tomorrow. Since Auntie Cassa won't be staying overnight. . ."

"I wish she would," Sandra interrupted, "so we could wake her up and all have breakfast together."

"Please stay, Auntie Cassa, we'd love you to stay. Please! Please!" This unexpectedly from Orla.

But Cassa had got the message: "Let's go along with your daddy's plans just for now, shall we?"

It had rained too much all day for a late visit to the pool. The girls went off to the den, and after a while the TV could be heard.

Cassa stood at the door of his study, the better to admire its magnificence. There was wood of some variety she could not name, although in Firenze there had been mahogany and walnut and rosewood and maybe other kinds of wood. This was an unshining wood made for the comfort of the volumes on its shelves and the ease of the writer at the big desk.

"You like my study?" This understatement of the spellbound look in her eyes pleased him enormously. "Welcome to my special place." He took her hands to show her around, drawing her closely to his side. "Satinwood, Cassa, from the East Indies . . . I saw it used in the Barbados, and I liked it. I kid myself that it is fragrant." At the large window overlooking the greenery of the garden, his arm encircled her and his head bent to kiss her. His handsome looks were irresistible, but Cassa knew she should resist. She slipped from under his arm, essaying a deterring smile.

"Dermot, I should not be allowed to forget that I am an old married woman!"

His answering smile was generous and indulgent. "As if I would ever forget!"

"And I won't forget either that you are married, too. Is that the reason why I am not going to sleep in this beautiful house tonight?" Cassa's gentle voice had always caught at his heart; he wanted her in his arms for talking as much as for caressing. He had seen at once that while her eyes and her hair and her delicate skin were lovely, she had failed in other ways. She was fragile now, whereas two years ago when he had held her under the portrait of Elvira, she had been pliant and yielding, and passionately eager.

"Come," he said, "sit by me and at least let me hold your hands while I bring you up to date with my life; and if you will let me into your recent life, I promise I will respect every word you tell me. Come, Cassa, I won't hurt you now. We both know why you ran away: you had tried to warn me about the terrible murder that Nicole was about to commit. I can say that because I have learned to live with the fact. In the garden of Firenze, I told you she was gone out of my life. I offered myself to you that day, Cassa, but again you ran away, and you married a man you hardly knew."

Cassa withdrew her hands. There were tears in her eyes. "That day you were still married to my sister, and I knew, as I know now, she will never let you go, and that is not to go back in time. I always knew. I made up my mind to marry John Gowan that day in Firenze with all those people milling around in our gardens. You said my sister had gone away of her own accord, but I'd never believe that. For that reason I have not returned to Dublin, much as I wanted to, wanted to be among familiar faces and familiar voices and wanted to see my nieces, the only family I am ever going to have because I. . ." Now tears were streaming down her face, and when Dermot took her into his arms, she hid her face against his shoulder. "You don't make much sense," he murmured, "but I think I understand you."

They lay together in the big armchair, letting the silence envelop them as the late twilight faded from the window. The need for comfort was mutual.

Cassa whispered to him, "What about the girls?"

He whispered back, "They'll have gone to their room; they read or play Scrabble. They'll come down later and coax Mrs Flynn to give them supper." His whispering voice was amused as he said, *"Portrait of the Whispering Conspirators."* John would never say a thing like that; antique pictures were to him an unknown world.

"I promised John that I would phone to let him know I had arrived," she said.

"There's the phone on my desk. Go ahead, and I'll have a word with the girls."

Melia's niece took the message on the phone. Mr John had come home and had gone out again. Aunt Melia had gone to bed. She hoped Mrs Cassa had arrived safely. She'd tell Mr John.

"Good night, Aggie."

"Good night, ma'am."

She reset the phone on its receiver with the contented feeling of resetting her other life at the end of the wire where it belonged; she was back home, or as near home as she would ever be again. If Dermot were to escort her upstairs, she might very well look from a bedroom window across the fields at Firenze – if it is still standing, she thought.

Dermot had come back. "They are settled down for the night," he said. "They always read in bed. They send you their love – you made a big impression on them, Cassa."

"Oh, please tell me what they said, Dermot."

"They both said that you are the nicest auntie they have and they think you are gorgeous and they hope to see you tomorrow. Does that please you?

She nodded, smiling. "Oh, that's good, because I think the same, Cassa." He extended his hands to lift her out of the deep armchair. "And I should add, you are much too light – Sandra is heavier than you are!"

"I am going to put on lots of weight now that I'm back in my native air." Cassa puffed out her cheeks so comically he had to catch her close enough to press his lips into her hair to hide how deeply he was moved by the gallant gesture. Her face had not changed from the perfect mould his memory cherished, but her frame was too slender. Had that country husband not noticed? Was he not worried to distraction? He had put her in a hired car and let her drive across the city traffic.

"I have put your things in my car, Cassa, and we are going to your holiday apartment. Tomorrow the hire company will collect the car, and while you are in my care I will do the driving."

What woman in Ireland, she thought, could resist the charm of Dermot's persuasive voice, the accent so dearly familiar to her after her time away? But Cassa tried. "I had big ideas that I would drive down to old haunts like Seacoast or Bray or," and now she smiled up at him, "maybe the Glen of the Downs. Or into Stillorgan with Sandra to buy the daily paper."

"All of those things, Cassa, but this is my holiday, too, and I wouldn't trust that little hired heap of scrap." Now they were into his car and had come down the drive on to the Stillorgan Road. Cassa wondered sleepily, did every man have this special relationship with his car? Did they know they did? Bentley or Mercedes, did it matter? I'm very tired, she thought, but shouldn't I ask where are we going?

"Back to Dublin, Dermot?"

"No, only as far as Donnybrook. Some years ago, I bought a block of apartments on Aylesbury Road. I reserve the penthouse for special guests."

Turning the car into the apartment block's drive, Dermot said, "I am going to tuck you into bed, and then we will talk a little. You are safer here, Cassa. I suspect the many battalions of Gilbey cousins have been coopted on to Nicole's Secret Service."

Cassa shrank back into her corner, but Dermot had the door of the car open and was helping her out. "I know, darling, I know. We have a lot to put right, but you can trust me. No need to be afraid, I promise you."

In the lift going up to the penthouse, he held Cassa close and warm and safe, and it seemed that the long months of freezing isolation must surely be over. Being with someone who had known her father; with someone who knew all her family circumstances; who had danced with her long ago in the garden of Firenze; who was settling her into bed and promising to come back tomorrow; who did not expect her to engage in . . . A light kiss was a relief . . . and someone had closed a door.

CHAPTER FIVE

John Gowan had been concentrating on his arrival home for the last fifty miles, not that he was wary of falling asleep; to Dublin and back was a long enough journey, but the actual need to be at home in his own house dominated his mind. It was a safe place to be. A mind could shake itself free of confusion in the mind's own dwelling-place. A mind that was cogitating back and forth when it needed to keep itself on the road was a mind that had no control. When he was a small kid, the local farmer used to trust his old horse to get him home from the pub in the town; the Bentley had horsepower but no sense of direction. Funny thing, that, he thought. Another type of confusion. The mind wandering backwards.

John was mighty glad when he drove out of the last street in Carrick, up the incline and into the yard behind the house. Beyond the wall he could see the river in its night-gleam reflecting into the many-windowed conservatory. In the kitchen there was a lone light, no doubt the conscientious Aggie waiting for the late traveller. There would be food on a tray. He locked the Bentley as he always did and walked back out through the gates. To hell with racking your brains all on your own in your own home where your great grandfather on your father's side had been born. Much good that did him now. He'd walk up to the golf club. He'd get pickled just for the hell of it.

There was some kind of a soirée going on in the club, hired out for the night, a birthday party for someone. Everyone in the town knew John, and he was welcomed in effusively. They were all at the stage of princely sharing with the drink, and yet another party-goer was just what they needed. One of the leading lights of the town was a bonus; they were honoured. The music was struck up again, and within minutes John was dancing, a glass in one hand and the other clasped by a young lady he had never seen before. As Melia would say when she heard of it, "What's the world coming to? A married man acting the bachelor!"

He could never afterwards say if he remembered X's birthday, much less enjoyed it, but for a couple of blessed hours he forgot that his wife had gone off for a holiday without a single thought of inviting him along. Some kind fellow dropped him home at dawn. The quick word had been conveyed to Melia Tracey, and she let him sleep off the few drinks. When she brought up some tea at midday, she was kind enough to say only the one sentence: "God knows, you needed that."

When he came downstairs, his memory of meaning to ring Cassa had returned. "Did I leave a note near the phone? I should have rung my wife."

Aggie was the niece who was in charge of the phone. "The note is there on the table, sir. Mrs Cassa rang this morning, not that long ago, sir, but Aunt Melia said not to disturb you, and the mistress left another number – it's on the table, too, sir, and the mistress said to ring tomorrow because she will not be there today. That's all, sir."

John wrote the new number into the phone book. He felt ashamed, but only defensively and only slightly. He said, "I'll be out all day, myself." He could always forage up some business. Last night there was the urgency of wanting to be at home. Today, anywhere else would be preferable.

In the office, Tom Frame had asked for an interview. In the previous couple of weeks of Cassa's decision to take a holiday, John had forgotten promising, the night he took them to dinner, to look out for a rental for Tom and Hazel in Sligo. They knew John had property in Sligo town. Getting a place to live would settle the date for their wedding.

"Still commuting, Tom?"

"Only at weekends, Mr Gowan. Hazel has started the job we were telling you about, if you remember, assessing the Leaving Cert history papers, and that'll keep her in Carrick for the next six weeks. We'll take a break then and decide if she'll go back teaching with the Ursulines. There is a possible teaching post in Sligo; she would like to keep on teaching after we get married, she says. Today I was wondering if you had had time to look up that list of houses or flats? You had mentioned. . . I could have a look during the week, in the evenings. . ."

Tom Frame's deprecating manner was a little unfortunate, like a man who hadn't paid his dues; it made you want to help him out. "Of course, of course, Tom. I'll get Joan to dig up that file of places. She will know where to put her hand on the very thing to suit you, and she will give you the details. The properties available may need a bit of doing up, I think – been neglected in the last couple of years, in fact since my Uncle Tim passed on." While bolstering up Tom Frame's hopes, John was actually thinking of the very pretty fiancée, her vivid features replacing Tom's bifocals. "Perhaps if you give me Hazel's phone number here in the town, it would be all the quicker to get the list and pass it on to her."

"She would like that, Mr Gowan. And she knows Sligo better than I do, being a local." Frame was writing the telephone number on a business card. "There!"

"Are you going back to Sligo today, Tom?"

"I'm on my way now, Mr Gowan. Joan wasn't sure if I should wait or leave a message."

"You did the right thing, Tom." John Gowan was slightly bemused by his own attitude to filling the gap of company left by Cassa's departure. Bereft was an excusing word he had never had occasion to use. It came to his mind now, along with relieved, and free to choose, and an appetite for cheerful talk unconnected with loss of any kind. Not necessarily talk with a woman, he assured himself, although a pretty woman could brighten the dullest day. God alone knew where Melia Tracey found all her sayings, but there was one she trotted out regularly: "A man's a man for all that." He did not pause to figure it out, but went in search of the addresses. He had recollected a neat house recently vacated on the near side of Sligo which might suit a young married couple. Perhaps Hazel would like to view it. Sure, asking would do no harm.

CHAPTER SIX

Into Cassa's dreamy state of contentment rang the phone beside her bed. That will be John, was the immediate thought, and she was in a business-like mood at once as if ready to deal with daily life. The caller was Dermot, and all the dreaminess of the night before came back into her voice when she answered his hello.

"Good morning, Cassa. How well did you sleep in a strange bed?"

"Beautifully! Wonderfully! I didn't realise how tired I was. I don't even remember getting into bed."

He let that pass. "May I come over in an hour, and we'll plan your first day of holiday? Or do you need more time to rest?"

"An hour would be just right, Dermot, and thank you for all your kindness. Please give my love to Orla and Sandra."

"After all the rain yesterday, it's a glorious morning and they are splashing about in the pool. They haven't even had breakfast yet. I hear Mrs Flynn calling them now. Do you fancy the pool, Cassa?"

"The sheer novelty of it appeals to me. Would tomorrow be time enough, Dermot?" Time enough to test out her energy against the teenagers, Cassa thought, with a slight return to what had become a state of misgiving for months since. . . since. . .

"Of course, dearest Cassa, and, in fact, that suits me fine. May I suggest a drive up into the Wicklow mountains, and perhaps lunch in Roundwood?"

With a hint of mischief, she questioned, "Not in the Glen of the Downs?"

His recollection was in the warmth of his voice: "Sweet girl! We'll save the Glen for dinner tomorrow. There's always tomorrow, Cassa."

Looking from the window, Cassa was back on well-known ground almost in the shadow of Donnybrook church. The torrents of thoughts seemed easier to endure than they had been for months, and under the shower she let them stream away. The running rivulets of clear water were taking the fears down underground, as if the kindly earth here in Aylesbury Road could absorb them in a depth friendly to a returned exile. Did I go into exile seeking a treasure I could never have had? When did Carrick become exile? Was it on the day Frank told me there was only silence? Did that silence translate into hope when the new life began to tell me that hope could be reborn, a nurturing all over again? Or did that longing for my own place, far away from the Shannon, begin the night of the earthquake? Was I truly set apart when John could not share his grief, so badly I needed sharing even with a brother . . . an exile since that night? Was I right in the belief that the new life was extinguished by the earthquake's fire! Just as Frank had gone into exile, so had I. Did he take the baby with him into exile?

She shut off the shower and with it the scalding reverie, but she continued the therapy deliberately at the mirror, brushing her short curly hair very briskly as if to brush out the invading thoughts: wasn't that "briskly brushing" one of Sadora's many Rules? "To banish ennui, my pet – it means boredom but ennui is a nicer word." Cassa really had come home, if only to be haunted by Sadora's ghost. She pouted sadly into the mirror the way Nicole always did when Sadora gave out the Rules about "pulling yourself together". So it seemed only proper to use a little make-up and to choose an attractive suit for going out with Dermot. Had she chosen to be less sophisticated for her husband, John? Why less?

Some other time, Cassa promised herself, some other time she would consider all these questions. Now, a handsome man would be on the doorstep expecting a pleasant companion. Still under the influence of Sadora's Rules, she told herself that this was her holiday and a holiday should set her up, restore her spirits and enable her to face her normal life again. There was Dermot at the door; her smile came naturally, for overnight Dermot had become special. They were sharing a little breakfast together and he was admiring her, not fulsomely nor flatteringly, but in sunny spatters of compliments tuning in with the bright morning light.

When they set out on their drive, the conversation was casually comfortable. With Dermot, his serious interchange of facts would come when he was assured of Cassa's situation. Had her marriage been a disappointment, a failure? In what way had she been affected by the death of the baby – physically, psychologically? Was she now recovered, or was she putting on a show to cover her distress? He remembered the words in Nicole's letter: "Cassa looked like death." She was still fragile many months later, and her fragility had touched him deeply as he had helped her to get ready for bed.

"I've never been on this road before," Cassa remarked, suddenly remembering the Bray road on a Sunday morning with Father Frank. A friendly priest on a first outing, so hard forgetting.

"No," Dermot told her, "this is not the Bray road; we can come back the other way. This is a short way to Rathfarnham and up through the Sally Gap. We can pull over there and maybe climb up to the Hellfire Club. Have you ever done that, Cassa? We are nearly there now."

"I hope you won't have to pull me up the hill," she laughed, "I haven't done much walking lately."

He took the chance. "Were you seriously injured, darling?"

She was a little surprised. "You mean by the birth of the baby?" When he nodded, she said, "No, I wasn't injured, if you mean physically?" When he nodded again, she added, "I tried to cope with the. . . with the sight. . . with the unfairness. . . with the uselessness of it all. I suppose I just gave up trying."

Dermot found himself in sympathy with her, totally in sympathy. Cassa had never been a fighter. She had been conquered in every battle by her bullying sister. The year in San Salvatore flashed through his mind. "Poor darling," he murmured, "Nicole never gave you a chance."

"Dermot," Cassa said very seriously, "don't be sorry for me. Nicole was gone out of my life when I married John. . . or I was gone out of hers. Selling Firenze and keeping the money was the final blow to our ever being sisters. Wherever she is, she will never forgive that sale – all the antique pictures and priceless things she was forever boasting about, at least the things I didn't take to Carrick-on-Shannon. I had that to ponder on all the time the. . . the. . . the baby was coming. . ." Her voice had lowered so Dermot had to pull over the car into the grass verge to catch her words. "What happened. . . what happened was my fault."

Quickly and without effort, the inquisition had been handed to him; she was inviting him into her confidence. Gently, he took her shoulders and turned her to face him. "Let me remind you, Cassa, that you and I share the same very precious memory: we both lost a child. I could tell you that I was to blame for my loss. The morning she went to London was the morning I should have locked her in her room for nine months. I knew and I did nothing. Pride? I no longer loved Nicole, I had lost respect for her and yet seduction still held sway in our bedroom." Now, male pride made him withdraw a little.

Cassa looked earnestly at his perfect features, and deeply into his hazel eyes, knowing she would never reveal to him, never in this life, that there was a possibility this mourned child had not come from his seed. Buried in the depths of her unwanted images, with the nightmare of her old friend Louise drowned in Caragh Lake, was the clear-cut picture of Nicole offering herself temptingly to Clive Kemp. Six weeks later Nicole was looking for an abortion. Years before, when Cassa was too young to know and Nicole was in her early teens, debonair tennis champion Clive Kemp was always there in the deep woods of Firenze. Sadora, who prided herself on the gift of words, had often remarked that Marjorie's nephew, Clive, had rather too abundant a male prowess. Papa never liked that type of remark. The Kemps were Gilbeys, and to Sadora that was uppermost. Others were expelled from the house and the tennis parties; Clive was uncritically accepted.

"We have both gone very quiet, Cassa. Are we going to climb up to this famous Hellfire Club? We may not see the devil, but the view is, I am sure, worth the trouble." He took a rug from the car. "When we find the view, we'll sit to admire it."

And that is what they did, Dermot's arm comfortably holding her against him, her slight body acceding to his acceptable warmth, not pausing for a moment to consider rights or wrongs for couples who were safely married. Dermot Tyson was today rediscovering a facet of Cassa other men had discovered before him: Cassa's nature was composed of feminine acceptance; men were made to be dominant, and the decisions would always be male. Her eyes of velvet brown, her faintly coloured skin, her close-cut hair were all identical with Elvira's portrait, except that in the portrait, Elvira's wonderful eyes betrayed that her sexual appetites were fully awakened. He held Cassa even closer; she had been through childbirth, but she remained acceptingly untouched. Her husband had taken her, but he had never taught her, never actually possessed her. Tyson exulted in that personal belief, resolving on continued prudent care never to overstep her feeling that she was in safe hands. She was in safe hands, he was resolved on that, but how long would this little holiday be? He could not ask in how many days would her husband claim her; no host could ever do that anyway.

"When we were little kids," he said, "and when my mother learned to drive, this was the Sunday expedition, the four of us scrunched into a Morris Minor. We got the story of the Hellfire Club every Sunday, and the dangers of gambling. Some local pedant had told them, in their pub, all about this place. Dublin yarns fascinated them. They are both from Galway, and Dublin remained a mystery in those days."

"Tell me the story your mother told her children on those long-ago Sundays, please, Dermot."

"Well now, I hope I remember it. Mum always started off those stories by reminding us that was in the days when the British Empire ruled over Ireland and the land was awash with lords and ladies and such people as earls – always a bad lot, those earls, she told us." Cassa felt as close to him as she felt when her papa was retelling the endless story of the Donnybrook Fair, while she basked in every syllable of Papa's voice and Nicole was always reproved for yawning. She snuggled closer and Dermot smiled down on her very lovely face. It brought them a unique amity to sit in harmony as if the story being told was all that mattered in life.

"Let me see," Dermot continued, "there was an Earl of Rosse who started up a gambling den in the Liberties in the city where huge sums of money changed hands among the upper classes. So many earls and lords assembled that they moved the den out to the Dublin mountains; space is needed for these great casinos, and this is the very space where they set it up, here on this hill known then as Montpelier Hill. So now."

"But, Dermot, you promised we might see the devil?"

"My mother always promised that, too – especially if any of us fell into the heinous sin of gambling. Apparently, Old Nick with the cloven hoof was a constant visitor out here. And highly thought of, so my mother said. She always pointed out the remains up there of the original gambling den, designed and erected in elegant cut stone by William

Conolly, Speaker in the Irish Parliament in 1727. . . or so she told us."

"Two hundred and sixty years ago."

"Almost." Dermot helped her to her feet and wrapped the rug around her. "Time for lunch, Cassa. Please don't go catching a cold. There's a stiff breeze getting up. Come, darling, give me your hand."

Tucked warmly back into her seat in the car, it seemed no more than beneficial for them to exchange a lingering kiss of gratitude, Dermot's fingers stroking her face and her dark-lashed eyes closed in pleasure.

CHAPTER SEVEN

In their married life there had neither been the necessity nor the opportunity for phone calls between John and Cassa, and although they were undoubtedly concerned for each other, the morning phone calls at eight a.m. became perfunctory. To John Gowan a phone call was business-like, an inquiry as to the state of her health, and a word of thankfulness that she was feeling well. This self-controlled approach did not encourage Cassa to enthuse about her outings with Dermot Tyson, offering merely that he had lodged her in this apartment which was quite comfortable. She waited for John to ask how she had spent the previous day, confident that he would want to know, but the phone calls were usually ended abruptly by his business calls on another line. Cassa accepted that calmly: this was the height of his firm's tourist year, and she knew he was in his element as the boss running the show. It was not in her nature to expect priority, ever, in any way.

Dermot's morning calls were different. He waited until nine o'clock to ring, and then Cassa settled back on the downy pillows to enjoy his tender concern for her health and her state of mind and her preferences for the day ahead. He had been candid about reestablishing his place in her childhood memory. The visit to the Dublin mountains to tell the story of the Hellfire Club had been a deliberate ploy, he told her over lunch that day.

"In the very early days when Nicole was sixteen, she often grumbled to me about you and your dad's infatuation with each other. His recital of the history of Dublin and the Donnybrook Fair went on for hours, she said, and she was the one who always got ticked off for her lack of attention."

"So that was why you told me about your mother and the Sunday drives? Did you make it up?"

Dermot smiled. "No, dearest Cassa, that was how it used to be on freezing Sunday drives, but I dug it up to get on the side of you that needs someone to share your memories of home and of the past and of Dublin. I could have gone away to make my own way in America – there was nothing here when I came out of college, in the fifties – but I never wanted to leave Dublin. The old place gets a grip on its citizens."

And an excellent marriage settlement had set him up very well, but he did not choose to tell Cassa that if she did not know it already.

"Why did I not know how much I would miss dear old Dublin when I agreed to settle so far away? The one thing I thought was that when Firenze was gone, there was nothing else here."

Dermot thought this a good moment for a question. "Going away with a man you had fallen in love with, wasn't that important, Cassa?"

"I never fell in love with John. I thought loving was enough, that loving was enough to construct a life in marriage. And, you know, Dermot, Firenze had become very lonely."

"That last night in Firenze, darling Cassa, if I had pressed your decision on coming away with me to Paris, would I have won you over?"

"Was that what you wanted, Dermot? I wondered for a little while. But there was always Nicole. To get safely away from my sister and the hospital became more urgent than anything else. . . nothing to do with selling the house that night."

He had turned the conversation. San Salvatore Hospital should have been his responsibility. He had plenty of time to admit to himself that once again he had been blinded by money, no less blinded than on the night he proposed marriage to Nicole when the woman he desired was Cassa. That night her father had stepped forward to take Cassa's name out of the transaction. The wily lawyer in Richard Blake was suspicious of the young suitor, and in another minute the money became the tempting issue of his proposal. He was blinded by his own greed, and had been punished for it, almost irretrievably. Across the luncheon table, he took Cassa's hand tenderly. Who would ever have believed that fate could offer again such a gift?

"The appetite of a little bird, Cassa. What about that promise to put on weight?"

She smiled with delight at his interest. He had become a new and interesting person, quite unlike the Dermot Tyson she had come to dread in the San Salvatore days. Was there ever such a person or was that ogre invented by her sister? Nicole had invented sinister people and sinister motives since ever Cassa could remember.

That was the first day, after lunch in Roundwood. Now almost a week had gone by, each day more relaxed and enjoyable. She had established a good relationship with Sandra and Orla; she could remember all their friends' names, and although she had not ventured into the pool yet, they did not tease her about it. She herself was a little taken aback to see herself in a sundress, realising that her arms and legs and bust were much slighter than she had realised. She tried to eat a little extra, more conscious of her appearance than she had been for a year.

"I was looking forward to our telephone call this morning, Dermot, but I was also thinking that your holiday must be nearly over."

"I am going to give myself a few more days," he said, "and what about your own holiday, Cassa?"

She hesitated. She would like to stay longer; in fact, no one had mentioned time.

"Would I be in the way for another little while? This morning when you come to take me out, could we talk about it?"

"Dearest Cassa, you would never be in the way – such a thought! We haven't really had a good pow-wow, have we? I'll be over to you in an hour."

When she had taken a final look in the mirror, Cassa carried the coffee tray into the sunny sitting-room, where there was a balcony and a view of the distant mountains. Questions had been hovering since the first day, but perhaps it was not fair to ask questions; maybe he was a heartbroken man whose wife had left him. Maybe Nicole was expected back from a trip any day now. Cassa had never understood her sister, but she had witnessed Nicole's utter possessiveness of her husband, and of every other thing in her life. The abortion remained a mystery.

It was, so to say, taken for granted that as in-laws they would kiss each morning on greeting. Cassa enjoyed the little fire ignited by Dermot's way of kissing, though it was not yet the volcano she remembered. John knew of no such kiss, and Frank's ceremonial evening embrace had best be allowed to fade into a dim twilight with all things safer to forget. Dermot's personification of good looks added immeasurably to the magic of his kissing. He had taken lessons from a mistress of the game, and now it was second nature. His tentative lips tasted Cassa's lips slowly, as if waiting for a flame to burn and light up the tremulous flicker of her response. For Cassa, it was pure happiness to enjoy this gently passionate kiss in the certainty that his wife could not walk in. Every day they had kissed in his study in Nicole's house, Cassa had shivered with fear of her and a sense of guilt. Here in Dermot's penthouse there was only a delicious holiday freedom from everyday living.

"This could go on all day," she murmured.

"You wicked little thing!" he laughed softly at her. "And you were the one to tell me to remember that you are an old married woman."

"But on holiday." Cassa, surprised at herself, drew him

47

down on the sofa, "and when I go back to Carrick-on-Shannon, this will all be forgotten. Convalescence!"

"And getting better every day!" He was charmed to find her so at ease with him. "So, talk to me, Cassa."

"There are a lot of questions you could not answer, Dermot – like, for instance, why am I not overwhelmed with guilt, or why are you not?"

"That's easy," he said; "because we are not, either of us, in Nicole's shadow."

"Let me take that slowly, Dermot. You are still her husband. She would never let you go."

"She was forced to let me go. We have a judicial separation. She wanted a Mexican divorce, but I don't believe in those decrees. By our Irish law, the separation is absolute and final. Please don't be hurt by this news, Cassa: it became inevitable. The girls are in my keeping; Nicole may not take them out of the country but she has full visiting rights. I have been waiting for an opportunity to break this to Orla and Sandra. Would you help me in this, Cassa, stand by me, even be there for me when I explain?"

Cassa was silent with astonishment. It was incredible. She knew, she had no doubt, that Nicole had never been a faithful wife, but did Dermot know that? For the sake of his daughters could he not forgive the abortion? Surely that could have been concealed and somehow patched up to keep the family together. A lot of questions now to be answered, none of which she had wanted to ask him; nothing actually about Nicole, but about the past, and about life, the way things turned out. Nicole giving up her husband? Impossible to imagine. She had ruled imperiously over her husband, a huge business, their home, their daughters, and over all the Gilbey relations. Over Cassa, who had longed all her life to stand high with her sister. . . over Cassa who was at this moment in the strong arms of Nicole's husband and even now very glad that she was nowhere in sight.

48

Dermot could read sad bewilderment in her face. "You have your own problems, Cassa. I think you must have guessed at mine already. No, don't cry, darling. Do you remember the night of your father's death? You let me dry your tears that night." Now he tried to tease her into a smile. "Your sister always said that you thought you could conquer everybody, even the nuns, with a few tears!"

Although Cassa dried her tears and tried to smile, it was a forlorn attempt. "The idea that Nicole has failed to make a success of her life is hard to take in. I am a worse failure than my sister. Orla and Sandra are her precious pearls, and they bear witness to her life." Cassa's voice broke. She moved away from Dermot, feeling in that moment a sense of disloyalty to Nicole, and to her husband John, and in some obscure way to Frank Gowan, buried in shattered earth thousands of miles away. "I am a useless person," she whispered.

"I am sure your husband would never let you say that, poor darling. I have known you since you were a small girl, and I won't let you say such a thing. Think of it, Cassa, I am the one who really knows your worth. Didn't I employ you, for God's sake?"

Cassa smiled, and then she laughed at the mock-serious face he was making. In a moment, she was back in his arms, and another kiss had brought a wistful happiness back into the sunlit room like a conjuring trick. John Gowan had once tried to explain to Cassa his belief that he and she had joined a circle, a truly fairy circle, in their coming together; and how he had feared that his brother Frank might cause the frail threads to snap before completion. She knew now there had never been a completion. She had known almost from the first night of their marriage and of his lovemaking. He had been a high diver on the topmost bar, assuming without words that her depths of desire would receive him. If only, she thought now, we had made the act of love before we had made the marriage vows.

49

"Cassa, Cassa, don't look so sad. I need you to stay around for another little while until I get my own life straightened out with my daughters. You will, won't you? They think you are so sweet. They are so full of sympathy for you."

Was this a disingenuous plan to have a family background against which to tell Sandra and Orla that he had shut their mother out of their lives? Was this the same man she had feared when she was employed by him and by her sister, who had taken pleasure in repeating his hateful messages, his humiliating remarks? Should she be on her guard? Her nieces could not have invited Cassa except at Dermot's suggestion. And why am I suddenly on Nicole's side? As Melia Tracey would say, "What did she ever do for me?"

"Dermot, knowing you as remotely as I do, I feel you could manage very well without my presence." Her usually gentle voice was shot through with a bitter regret.

He was taken aback by her tone and by the way she walked over to the window as if she had suddenly noticed the view. He wanted her by his side when he told the girls, but he wanted much more than that. He wanted to draw her into his life so that she would forget the country husband in Carrick-on-Shannon. Instinct told him that there was something amiss there, and he had been on the winning team with Orla and Sandra. Her response to them was adorable, but perhaps it was only a holiday mood. After all, the Cassa he knew was a Cassa he had set up in his imagination a long time ago, a Cassa he had let slip away and must bring back.

"Dearest Cassa, I wanted to take you somewhere special today. . . please turn around and look kindly on me. . . ah, that's better, please think well of me."

"You know I do. It's just that sometimes when you say something, a lot of bad old memories come rushing out of the air and I start feeling guilty. This morning, before you came, I felt better than for ages, more like I used to feel in

Firenze when the worst thing in the world was my mother's Rules. I've never really escaped from them. . . . the silly thing is that when I obey the Rules, I feel better."

"What Rule did you obey this morning?" he asked. Nicole had kicked against the Rules when they were young, and Cassa had often been frightened should her mother Sadora discover the lying evasions.

"What Rule, Cassa?"

They laughed together when she told him, "The Brushing the Hair Briskly Rule." And suddenly their special atmosphere returned. It struck Dermot that he had been living in the Blakes' lives almost half his own life, as familiarly as in his Tyson life.

"Aren't you curious about the special place we are going to go today?"he asked.

"I thought we were fixing up to have a family meeting with Orla and Sandra." Not that she was anxious for this event with its probability of children's tears.

"That'll come tomorrow. First, for today! When were you last in Galway? In Galway city?"

"I've been there," Cassa said, "but it's so long ago, I've forgotten. But how could we go there and back in one day?"

"Oh, I'm sure we could," he said lightly. "In a Merc, of course."

"Didn't you tell me that your parents are from Galway?"

"They are," he said, "and if you are interested, I'll show you the little house I was born in."

"Why did I always think you were a Dubliner? Your accent is the same as mine. I suppose Carrick-on-Shannon is so close to the north of Ireland, they speak differently. I will get used to it in time."

"We got the pub in Donnybrook when I was one year old," Dermot told her. "My mother's uncle, who never married, left it to my father. When he was young, Uncle Joe emigrated to the States and made enough money to come

51

back and start up the pub. So I am almost a Dubliner, too. Came here when I was only one, two brothers before me, and after me came my sister Della; she is the real vintage."

Cassa was very happy with this family talk, lightly careless. In the last day or two a slight guilt had oppressed her. Where had she suddenly found the right to enter into a flirtation with her sister's husband? Was it flirtation? Or where had she found this new fluency with any man, she who had sunk into herself for months past, unwilling to talk and reluctantly thinking that everyday happiness had disappeared out of her life. To make conversation with her husband John and with the household had become an onerous duty in the endless monotony of time.

"Galway is different," Dermot said. "Not that I'd want to live there, but there are a few places I'd like to show you. What do you say, Cassa?"

Suddenly the romantic notion of Galway Bay and the western mountains became a desirable planet on the edge of holiday-land. . . just a little further on.

"Beautiful! Gorgeous! Wonderful!"

They called in to say goodbye to Orla and Sandra and Mrs Flynn, promising to be back home again within the week. The girls were very affectionate, hugging Cassa and telling her all their plans. They were excitedly looking forward to a big twenty-first birthday party for one of their cousins.

"Auntie Cassa, you must remember Rebecca. She's Auntie Janet's daughter; she's the eldest."

"She used to have big thick glasses, but now she has contact things," added Sandra.

Cassa smiled, but she remembered little about the Gilbey cousins. They had all grown up in the long years of Sadora's illness. They had been Nicole's friends, never hers.

CHAPTER EIGHT

Galway
13th July

Dearest John

You'll have been wondering why you got no answer to your morning phone call, and please forgive me, but I was halfway to Galway before I remembered that I should have rung you before I left. Coming here was a sudden decision to take advantage of being on holiday with Dermot to do the driving. He is a much nicer person than I ever expected him to be. Apparently (although I find it hard to believe) Nicole and he have split up and she is in America.

I must have needed the change and the holiday. You'll be glad to hear that I am so much better, eating and sleeping, and I hope putting on some weight – you had used the word "skinny" and you were right, as usual.

Dermot and I had expected only to go as far as Galway city, but we were both carried away by the scenery – I never remembered it being so beautiful. Last night we stayed in a place called Renvyle, and the view from my room was something to dream of. We had tea in Kylemore Abbey, and there were some nuns – never my favourite people!

When we get back to Galway we will stay one night in the Great Southern Hotel. I think you stayed there last year when you went to the Tourist Board meeting, didn't you?

The real point of writing is to hope you are in top form. I am sure you are terribly busy with the weather so right for cruising. My fortnight is nearly up, so when I get back to Dublin, I'll be on the phone and I hope you will be into your Bentley and on the road to fetch me home.

Love from Cassa

John Gowan accepted Cassa's letter at face value, and he was satisfied enough. He was, as Melia Tracey told him every day, "run off his feet". It was easily the best season he had

had for years. He was glad to hear that his wife was returning to her normal placid self, and as he had the barest of memories of the Tysons, it was equal to him who was driving the car for her to see the wonderful scenery. His brother Frank was the much-loved friend in whom Cassa had confided all her secrets about her sister and the awful hospital and the holy nuns – she had a bad time with nuns even in the maternity ward. He threw that memory out of his mind very quickly. By nature John was not a theoriser but rather a negotiator, who was prepared to go a certain distance and even retrace where necessary; after that he accepted a dead end. He reread Cassa's letter; she would come home in her own time and there would be no more weary silences leading to a loneliness that he had never imagined.

His mind had tuned in to a cool, healthy friendliness with Hazel. He had taken her over to Sligo to see the house which might be suitable for newly-weds, and it had been an enjoyable few hours. She had liked the house, but according to Tom Frame, something more central would suit him better . . . and with a lot less garden! John told Hazel about his possible plans for Uncle Tim's old place, and she said she would like to see that area – maybe they could take a picnic. . .?

"If you need to give me a call to fix a day, you'll get me in the book." Easily, then, he knew where to find her, in her garden flat in Summerhill. . . twice in the first week, and open house in the second. On her table she had hundreds of Leaving Cert History papers to mark and a very efficient system for doing so. "The door is open!" she called out when his car pulled up, not lifting her eyes from the exam paper until she had set down her marks.

"Suppose I were someone else?" he questioned the first time he called.

"Someone with a shotgun?" she laughed at him. "Don't worry, I'd know the sound of that car any time!"

That pleased him. "How's this job going?" The same question each time and the same answer: "Sure these kids haven't a clue!" Things between them had been casually personal since the first day. Her fiancé came over from Sligo at weekends, but Tom's name seldom got a mention after John's first call, and now they accepted each other.

"I had a letter this morning from my wife, Cassa," he said. "She expects to be returning from Dublin. I'll be going down for her."

"Oh, I'm sure you are delighted," Hazel smiled up at him; "it must have been lonely for you." Under the dark arch of her eyebrows, her grey eyes were candid.

"Luckily, I've been too busy to miss her; it's the best season for us in the boat business, the best for years. Just as well for Cassa, some of her family have been looking after her. When I got the letter, I suddenly remembered that the two of us were going to make a run up to Colgagh."

"And I was going to bring a picnic. But don't worry about it, maybe some other time. Unless maybe your wife would like to go, and maybe Tom? We would both like to meet Mrs Gowan. Tom told me she is very beautiful: he saw her with you in the car just before she went on holiday, when you were both in Carrick."

"That's right." John laughed when he recalled for Hazel his insistence that Cassa practise her driving before she could drive a hired car in Dublin. "I needn't have worried," he added. "Apparently her brother-in-law took her off to the west of the country."

Hazel noticed the slight edge to his voice, and she hurried in with a suggestion. "I would love a little drive in your Bentley, half an hour just, it's such a lovely day. Up around the lake, perhaps?"

"There's nothing I'd like more. Up around the lake road before the sun goes down and the water goes dark – the tourists' favourite time of the day. You must deserve a break,

Hazel; those scribbled-over papers look terrifying. You'll have observed by my gross ignorance that I never got as far as Leaving Cert."

She wanted to comment that he was none the worse for his loss. He was a man of singular attraction, in his appearance as well as in his stature in the town. Hazel felt a compelling power in him. Knowing that he was securely married and that she was engaged to a decent man should keep all untoward ideas in abeyance. Or so Hazel hoped. . . against a self-preserving instinct that warned her not to get carried away. It had all happened before when she was a college student on a working vacation in Boston. . . a first love affair had opened up a world of romance, and a future of wealth and privilege. She had three enchanted summers on Cape Cod, until there came a certain Labour Day when all her summers ended in a five-hour flight of streaming tears.

She always remembered her father's words when he saw her face in Shannon Airport,

"Cheer up, alanna, no gain grievin'." On another occasion he had said, "You're safe enough with Tom Frame. He's a steady goin' fella." Her father's attempts at sympathetic wisdom were always galling.

Surely, Hazel reflected as she pulled the door of the Bentley shut, surely there are some things I can have both ways. Sitting beside John Gowan, Hazel was sure his famously beautiful wife had it all, both ways and every way. She concentrated on the evening glory of Lough Key and the myriad sailing craft replicating each other in the calm water. Her voice aimed at being inconsequential and gay, never inquisitive.

"With all those dozens of cruisers out there, how have you the energy, or the nerve, to be out of your office, off your phone, wasting your precious time out here?"

"Around about six o'clock, I got the notion that it would

be a nice idea to share my dinner with a talkative woman, if she is sure no one would object and if she has the time off from her learned papers."

"Talk about an inferiority complex. You probably know more history than I do – at your age!"

"The history of the sailing-boat, is it? Have you a few questions on that? The weight in water of a three-berth? You don't know."

"I'll do a bit of research and we'll have an exam." They had rapidly reached this point of easy quipping, and for John it was a blessed relief. To escape the remarks of Melia and her nieces about everything from the weather to the absence of Cassa, he had been locking himself in his study in the evenings with the day's figures and a bottle of Jameson. The Jameson would have to come to an end with Cassa's return. Just as well, perhaps.

"So, what about you, Hazel? Would you join me for a bit of dinner? You must know a few nice places where you go with Tom."

She gave him a bright-eyed glance: "And save up to get married at the same time? And buy a house and go on a honeymoon? But we did go out to dinner on my birthday, and maybe you know the place: the Nashford Arms this side of Mohill? It's fairly new, I think."

"Never heard of it." John was all in favour of new places for the tourists. "It's an odd name, sounds more like the Fresh Food Arms with a gnashing of teeth." Cassa would never have indulged that sort of a joke, but it sent Hazel into a fit of giggling laughter. How young she is, he thought. So many years ago since I had to save up for my dinner. . . how young and how very pretty. "I think we are on the right road for Mohill."

The dinner was very good, and they kept up the joke, calling the cutlery the gnashery and making chat in lieu of any more serious communication, both aware it was safer to keep the other at civil lengths, but, in spite of their awareness, each making inroads into the other's need.

"Tom and I got engaged on my birthday," she told him, "the night we came to have dinner here. He proposed and I accepted; we met last Christmas."

"And when was your birthday?" John asked.

"It was at Easter, in March." So she wasn't that long engaged. He wondered why she had set her cap at Tom Frame; somehow they did not match. Yet she must have encouraged Tom, a reticent character at best, surly enough on a bad day.

"Had you got tired of teaching? I understand that teaching is a tough proposition nowadays."

"Oh, I think it can be, and there are days! But I love it. I teach English as well as history, and I am learning a lot as I go along. I hope to go on teaching after we are married."

"I thought women liked the idea of being at home, and kids and all that!"

"Maybe they did long ago, but it can get boring! My mother hated it; she had five of us and no help, and she was often very frustrated. She had hoped to be a musician when she was young. All her family were in the music business, and she used to play the fiddle at weddings to make a bit of money to help with our education." Hazel smiled as if to make up for a doleful story.

"I hope there were lots of weddings for her," John said sympathetically.

"Well, you know, weddings and country occasions. She died four years ago, just when the youngest of us was ready to leave home," and again she smiled.

He liked her smile; her practised attempt at bravery would deceive no one, but the little bit of theatre appealed to him. It gave him room to climb down to her level. He knew very well he had spent several years climbing upward to his wife's level, and lately he had felt the strain. In Hazel's company it was easy enough to postpone the wishful hope that Cassa would come back from Dublin as serene and trusting as she had been in the early days. As he opened the door of the Bentley for Hazel, the thought came that postponing was almost over.

"We were nearly forgetting about the picnic to Colgagh," he said. "What about tomorrow? Can you get away from all those papers for a day? I could pick you up early."

"Of course I could, but not too early. I will have to put the picnic together. With a bit of luck the local shop will have the necessary."

"But I could get some stuff down town," John offered, "or on the way."

"No, my friend, it was my idea and I'll prove I meant it." Her voice was gay and happy. When they pulled up at her flat, she stood by the door to say goodnight, her hand extended. There was some sort of a trailing plant on the wall behind her head, and in the darkness there hung a fragrance.

"That's nice," John said. "What is it?"

"It's called woodbine," she told him, recognising joyfully that he was reluctant to go home.

"Now that's a strange thing," John laughed softly. "When I was a kid, my Uncle Tim smoked Woodbines, but they never had that gorgeous perfume."

"My father knew your Uncle Tim long ago in Sligo," she said.

There was an appealing attraction in her young face, and he welcomed their sharing of a remote past which was special to him. Suddenly the handshake became a hug and Hazel was in his arms, and he was kissing her as hungrily as if he had been starving for years.

Then he was apologising and holding her closer and caressing her thick dark hair and apologising all over again. . . Not for a moment had he intended to take advantage. Hazel in return was murmuring the phrases of

understanding while her lips against his face were soothing and sweet.

Then she was gone and her door was closed.

In the car, he remembered Colgagh. Would the picnic be
on or off? He felt as unsure as a boy on his first date. He had
never meant to, but had he frightened her off? After all, she
saw him as a married man of mature years. . . Tom Frame's
employer.

He would phone her when he got home, he would say
sorry again, and perhaps she would forgive his hasty
response to her murmured thanks. That was what it was,
wasn't it? A hasty response? On the phone he would say. . .
say what. . . that he had been. . . been what. . .?

By the time John got home and lifted the phone, he knew
he would ask Hazel for the day in Colgagh. And he did.

CHAPTER NINE

It was as if they had been on a month's holiday and not merely a matter of days with nights in between, nights of few enough hours because they had talked until long after midnight. Cassa, born with a respect for the male point of view, listened to Dermot's outlook on the happenings on the news; simply having him chat with her seemed a compliment which gave her insights into the man himself. John Gowan did not share like that: his business affairs were a male mystery.

They were at breakfast early for the journey home with some planned asides for more sightseeing. Dermot, always claiming to know Galway inside out and upside down, had remembered places Cassa had never heard of and would absolutely love to see, or so he said.

She was beginning to examine her conscience in his regard, for she found him relaxed and considerate and, dare she think it, a lovable person. It had been less easy from the second day of this necessary holiday to remember herself as a recently depressed woman, grieving silently for her sad inability to cope with the life and the people to whom she was committed. And she was committed, her mind admonished her even while she enjoyed Dermot's morning kiss at the breakfast table, even while she noticed the little waitress admiring Dermot's good looks. He was as splendid now as he had been on the day of his wedding to Nicole. Was that almost sixteen years ago, she asked herself, the year she had done her Leaving Cert? But, no, it must be more: she was only eighteen then. Dermot had not aged, and she dreaded to think what those years had done to her. It was deliciously reassuring when Dermot fussed over her, openly and in his clear voice.

"You must have slept well, Cassa. You are looking terrific

this morning. Let me choose breakfast for you." To the little waitress he said, "Have the bacon well grilled and the eggs scrambled with cream, not with milk." When she had tottered off in obvious astonishment, he directed his brilliant eyes on Cassa's smiling face: "No quailing at the thought of a good breakfast, sweet girl. You promised to grow big and fat."

He relished their shared merriment and wished he could extend their time together. She had told him that she should pack up: it had been two weeks, and wasn't that the usual length of a holiday? He had hesitated to persuade her, fearing that to force himself on her in any way would serve to remind her of her own obligations in that country town in Leitrim.

"Remember I told you I would show you the little house we had before we came to Dublin?"

"Where you were born, Dermot?"

"It's a fair few miles further west, Cassa. Would you be equal to that? Some mountains have bad roads, nothing much done on them for years. Would that be asking too much?"

"Of course not, Dermot!" With Dermot at the wheel of his Merc, precipices and landslides would be no bother. So off they set for Clifden. The scenery was so unexpectedly wonderful in the full sunshine of a July morning that they had little talk. Now and then, Cassa appreciatively laid her hand over his hand on the wheel, and there were times his hand found hers when the rocky road was safe for a mile or two.

"We've seen nothing yet," Dermot promised her. "When we get on the Maam Cross road, then you will realise you are in Connemara: first the Maumturks, and from Recess on to Clifden we'll get the panorama of the Twelve Bens. We're lucky, Cassa; there will never be a better day to see the peaks. I've been over here in thick fog when there was nothing to see, and it was easy to understand mass emigration." His tone was a little sad and a little humourous. "My mother remembers the fog more than the sunshine."

"But then," Cassa reminded him, "when your mother was a little girl going to school, it was autumn-winter-spring, not always like now."

"She never asked to go back. Her idea of a holiday is in the south of France."

Cassa had seen his mother on the day of the Firenze auction and had admired her appearance and the affectionate way Dermot had taken her arm. He himself had looked very severe. No need, she thought, to mention that day.

"I want you to be very, very impressed," he said, "when we get out beyond Maam Cross. One place in the world that Nicole couldn't bear was Connemara. We always seemed to get into a ferocious argument as soon as we hit Maam Cross. I wanted the girls to love all this part of our country, but they never got the chance. She took them to Donegal once to my sister's hotel, Port Salon – that was the time your father died. She hated that place about as much as Connemara."

Cassa remembered only Papa's cold dead body, but when Dermot spoke openly in that friendly way, she felt included in the family history. In Carrick-on-Shannon she had often felt very lonely in a sort of self-pity which she despised in herself. Cassa gathered her thoughts together. This was a special time today for rejoicing. . . a few days given to her quite accidentally and for which she felt immense gratitude. She had discovered in Dermot one of those unique people, a man who couldn't do enough to please.

The overwhelming, rugged, colourful splendour of the Connemara mountains was far more than Cassa could have expected, and she was wide-eyed with wonder. Dermot pulled over at the gaps in the road, driving more slowly than he usually did, so that Cassa found the words to express her feelings at the beauty around them, mixed up with a loving appreciation and a gratitude for having been brought to so much magnificence.

Dermot quite evidently felt that she had made up for her sister's lack. His voice had mellowed, and his smiling lips almost made Cassa wish this was an occasion for a kiss. "Now when we are coming into Clifden," he said, "I want you to tell me that this is the nicest little town you have ever seen. It is perched on the rim of the Atlantic – I put it there specially for you!"

And Clifden was immediately special for Cassa, too, so special that she hoped no great hurricane could ever swoop and bear it away. It was, as Dermot said, "just perched", chapel spires and church towers vying with the taller houses for sky-space against the tumbling ocean. When the car pulled up outside an unexpectedly grand hotel, Dermot had a question for her.

"Are you a good sailor?"

"Well, I think I am. There's a lot of cruising where I live, and I've never been seasick, if that's what you mean. Still, that is all canal and river, not the real sea."

"Would you like a motor-boat trip of the islands? We could get a boat out at Errislannan – in fact, I keep a boat there. But the motor-boat trip from here is more comfortable, and I see one is due to go out in half an hour."

Cassa never questioned his arrangements, never wondered how long or how far a trip would be. When he booked them into the hotel, she was glad of a wash-up, a change into slacks, a critical look at her face and hair. The mileage back to Dublin was in Dermot's hands. The sea view from her window was the most wonderful view of all this day.

Dermot was standing at the door. "All set, darling Cassa?"

"Dermot, have you seen that view? Look!"

He did more than look: he took her in his arms and held her as they stood at the window. "With a bit of luck, my dear

Cassa, this evening you will see the most wonderful sunset you have ever seen, a western sunset outlining all the small islands."

Cassa did not tell him, but she had some experience of sunsets, one she had not forgotten on Lough Boderg in their cruiser, when Frank had come very close to much more than his formal embrace. Quite suddenly that memory fell away into the past year with a lot of other memories, and she saw herself turning to Dermot, going closer and deeper into his arms, cherishing his kiss. She heard herself whispering, "You are so good to me, Dermot. I am so glad of you."

"And I am of you. I think you know that, ever since you were twelve years of age trying to get yourself killed outside Donnybrook church. Did you know I used to go into the paper shop just to admire yourself and the lovely Louise?"

Cassa pressed her face against his jacket. Louise had not vanished with the other memories. "Thank you," she whispered.

"Is this your warmest coat, Cassa? Best to wrap up out on the ocean."

They both knew, and acknowledged it in their fond exchanged glances, that their expedition to the islands would be a great page in their books for years to come, that first page of courteous references and memoranda of gracious thanks found in important books. The big motor-boat was crowded and noisy, and their situation necessitated Dermot's arm about her shoulders and his head bent close to hers as he named the islands so intimately into her ear that the names seemed inscribed: Talbot, Eashal, Inishturk, Omey, Cruagh, Friar Island and High Island. On the wild sweeping return, he told her tenderly, "See over there, my darling, that's Errislannan, where I have a boat and a small shack. Will I bring you there some day?" She was nodding enthusiastically.

As they walked hand in hand up the pier, both still enraptured by the islands, Cassa said to Dermot, "It's the strangest sensation, but I am hungry, really very hungry, for the first time in a year!"

"That must be what is the matter with me, too! Absolutely starving!" And Dermot whirled Cassa around on her heels, executing a bow like a dancer. "It looks as if we must find a place for a good dinner. But, Cassa, may I suggest you take a little rest before dinner. And perhaps a little drink: wine, sherry, gin and tonic? You've done a lot of travelling today for a recuperating lady." He knew very well that she liked his affectionate smile, and her black lashes closed shyly over the brown eyes as if to hide his reflection. "Look at me, Cassa – ah, that's better."

Dermot opened the door of her room. "So, Cassa, what'll it be? I recall your family always had Croft Original in Firenze in the times I was courting Nicole."

"Imagine remembering that. Were those happy times?"

"Not really," he laughed. "I was terrified of your mother."

"So was I," Cassa told him, "and with good reason. I wasn't her favourite."

"You should have been," he said with great loyalty. "You were mine."

Cassa had been told something about all that, through the solicitor via Nicole. She let the whole thing slip away, now that she needed Dermot's loyal friendship – just that, she assured herself. "So, that particular sherry, and we'll drink to better times."

"I'll freshen up," Dermot said, "then I'll bring the sherry and then we'll discuss dinner. I'll have them send up the menu. How about that? We'll meet back here in twenty minutes, Cassa." He wanted to scoop her up. She seemed so vulnerable standing there, so defenceless. He closed the door very quietly.

Cassa took a few things from her overnight bag. She had

not reckoned on a prolonged stay, but she had a change of underwear, a silk dress in case of an unlikely heatwave and the delicate negligee which had been her father's last birthday present and which she kept always in his memory. Occasionally, Melia Tracey had mentioned the joys of a shopping spree, and maybe that is what she should have done to cheer herself up. Maybe. Events had taken over and her interest in any apparel had dwindled away.

After the shower, she stood at the mirror in her underwear, almost marvelling at her slimness. The pretty negligee was always flattering, so she put it on and set out her make-up. She would try to look like an elegant dinner guest. She lay back on the pillows, a little tired after the day in the sun.

When Dermot returned with the sherry and the menu, Cassa was fast asleep. He stood and gazed down at her beauty. She was always defenceless and now more than ever before. To lie beside her and pretend that he, too, was tired and sleeping; to curve his body against hers; to be there for her when she awoke. . . His hands moved to take off his jacket as if her loveliness were on offer. Then Dermot stepped back. He drew the brightly coloured duvet that had been pushed aside up about her shoulders, switched off the light beside the bed and moved away. Without looking back, in fear of his own second thoughts, he closed the door of her room, and then he began to breathe again.

CHAPTER TEN

There is always that special bright morning when the weather report is good, people are at hand to help, there is music around every corner, and the future is assured. That is a day to beware of, a day when it were better not to have set out at all. In the simplest of life's designs and in the most complicated, the day of flourishing trumpets is a day not to be trusted.

Cassa was awakened by Dermot's phone call beside her bed; his voice was light and happy.

"Sleepyhead! How are you this morning?"

She knew instantly that he had come to her bedside the night before and left her there in peace. In the motorboat, she had had, for a moment, a kind of intuition that the coming night, perhaps the after-dinner talk, might open up their thoughts about their situation. Well, she had been mistaken, and he was her good and caring friend.

"Oh, Dermot, did I let you down badly last night? Darling friend, I am really and truly sorry, and after the lovely day you gave me. I never meant to fall asleep and ruin your night. Please tell me that you had a good dinner."

"I'll give you fifteen minutes to join me in the dining-room. Beware – I'll fetch you down in that lovely nightdress if you are a second longer!"

"Dermot, are you trying to make me blush?"

"Yesterday you were starving, Cassa – by now you must be ravenous. Come quickly."

After breakfast they walked across the street in Clifden to see the small terraced house in which Dermot Tyson had been born. It was one of their shared moments in which their eyes met in family unity, and perhaps blinded by the marvellously blended light of sun and sea and gorse, they were propelling each other into a relationship amorously desired by one and sternly forbidden to the other. Cassa knew all about a forbidden relationship, and she struggled against the thought of being doomed again, this time by her own will. It helped a little to take Dermot's hand and feel his warm reassuring grasp.

"Tell me, Cassa," he asked, "we have access to each other's moods now, haven't we? What is it?"

She tried for a bright smile. "Now don't laugh at me when I tell you. We have a housekeeper called Melia, and when you have lived with her for a year, you forget how to have private thoughts. She is not unlike my mother, Sadora, who believed in her own gift for words. . ."

"Don't I remember. And could she put you down! Go on about this Melia person. Tell me those secret thoughts."

Now Cassa laughed outright. "Everything in Melia's life has a set phrase; she has hundreds of them. Just now I found myself being a Melia: I had two phrases, I was being Queen For a Day, and I was Cooking My Own Goose." His sparkling eyes told her that he understood very well what she was trying to tell him.

"You know," Cassa said, "I have just remembered that you promised a glorious sunset last night. I missed that."

"And you would like to stay another day?"

"You know I would, I never dreamed the west was so glorious. I should love to come back some day, but perhaps for now I should be contented. We were only going to have a quick look at Galway, to round off my holiday. Wasn't that what we told Mrs Flynn?"

"I rang her this morning, Cassa. Sandra and Orla were still asleep, but all's well, she sounded in good form. I will phone later if we have decided, darling."

"Shall we say that we have decided to set off now? Let's just have a coffee and get our things in the hotel." Cassa was glad and equally sorry when he agreed.

They had set off on this little holiday as good friends quite attracted to each other . . . perhaps, Cassa thought a little confusedly, they were more affectionate than the usual run of friends, but then they were actually related by marriage. Now they were getting back into the car in the unmistakable attitude of a comfortable, settled couple, richly uncaring of approaching middle-age, a little while to go before they would admit to having fallen in love, one of them perhaps toying with the dream of total union, the other on the brink of. . . what? She knew very well that the Cassa who was concealed beneath the jaunty atmosphere generated by this man was a Cassa afraid of her own shadow . . . afraid of wrongdoing and afraid, too, of that awful silence of the heart to which she had been sentenced by Frank. Concentrate on the pleasure of Dermot, she told herself, just for this one journey, just for this one day.

"Is this the best moment to start telling you how very grateful I am for this beautiful holiday, Dermot? I never expected you to be so nice. I was in awe of you for years."

Dermot Tyson was not in favour of driving on main roads while getting stuck into an argument, but there were a few questions he would like to ask, questions to put out of the way before Cassa was at arm's length and admiring the scenery again.

"I know," he glanced at her with a smile, "and I often wondered why the auctioneer gave me the picture of Elvira. Was I to take that as a promise? A pledge of remembrance? That day in Firenze I told you that Nicole had gone out of my life, and you were not married then, Cassa. I drove past the gates of Firenze every day, hoping that perhaps you would be there for some reason. I continued to hope until you sent the invitation to your wedding. You never thought for a moment, darling, that the Tysons would turn up in Carrick-on-Shannon."

"No," she said sadly, "but I had no one of my own there."

"I was very angry about the marriage; perhaps I should have written good advice to you."

"Oh, how I wish you had! I made mistake after mistake, and I could have done with advice and a bit of family wisdom."

Dermot drove to the left and pulled up. "We'll have a break," he said; "I got a couple of flasks and some sandwiches from the hotel. There, Cassa, set them out on this paper plate and I'll pour out the coffee. There's a carton of milk and packets of sugar."

They moved into the back seat of the car to have their picnic.

"Not only are you a genius, Dermot," Cassa told him, "but you are the kindest man in the world – and the most efficient!"

"And the most hygienic," smiled Dermot, gathering up the remains of the snack. "Do you realise, sweet girl, that we are miles from a house or a pub, practically in a wilderness. How about that talk we could have before we face the world again?"

Cassa's voice was full of doubt and down to a whisper. "If *my* world could end this minute. . ."

Dermot placed his fingers under her chin. "No, you don't wish that, dearest. You want to see me again next week; you want us to go out to dinner and to the theatre; you want me to buy you special gifts; you want me to phone up every morning. Most of all, you are curious to see what I have done with the portrait of Elvira, and you would like to know what having Elvira means to me. . . me, Dermot Tyson, of whom people think I have everything a man could possibly desire. Don't you think that, sweet girl?"

Now she smiled for him. "My father certainly thought that. I think he was envious of you. 'That fellow will end up a millionaire,' he used to say."

"And he was right. Lawyers seldom have a head for

71

business, but he looked after you, and I am glad of that. Has your husband looked after you, Cassa?"

That was an important question, one of the questions to get clear. Was Gowan, as Dermot suspected, a fortune-hunter?

"If you mean, has he embezzled my riches from the sale, no. That money has scarcely been touched, apart from paying for the removal of the furniture from Firenze. It is in my name in the Bank of Ireland, and the furniture itself, all that was not sold, is in the house in Carrick in case Nicole looks for that, too. I have never got rid of the frightened feeling that Nicole will come after the money, the pictures and the cabinets, and Papa's desk: she asked him for that desk, from time to time, when my mother was paralysed, the big desk and other things. Those years were endless; I never saw you then."

"Forbidden! Forbidden! Forbidden to mention the illness, or you. To try to introduce the idea of help or a holiday or a gardener always started an enormous shouting row that went on for days. You would never have heard of Louise's death, although she made a big story about your visit to the professor-husband at the funeral. No, no, Cassa, she never hesitated to take your good name away – I realised that in time. She used to rant on and on about a sick priest."

Now Cassa hid her face in her hands. Not even to her husband John had she revealed the depths of her desirous adoration for Father Frank. John must have known when their estrangement began after the earthquake in Peru. . . she and John had equal shares in Frank, but there was no possibility they could share *him*, not even his memory. It was then she had no more interest in the coming of the baby. Not no interest, more a lack of courage, an inability to face into a future where Frank's space of love would be filled up by a new life, a space she thought could never be filled. . . So it had turned out, both lives were gone, swallowed up in two deaths obliterating the need for everyday desire.

Strangely, Dermot Tyson had stepped into all her secret areas of desire, and he was assuming that she had always known he could do that. Had she known that? Was his face and name always impossible to forget since the day he held her so close she could hear the beating of his heart as they danced at her sister's wedding in the garden of Firenze, and afterwards, and afterwards, and afterwards. It seemed like that now, a keeping at bay.

Dermot took her hands from her face. "Please tell me, Cassa. Who was this sick priest? And why did you say you never fell in love with your husband?"

"What happens if I can't answer these questions? I may not be able to. . ."

"What happens is that we drive back to Dublin and we say goodbye. Is that what you want, Cassa?"

"No, Dermot, no. . . but I have no right to say no."

"I give you the right. Now, tell me why you married a man you did not love. Now, Cassa, now – we have a long way to go before we see the Dublin mountains . . . Please, Cassa."

She was very hesitant, close to a tearful breakdown, unsure why she should uncover her naive loves and hopes and fears to a man who could forget her tomorrow. What made me so uncertain as a person, unable to know myself, she thought in despair. He is as near as I have ever felt to a man, nearer by far than I have ever felt to John with whom I try to be on my best behaviour. And to Frank? The word "sacrosanct" always stood between us, and sacrosanct won in the end.

Cassa sat up straight and fixed her eyes on the landscape.

"There was never a sick priest," she said slowly and with an innate dignity. "Nicole's words were always derogatory. There were two brothers, and when I needed friends in that terrible hospital – oh, Dermot, you'll never know how much I needed friends – they befriended me. When I ran away from you and from that awful job, I ran to them. I could not face the thought of going to London with Nicole, and there were a thousand reasons for that. Suppose the event had brought about her death? That last night in the drawing-room in Firenze when you kissed me passionately, that was the first time a man had ever kissed me. You were the handsomest man in the world, and you were my sister's husband. Above every other thing on earth, I feared my sister that night. To marry was safe. The priest did not break any vow for me, and now he is dead and buried far, far away. The foremost aim in my whole life, since the very beginning, has been to be safe from my sister. John makes me feel safe and secure. He is undemanding. Both brothers were lovely men, but I found out that loving is not enough. I am sure being safe from Nicole is an unchanged aim. . . it dominates my life." Now the tears slid down her cheeks, but she made a last, courageous effort to see the humourous side of her tragedy. "I guess I've cooked my goose now."

Dermot found nothing more to say. He knew that a lot of blame was his own responsibility. He held Cassa in his arms, and without a word or an action she was comforted. She was aware of a bleak future somewhere ahead, but she could indulge herself in his caresses for an hour of bliss until they decided they must get back on the road.

After Mullingar, Dermot proposed a stop at a little pub he knew near Clonard.

They were at peace with each other in the pub, but somehow the confessional talk had tired them more than they admitted. It was the plan that Cassa would be left home to her apartment and they would meet the next morning. Together they would tell Orla and Sandra about the judicial separation. He was insistent that Cassa be there because, he said, the girls were so fond of their Auntie Cassa. If there were tears, she would help to console them. She was reluctant. But she gave in.

Aylesbury Road had assumed a comfortable familiarity.

There was an opulence about it that Cassa found congenial, almost like coming home to Firenze a year or two ago.

"Thank you for putting me up here. I shall be sorry to leave," she said. "I have loved being here."

"I am going to ring the house to tell them I shall be home shortly." He winked boyishly at Cassa. "Shortly is an indefinite duration of time as no one knows how faraway I may be." Then he dialled.

Cassa had been admiring the look of him as he stretched out in the armchair, and when the phone was answered she could not but be surprised at the range of angry expressions crossing his face. He could scarcely get a word in with the staccato echo out of the phone of the two girls talking together and most excitedly, sounding as if their voices were pitched one against the other. Was there something wrong, something gone amiss in the Tyson household? There were fully five minutes of the phone call, and at last he got to speak. "Yes, yes, yes!" he shouted, and then he lowered his voice. "I will be home shortly. Just hang up the phone."

Her deepest instinct warned Cassa that this was doomsday.

There was no doubt but that Dermot Tyson had lost his temper. It took him an effort to control his voice. "Apparently Rebecca Gilbey's godmother came all the way from America for her twenty-first birthday party. Yes, Nicole. And apparently she made a big fuss of her daughters, becoming their doting mother all over again. That's not the worst of it. They told her all about you being down in Dublin, and, Cassa, worse still, they told her that I had taken you off to the country for a holiday. The righteous Nicole was very concerned that I had left Orla and Sandra to the mercy of Mrs Flynn, and she is coming back first thing in the morning to make sure that they are safe! Cassa, they were both talking together, and they were overjoyed to see their mother and to know that she loved them the same as she always did. . ." He had raised his voice, an exasperated voice, an angry voice, an indignant voice. There was more, but Cassa could not take it all in, only the bare fact, and maybe she had always known it. Being thousands of miles away in America did not mean a single thing – Nicole would be wherever Nicole wanted to be.

She heard herself pleading with Dermot to go. "Go home now; your daughters need you to be there. Now, Dermot, please." And finally he went, and she had no idea what he said as he went out of her door.

She waited for the sound of the elevator, then she picked up the telephone and asked the operator for the number of the Gresham Hotel, the hotel where she had had lunch with John the day she arrived in Dublin. No other name came to mind. She booked a room for the night, then rang to book a taxi as soon as possible. Tomorrow morning she would be early on the road north-west; she had done it before, she could do it again. It took ten minutes to gather together her clothes. As if she were someone else, a person who might be shivering with fear but without the faculty of thinking, she went down in the elevator to wait for the taxi.

Within another few minutes, her taxi had turned the corner out of Aylesbury Road.

CHAPTER ELEVEN

The single room was comfortable and quiet; there was a phone beside the bed and a bathroom en suite. Returning to Dublin had reminded her of so many things in childhood, and now one of Sadora's Rules came to her as she viewed the room: "Take time to compose yourself, Cassa. Time!" So she sat down in the neat armchair. She supposed that all adults in a near panic remember their mother's words of warning, but Sadora had made such a big thing of it – like Melia and her string of warnings. No, keep away from Melia, she thought, settle other things first. It is too late tonight to ring Carrick, and if John is in bed, would he want to be told that once again I have run away? He has probably had a hard day in his office. . . and do I really want to hear what he might have to say? No. Should I ring Dermot? Well, that's different. Should I? Will I? She realised that her hands were still shaky, her breath was catching as if she were running in a race. Should I ring Dermot? This is not what is meant by composing yourself. But he has been so good and sweet and kind, maybe a little phone call? No. No. And No again.

She looked across at the en suite. I'll have a bath, always my refuge when I came home from the awful hospital. Yes, an hour-long bath. After all, I should think about this escape, which is different from the last time I ran away. Those things I had to worry about then in San Salvatore – the nuns and the women and money – are not there to worry about any more. I have been in Dublin nearly two weeks and I haven't spent a penny. All the money is still in my wallet and a chequebook besides. It took a while but that thought helped her to sleep at last.

In the morning, Cassa dressed with care. When she rang the solicitor, Dick Boyce, they made an appointment for eleven o'clock, after she explained that she was in town for a day only. He expressed pleasure at the prospect of meeting her again, and Cassa smiled to herself. She had not made much impression on him before the selling of Firenze, but now he was ready to bend the knee. To call on him was an instinctive gesture: there were a few questions to ask, but to have his continued contact in Dublin would be perhaps useful in the future. He had served his terms with Cassa's father, in the legal firm owned by the Blakes for generations in the same old Georgian house on Stephen's Green familiar to Cassa since her grandfather's time.

She paid her bill at reception in the Gresham. There was a note for her from the manager: he remembered her coming with her father and hoped if she were free, they might talk over old times, perhaps at dinner this evening. Cassa was pleasantly surprised. "Small world," she said to the girl at the desk. "Please convey my thanks." She arranged to collect her things later, but she did not think she would be staying another night.

Her father always said that everyone in Dublin knew everyone else. Certainly her father in his day seemed to know everyone in the city, and she wished he were still here nodding affably as they walked along. What would Dublin in the eighties look like to my father compared to the Dublin of his youth before the First World War? Maybe this dear old Grafton Street would look much the same to Papa. It has a lot of the same shops, and I've missed it in the last three years, only now I know how much I've missed it. Her father never passed Clarendon Street without paying a visit to the church, so Cassa turned into the small street and paid her visit in loving memory. The church looked cavernous and gloomy, although somewhere in a far chapel there was the familiar sound of a low-key mass. When she knelt down to offer a prayer, she noticed a sign hanging on a confessional: Ring the Bell for a Confessor.

She had thought about her conscience several times in the days of her holiday. Suddenly she remembered back more than twenty years and her father pointing to this sign, and smiling down at her, "Will we go to confession, pet?"

"What sin would I tell, Papa?"

And the way he smiled, his loving amusement. "Aren't you the luckiest little girl in the world?" Her father had never rung the confessor's bell, and they had walked out of the dark church into the sunshine, and he had bought an ice cream for her to eat in Stephen's Green. A vivid memory. Maybe it happened many times when she had summer off from school and their yardman brought her to the Donnybrook tram and Papa took her home in his new car. Nicole never came on those expeditions, but then Nicole was four years older and always very grown-up.

Like her father before her, Cassa felt no inclination to ring the bell; her thoughts revolving backwards for a priest would confuse the effort to speak her mind to the solicitor. On now to Stephen's Green, and into Papa's old office.

As Dick Boyce recorded in his diary later, he had expected the woman he had seen after her father's funeral: good-looking but dragged down with worry, not too well attired and agitated in her manner. Now, not to exaggerate, he could say that this woman today was in the flower of womanhood. He had missed his chances there, and her father had (well, almost) entrusted this lady to his care as he was the senior solicitor in the firm. Boyce distinctly remembered dismissing her as a spinster destined to end her decaying days in an ancient mansion for the up-keep of which the same father had not left sufficient hard cash, only a load of old bonds taking years to mature. Dick Boyce knew Richard Blake's sins of omission, and the old phrase about wine, women and song was made for Blake in his heyday. A brilliant legal brain, he would have to say that. There was enormous surprise among the legal fraternity when the

79

Blake property was put up for auction and fetched the massive price it had fetched two years earlier – the first of the big estates on the south side of Dublin to sell for development. Yes, the first. He himself had done all the legal part of the sale, but this lady had employed an agent, name of Gowan – a big country gentleman. A country auctioneer, he had supposed.

The little solicitor was fussing around with a chair. He had told her three times that he was delighted to see her, and he was settling his necktie and adjusting his waistcoat. Cassa found that she was not in the least concerned. The enchanted days in Dermot Tyson's company had wrought an effect on her, and she was becoming aware of it in a new confidence. Walking up Grafton Street, she had walked away the long years of being a daughter and the brief years of trying to be a country wife. She had almost been on the brink of a love affair with a very handsome man.

The effusive greetings were over, and the solicitor's office was calm.

"Have I still a place in your filing cabinet, Mr Boyce?" Cassa enquired pleasantly.

"Oh, but certainly, Miss Blake. I had my secretary take out all your documents in case you had enquiries." He patted the papers on his desk.

"I have been married for almost two years," Cassa told him. "My married name is Gowan, and my address has been in Carrick-on-Shannon. I would like to keep the name of Cassandra Blake in my legal affairs, and that is one question. Would you deal with that in due course?"

"Unless your husband made a formal objection, there is no difficulty, Miss Blake."

"I shall consult with him, but for the moment all my papers are in the name Blake, and I will let you have my request in writing. I may take it then you will act for me in all legal matters. There is a second question, a family matter.

Has my sister, Mrs Nicole Tyson, any hold over my financial affairs?"

Dick Boyce found it necessary to clear his throat and attend to the proper set of his necktie. Two years ago, he had suffered a financial loss from this lady's sister. He was unwilling to say much.

"You may or may not know, Miss Blake, that after the finalisation of the second sending-for-probate of your late father's will, Mrs Tyson removed all her business out of my offices, out of my care, so to speak."

"To the best of your knowledge, Mr Boyce, has she any access to the legal state of my own affairs?"

"Not unless you, or your husband, have made her privy to such."

"I have not seen her nor communicated with her since the last day I was here in your office, Mr Boyce. If she did not settle your bills for the legal work done in relation to my father's will, then I will do so now, and I will settle my own bills with you now. We will start afresh, and I will have the satisfaction of knowing that our names, hers and mine, will never appear together in your files."

Dick Boyce's angular face permitted itself a flat grin, probably of satisfied relief. He had submitted a full account after the sale of Firenze, two or three times, with no result. His legal work on the sale had been taken care of, but not the prolonged sessions on the continued rush to probate afterwards. He had no way of knowing that John Gowan had considered those legal bills were down to Nicole; nor could he have known how, in the dreary months of inaction after the dead-born baby, Cassa had begun to wonder where all the bad luck was coming from. "I never knew you were so superstitious, Cassa! Bad luck? Things just happen!" Sometimes John made teasing comments which grated a little: sensitive would have been better than superstitious. It was somehow patronising when he used the word "Women!" as a joke.

"I was not very well recently, Mr Boyce, and if you will forgive me for saying so, I had no experience of business. You will remember my father was very protective, and after his death, Nicole looked after everything."

Dick Boyce remembered her extreme surprise and apparent reluctance to accept the provisions of the will, that she alone had inherited everything. He remembered, too, her sister's violent anger, which had been forcibly expressed in his office more than once.

"Nicole will never forgive me for the sale of our home and for lodging the money in my own name. I know she will not, and while I stayed away and kept quiet and while she stayed in America, I had a chance. Now I am afraid, and that is the reason I am here in your office. Should things go wrong, I will ask you to act for me."

"What do you think could possibly go wrong, Miss Blake?"

"With my sister, Mr Boyce, things have always gone wrong, and I have never known why." The solicitor rustled the papers and changed the subject. "As you are here, Miss Blake, there is a small matter of the other bonds left to you, and to your sister, by your grandfather who founded this firm. Your sister took her stocks and bonds with her two years ago. Yours are still here untouched – these are the shares on which you draw a small income. If you wish to take them and lodge them in your bank account, they are here. I believe their value has greatly increased in the last year."

"Is that a matter you could deal with, Mr Boyce?"

"Certainly I could. Is it the Bank of Ireland?"

"It is, in College Green. In fact, I have never used the chequebook. I was not married at the time the account was opened, so it is still in the name of Cassandra Blake, and, as we have agreed, the name will remain unchanged."

There was a certain amount of mystery in all this, Dick Boyce reflected, but it wasn't up to him to question it. Miss

Blake had brightened up considerably, and she appeared relieved and at ease.

"I am writing my home address here for you as I have no card, and there is one more thing I am hoping you could ask your secretary to do when I have filled in these cheques for the debt due to you. I should like to hire a car to drive home."

Boyce glanced at the address: County Leitrim. "That's a long drive, Miss Blake; surely there is a bus or a train?"

"I like the idea of driving," she said. "I have always liked driving; it settles the question, you see."

He didn't see, and it seemed a daft idea, but the expense was not for him to decide. "There is a reliable car-hire firm in Dublin airport," he said. "I often use it for clients from abroad. What about a taxi to the airport? I can arrange that for you." The taxi would also pick up her things from the Gresham. Now the little solicitor was rewarded with a delightful smile, and her dark brown eyes were full of gleaming light. She stood and walked to the full-length window looking out over Stephen's Green. "I always loved coming into this office to visit my father," she said in her gentle voice. "This brings him back. I miss him so."

CHAPTER TWELVE

There was no answer to John's phone call; he tried a couple of times, but evidently she had not returned from her trip to the west with the brother-in-law. He had wanted to tell her that he would be away all day, that he was going over to Sligo and up to Uncle Tim's old place in Colgagh. He would mention that Hazel was coming along. He would tell Cassa that she would like Hazel, who was a teacher in the Ursuline Convent and was safely engaged to Tom Frame who was in the office in Sligo town. It occurred to him to tell her also that Tom and Hazel and Hazel's sister would all be meeting for dinner in Sligo after Colgagh. Cassa would surely remember about the previous dinner and all that had happened on the day Cassa first decided she would be going to Dublin. Had he told her about meeting Hazel for the first time? Her name was mentioned, or was it? Did he know her name before he met her?

All of this was a carefully prepared preamble to his proposed enquiry as to when his wife would require him to go down to Dublin for her return. Now, he wondered, should he go into his office and alert them to keep him posted as to whether Cassa would be coming today or tomorrow? By nature more courteous than curious, he hesitated for a moment and then put down the phone.

"Aggie, were there any calls I haven't heard about?" Aggie was Melia's niece and regarded the phone as her special charge. Her vague look was an answer.

"If Mrs Cassa calls, this is the Sligo office number here on the notepad – I'll call in there just in case." Aggie liked very much being in command of calls, and she would never forget a message.

He was not in high favour with Melia, so he bypassed the kitchen on his way out. As he revved up the Bentley, he glimpsed Melia's face through the window, an anxious look. No doubt she "was readin' it in the stars", her own notion of her prophetic powers. Very deliberately, John shifted her weight of unspoken criticism off his head. He was taking a day off. That was all.

Hazel was already out at her door with a picnic neatly stored in a basket. "I heard the Bentley coming round the bend in the lower road," she greeted him. John noticed that everything about her was shining: her eyes, her teeth, and her black hair brushed into a thick ponytail. She looked young and very pretty. "The thought of hours spent bowling along on these wheels got me out of bed at dawn," she said. "I was hoping you hadn't had to change your mind. Maybe Mrs Gowan coming home today?"

"No change, Hazel. I made all the necessary phone calls. But tell me, what's so special about the old Bentley? I mean, special to you?"

She settled herself comfortably into her seat. "You're fishing for compliments, but I'll tell you, John. In the Bentley, I feel like a queen. In fact, I feel like the Queen of England sitting in state, inspecting my lands and properties and estates and castles – look, there's a castle over there!" She pointed out a well-known landmark.

"The queen can't be too happy today wherever she's sitting," John remarked, "with the things that are going on today over the border. According to the radio this morning. . ."

Hazel leaned across and put two fingers on his lips. "Not today, John. I get the North from everyone around here, and when I am at home my father drives me batty with his endless analysis of the historical contention, as he calls it. I teach history, but to listen to my father, you would think I was still in first class learning my ABC."

They both burst out laughing. "I must meet your father," John said. "I won't say another word about politics."

"Is that what they call it?" she rejoined, still laughing. "Politics! Democracy! Sectarianism! Terrorism! Give me a break."

John Gowan was learning from this young woman: her exuberance was catching and heartlifting, and she was so very good-looking. They chatted away easily about the little towns they passed through, about the lake-lands revealed by a curve in the road, about the poverty both hidden and shown in the empty fields. They realised in each other their sympathy with this part of their native world. Cavan and Leitrim were slowly emerging from the long sleep of emigration and unemployment. John knew his history from the instinct of times lived through, and he enjoyed very much the telling of it through the eyes of a student. When they fell into a contented silence, John suggested that Hazel play a tape of her choice. She put on a tape that John didn't know, and he realised that it must be one of Cassa's. Familiar music never recalled Cassa, who had often quietly closed the door on the songs and sounds from Melia's kitchen; indeed, she had often retreated to the bedroom, or down to the jetty by the river. She never hummed along as Hazel was doing now, quite contentedly, he thought.

They had left Sligo town back on the main road, and the next stop would be Colgagh where John intended to regale Hazel with stories of his Uncle Tim's eccentricities. Her responsive laughter had begun to be enjoyable, endearing; he wanted more of it, although he had not until now quite understood the effect of this girl's company.

"Where shall we have our picnic?" Hazel asked.

"In the car, if you like. The wind out here is usually blowing a gale. Or we can go into one of Uncle Tim's old houses. There are fold-up chairs in the boot."

Soon they were setting up the picnic in what must have been a farmhouse kitchen a hundred years ago. They moved the chairs under the window, where there were no panes of glass but a view of breathless grandeur with not another house on any horizon.

"Did your Uncle Tim actually live out here?" Hazel asked in wonder.

"Maybe when he was very young, but the family moved in the grandfather's time. My mother never lived here, but, according to Tim, her ancestors are buried here. There is a graveyard further along. They moved into Sligo when it was a village, but Tim spent all his time out here. He had an old bike and eventually an old car, and when he was a middle-aged man he had a succession of great cars. He loved this place."

"And what about his wife and family?" Hazel wanted to know. "Were there neighbours in those days, a little shop – was there a school?"

"I used to ask those questions, too. There was an English lord owned a lot of land around, and he found sheep more profitable than people – you'd know that from your history, I suppose, Hazel?"

"I was brought up in Sligo town, and my mother and her mother before her. And whatever you may have sneaked out of a history book in the local library, it was not considered politic to know much about the lords or the gentry, much less criticise them. Not in the town of Sligo. They were the landlords and every man's employer. They are mostly gone now, but even twenty years ago my father knew when to shut his mouth." She laughed a little at this idea. "We have some arguments, my dad and I."

"I was brought up in Monaghan," John said, "and I never knew my father: he was drowned – out fishing."

"Did your Uncle Tim fill in for your father?" she asked with sympathy.

John had wondered about that sometimes. "He never married anyhow. I remember when I was about twelve, I got the idea he was trying to fill in, not for me, but with my mother, for my dead father."

"That was a tough thought for a twelve year old. What happened?"

"There were three of us," John said slowly, reluctant to delve into that past, "and we used to put bets on it, my older brother and my young sister, when we'd see him shuffling into the kitchen with his cap in his hand. I always swore he'd ask her, because I wanted him to. He was a kind old geezer. Frank wished he would but thought he wouldn't have the courage; but Deirdre, she was the youngest then, always knew he wouldn't get anywhere, so she always won the bets."

"Were you his pet?" Hazel asked.

"We didn't see him for years: he was off making money with a tractor business, and then he got interested in the cruisers. When my mother married, he came back. He must have needed someone, and there was only me, then."

Hazel saw he did not want to make a long story about himself, so she let him ramble on about the decent old guy who had left him stacks of money and this wild property of land in Colgagh.

"Let's go out and walk around the fields, shall we?" Hazel suggested.

Glad to escape the prospect of sorrowful talk about his mother and his childhood, John was more in his element envisaging his great plans for using the land for holiday homes, for guest houses, even for a couple of hotels. He was surprised at Hazel's enthusiasm, her absorbed interest and her valuable suggestions. Today the weather was broken up by scudding clouds, so John tucked his arm through Hazel's as they trudged across the fields for a closer look at the Atlantic away to the western limit of the lands.

"If it were a really hot day and we fancied a dip in the sea," Hazel asked, "would it take long to walk to the shore?"

"If we had a car, there is a road of sorts a mile on up and three miles down to the sea."

"But you wouldn't take your Bentley down a road-of-sorts." She made a funny little face at him.

"No bloomin' fear!" He gave her arm a big brotherly hug. "And you wouldn't let me if you saw that old road. You think too highly of the Bentley, don't you now?"

"But, you know," she said looking up at him, "if you begin to plan for holiday homes out here, a road to the beach would want to be the first thing on your new map, a road with a name like you see in other seaside places: the Sea Road for instance, but a better name than that."

"When that time comes," John was pleased to tell her, "you will be the one to decide the name. I can see you now, breaking the bottle of champagne over the bronze plaque and declaring this new estate open."

"And I'll be the one to buy the first house. This is the very place I would want to live and bring up my family – always providing you had made a good road down to the sea!" Hazel was looking all around the empty landscape. "Not too many houses, John, more a village than a tourists' paradise, please."

"But enough to make my fortune, surely?" John teased but he appreciated the impression she was creating. "You are right, you are absolutely right. Having been in tourism nearly twenty years now, I have seen the original ideas blown into shapeless ugly environs, often with the wrong mix of people."

"The family home in Enniscrone, where we grew up, is still untouched, and the area is only full for a couple of months in the summer," Hazel said a little sadly, "but Maura – you met my sister the nurse– told me last week that the local Council have plans."

"The trouble is," John told her, "when there are no plans, no moves to implement new things, then the old ways fade away and the people who lived there go away. Just look here: once a country place where folk raised families."

"They left, and they leave, because of hardship – this is the teacher talking." Hazel was smiling again, "And you are going to change all that, same as you did with the cruisers in Carrick!"

"I wasn't the only one who saw a future in the cruisers; I wasn't the first, and I am still not the biggest. We all see a future there. But lately I am getting the ambition from somewhere, I don't know where, that I should spread my wings before I get too old."

"How old are you?" Hazel asked in her direct way.

"I am heading for halfway, to fifty," he said. "Probably as old as your father."

"My father is nearer seventy; they had to wait for years before he had claim to the land to make a living. He knew my mother since she was fifteen, and she waited for him. I often wondered why. He can be a cantankerous old devil, and she was a dear, lovely woman. I once had the temerity to tell her she could have done better, but she said he was all right in his own way, and anyway when she was a girl there wasn't much choice."

They were walking back to the old house. John felt a tender sympathy for the young woman. In the same way he had kissed her goodnight, now he bent and kissed her again, holding her head against his shoulder. There was nothing amorous in the kiss; she drew only comfort from it. Then she disengaged herself and gave him a long grateful look from her friendly grey eyes.

"Time we were on our way, John," her clear, happy voice rang out against the wide, lonely spaces of the rough fields. "Before we meet Tom and my sister, we could take the long road close to Lough Gill. I'd like that if you think we have the time."

In the hours of twilight, the lake closes in mysteriously.

90

The overhanging branches of the island trees reach out into the water, and the water is stilled as if quietened by the silence of fading light. Mysterious people like poets and archaeologists have sought shelter among the trees, built little fires, meaning to stay all night, or perhaps for ever. Tradition has it that the islands do not welcome strangers, that such folk were never seen again.

"When I was a kid, I often asked to go over in a boat and explore the islands for myself, but Uncle Tim forbade it, absolutely. There was 'something' over there worse than magic, he said. He had a great respect for magic."

"Perhaps your Uncle Tim thought you would be drowned in a little row-boat. Perhaps you were a very nice little boy then, a well-mannered child, and he was very fond of you."

"He'd have given me a good clout," John told her, "a right thump!"

"Thumps hadn't gone out of fashion when I was a kid either," she told him. "Kids nowadays get away with murder – the schoolteacher talking again, sorry."

They arrived at the hotel exactly on time to meet Tom in the lounge, and Maura came in directly afterwards. As Tom and Hazel exchanged kisses in greeting, John happened to notice that her eyes were wide open, and he wasn't sure if one should notice a thing like that. There was no problem with the chat because Hazel was full of the big adventure of the day, the discovery of Colgagh. John encouraged her to tell a little about the future possible plans for the holiday homes. The dinner ended on a high note of enjoyment, as if they were four old friends happily dining together. Maura and Hazel had a little talk to one side about their father who was improving in the hospital, while Tom Frame passed a few solemn words to John about the exceptionally busy times they were experiencing in the Sligo office.

Finally they were all out in the front saying goodnight, and John and Hazel saying goodbye to the pair who must fare off into the night for their return to Carrick-on-Shannon. With a slight sense of shock, John Gowan realised that the dinner was only a delaying tactic, that he was actually waiting to be alone with Hazel in the comfortable seclusion of the car. They enjoyed each other's company, there was nothing wrong with that. He hoped the pleasure was mutual. Perhaps it was. . . as she put her hand down to take the seat belt, she looked up into his face, and in the dark her eyes were shining.

"Is it all right with you, John, if we have soft slow music all the way back to Carrick?"

"Of course, Hazel. Choose whatever you like. We won't be going so fast; I didn't know it had got so late. Thank you for a terrific day, thank you very much."

She laid her cheek against his arm. "Thank you." The music was forgettable, but the warm softness of her face against his sleeve touched off a sensation of desire. Not for a moment did he question his right to this unexpected enjoyment. When at last the car stopped at the door of her flat, she turned fully into his arms in a loving gesture of gratitude.

"Would you like to come in for a coffee, John?" she asked.

There had been the kisses of last night, and there had been a whole long day in this beautiful young woman's company. . . enough time to have the cold embers in a rejected heart raked over and seeking for a lighted taper, as if a man needed the excuse of time to find himself in a rapturous exchange of seeking lips and exploring hands.

In the rich man's mansion on the other side of the world, Hazel had learned to excite and gratify. Eighteen and unawakened, she had given herself completely to first love with a world-famous man who could claim to have written the dictum of dalliance along with all his other books. Too late she remembered that he had told her his first precept in their first embrace: "There is no for ever." Tonight she added the satisfying knowledge of being essential, being

92

hungrily essential, manna in the desert. Nobody had taught John Gowan the laws of lovemaking; this tidal course would take so much delicious time. Was he ready for an affair? He had scarcely mentioned his absent wife, nor had she said much about Tom Frame. Tom knew his place in her world, a candidate for husband material. . . fairly well aware that her very limited response to his lover-like attempts were in keeping with his own ideas of avoiding sinful temptation. Hazel knew and Tom Frame knew the niceties of the waiting game.

With John Gowan, handsome and rich and attractive, she would enjoy playing the courtesan. He was not fully aware that he must make the running, and tonight she could hold temptation at a high level. After all, he was a married man; he ought to know the ropes. To Hazel, it was obvious that he did not, that he was grasping at his initiation. Procrastination in pursuit was a wile her mentor had taught her. Enjoyable? Just that, no more. She had made the mistake of falling in love ten years before. Never again.

John Gowan was not a man for analysing his needs, nor did he feel the necessity to repress them. A very personable young woman had become available to him in a natural way that was easy to understand; there was a mutual desire which was convenient to a man in his position, deserted temporarily by a wife who had become rather distant and perhaps unforgiving. He was prepared to give Cassa time, but while he was waiting he would take up with the temptation so engagingly offered. In fact, over a week or two John Gowan had become addicted. Hazel had become a habit.

It was two o'clock in the morning when John Gowan pulled in to the yard behind his house. A hall light had been left on, and there was a dim light in his own room. He walked down to the river: not exactly disturbed, not exactly confused, certainly not agitated, nor would he say pleasurably excited. Or would he? A bizarre frame of mind, a bit dishevelled. A phrase of Melia's would suit: "Yer man isn't himself."

He could see the trails of moonlight behind the clouds. Moonlight and Cassa were never far apart; she always called the moon the Goddess Flacthna. He had told her that name when she first came to Carrick. Another phrase of Melia's was "smote with guilt", but no uneasy guilt would ever be in the air around his wife. Cassa was a woman set apart.

The trouble with staring into the River Shannon, he thought to himself, was that it hypnotised you. He might as well go to bed as stand here. Stuff the confusion!

In the bathroom, he thought briefly about a shower. That would wake him up and he would start the usual worry about the absent Cassa... what to do... how best to please... what gifts to bring. All his intense caring had turned into fretful worry. He washed his hands and rubbed the towel over his face. It was nearly tomorrow anyway. His bedroom door was slightly ajar and the light beside the bed had been turned down low. In his bed lay his wife Cassa. She was deeply asleep, relaxed and lovely. One slender arm lay outstretched across his side of the bed, as if in invitation. Two years ago he had found her thus, a sleeping princess in a guest house in Longford.

Overcome with a bewildering mass of emotion, John backed out of the bedroom. Down the corridor was the room where his brother Frank had slept, now always kept in reverence by Melia and the nieces. John flung himself on the single bed, like a man ousted and exiled from everything he had ever known.

CHAPTER THIRTEEN

Every window in his house was lit up, and the hall door was wide open. There were no cars on the drive, but Dermot left his car on the road outside the gate, in case there might be cohorts of Gilbeys arriving at any moment.

Orla and Sandra rushed out to meet him. "Daddy, Daddy, you are just in time. Mummy was just about to go, she said you must be staying out, but we told her you always come home – quick, quick, Daddy, come on in!" They were both very excited, talking together at the top of their voices, and Sandra was almost in tears with the anxiety of waiting. "Hurry, Daddy! Hurry!"

Dermot walked into the lounge. Nicole, standing at the long mirror, swung around and almost screamed, "Where is she? Where is my sister?"

He knew this mood of old. She might have been controlling her temper but was ready to let it snap. If he made the required response, she could leash the fury and purr like a kitten. Let her rip, he thought.

He turned quickly, ushering his protesting daughters out into the hall and closing the door sharply. Then he looked at his ex-wife, from head to toe. The impression she made was an image of luxurious beauty, in full flight, ready for a madly spitting row; or if cajoled, ready for an extravagant scene of passionate abandonment to anything and everything sexually in excess. Always in excess.

It took three seconds to say, "What?" If she could claw his face, she would. He had come to know that look in the days of their legal separation, her long red nails at the ready.

"You've been sleeping with my sister for the past week and you have the nerve to say 'What!' You have been using my sister as a whore!"

Quite obviously the Gilbey cousins had kept tabs. "I

95

thought whores got paid for it," he said coolly. "You think nothing of calling your sister a whore?"

"She's such a fool," Nicole raised her voice, "you'd take it for nothing. Where is she? I know you brought her to this house. I know because the girls told me. Where is she. . . is she out in the car?"

So the Gilbeys didn't know everything.

"Stop staring at me!" Nicole shouted. "You've seen me before. I demand to know, where is my sister Cassa? Where is she at this very minute? Tell me now! You had her in this house. . ."

Dermot interrupted her abruptly. "This house is my house, and everything in it right down to the floor you are standing on is mine."

"I should never have signed it over to you – you have. . ."

Again he interrupted her shrill voice with some ferocity: "Signed it over? I bought it from you! And at a price! I own it, and I will have whoever I wish to have in it. Get that?"

"So you admit it! I could not believe my ears when Orla told me, and Sandra did too, that you have had Cassa here and you have been gone out of here with Cassa, gone for days, and now you have her here, or somewhere. Where? What about her husband? Have you told him where she is and where she was for the past week? And where were you with her? You can walk out of here and leave your precious daughters with a servant, while you take my sister from her lawful. . ."

Dermot Tyson recognised this habit in his once-so-desirable wife: she was building a case, in which everyone would be implicated. He had not forgotten the case she had once built about Cassa, until he had persuaded himself that Cassa was having an affair with a priest, a sick priest. . . and there was a suggestion of abortion. Nicole never ran out of words. She just went on to the next implication every time another penny dropped into her mechanical brain. He heard her without listening, and this time it was different because this time his silence must defend him against the truth she or her awful Gilbey cousins might stumble on. It would never have occurred to him to warn his beloved daughters, "Don't tell about Cassa." To say a thing like that was beneath contempt. He was a free man. Nicole had no rights – she had sold them all for his cash – but Cassa must be protected. Cassa was the prize he had determined on, the prize his own greed had previously deprived him of. He believed that he was being given another chance, that Cassa needed him in the same way Orla and Sandra needed him to be there for them. He must be there for Cassa: her fragile loveliness had taken a grip on his every sense.

Mrs Flynn had heard similar rows before the mistress took off for America, and before that (and not only with her husband), but that was their own business. She shut the kitchen door with a loud bang and turned up her radio to full volume. She didn't take any notice of the girls standing outside the lounge door.

The younger one was in tears. Daddy usually chased them up the stairs at bedtime – that was great fun – and often he stayed for a chat about their day. He used to read a story until last year, and Sandra had loved that; some things got lost as you got older, which wasn't really fair.

Orla thought they had better go upstairs: "Daddy wouldn't want us out here listening."

But Sandra wanted to listen in the hope that the good part would come, and Mummy and Daddy would be friends again and go to bed together. "They used to make up, so they did," she whispered tearfully. "They used to laugh the next day."

"It's different now," Orla said. "There's some reason Mummy went to America. I heard Auntie Janet tell Auntie Audrey, something about secrecy."

"Listen," Sandra said, creeping closer to the door. "I

think they are fighting about Auntie Cassa. Mummy is saying. . ."

Orla wouldn't listen any more. "They were always fighting about Auntie Cassa. It was the same before Mummy went away. It was always the will or the hospital." She pushed Sandra towards the stairs. "You can stay there if you want to, but I'm going to bed."

Tearfully, Sandra stumbled up the stairs after her sister. "I wonder what it was that Auntie Cassa did wrong? Mrs Flynn told me last week that Mummy and Auntie Cassa are blood sisters. What do you think that means?"

In the bedroom, Orla pushed her sister into the bathroom. "It means that you had better wash your face; it's all smudged. Daddy will look in, so please don't make things worse with your silly questions."

"Only just tell me," Sandra pleaded, "will Mummy look in? Will Mummy be staying with us tonight?"

Orla, who was older than Sandra by two whole years, shrugged her shoulders because first, she didn't know, and second, she didn't want to start let Sandra talk her into crying. She thought it would be unfair to take sides, but she really did love her daddy, and she knew Sandra did, too. But what about Auntie Cassa, she wondered? Where exactly did she fit in?

"Now, look here," Dermot interrupted forcibly again, "apart from everything else, I'm very tired – I'm actually falling asleep. I'll phone for a taxi for you." His voice was louder than he had meant it to be, but it was the truth. He was jaded after driving from the west.

She was screaming at him again. "I didn't say I was going anywhere!"

Automatically he shouted back, "You can't stay here!"

Now she didn't glare at him, but cast her gaze around the room in sudden sorrow. "Why can't I stay here? What is the reason why I can't stay here? My children are here and they have asked me to be sure and stay and be here in the morning. Mrs Flynn made me very welcome. I'm sure she has a bed made up for me. Why not ask her?" Dermot observed that Nicole was becoming craftily courteous, climbing down to a charming civility; in another minute she would have Mrs Flynn into the lounge, and maybe the children also. It was a scene that had been enacted several times in the months before the final split. All would be arranged for accommodation, and then in the middle of the night, she would transform herself into an alluring temptation, very beautiful and very sexy, and utterly generous to a man in need then of generosity. And in the morning, she would be glitteringly boastful: "I can always work the oracle for you, my darling!"

But the split was over and done with. No going back. No irresistible temptation tonight. He didn't have to steel his heart, or his flesh. That was taken care of.

"Very well, Nicole, you may stay for tonight. Make your own arrangements with Mrs Flynn."

Her radiant smile was something to behold. "Shall we drink to that, my old darling?"

His answer was short and decisive: "You know where the drinks are. I seldom drink any more. Goodnight."

He was gone before she could draw breath, but her smile remained in full consciousness of her own power. He had given in. She certainly did know where the drinks were, and a few snifters of brandy would perk her up for the interview with Mrs Flynn, who had not, by any means, been as obligingly servile as Nicole had trained her to be. As a child, Nicole had taken example from Sadora's attitude to staff.

Dermot Tyson went up to say goodnight to his daughters. Sandra was curled up under her eiderdown, her hair all tousled; she was fast asleep. Orla was patiently waiting for his goodnight kiss. She wanted to tell him in a whisper that he was the greatest daddy in the whole world, but the whisper got caught somewhere. He knew, she was sure he knew, because he gave her a great big confidential hug as he tucked her in.

He turned on the lights in his own bedroom and left his door slightly open. Going down the stairs, he heard Nicole's voice in Mrs Flynn's kitchen. The voice was as imperious as ever. He slipped into his study, closing the heavy door without a sound, and then securing the double lock. There was a similar lock on the glass door, and within minutes he was out into the garden, down the grass verge and into his car.

His whole being lit up with the expectation of seeing Cassa again, the one person on earth who would know the ripped-out desperation Nicole could cause, and who could sympathise. Maybe she would take him into her arms as she had when her father died, maybe let him lie by her side all night long. He conjured up a happy picture of their sharing breakfast when the sun dawned through the east window of the apartment. He realised how late it was as he turned into Aylesbury Road, and there was not a light in the whole block. He had his own keys of the entrance, and the lift worked smoothly.

Very gently he opened the penthouse door. Cassa would have gone to bed when he had to go home. Her long day on the road would have tired her, too. This would be his second time to come on a sleeping Cassa. . . so small in the big bed, so delicately lovely.

Cassa had fled. Defenceless as he saw her and as he wanted her to be, she had fled. Somehow, while she had allowed him to do every little service for her, to cosset and pet her, to put her to bed on that first night, she had been completely capable of flying off into the night. Dermot put on all the lights and searched, but there wasn't a scrap of paper to explain. Surely a few words of gratitude if not of explanation?

Understanding came very slowly. He had acknowledged to himself that Cassa had married the man in Carrick-on-Shannon to be safe from her sister. She had told him that even now a terrible fear of Nicole dominated her life. He could not recall what last words he had said when he was leaving her a few hours ago: some sort of instruction; some sort of plan? All he could remember now was the expression on her face when she realised that Nicole had come back. They could so easily have walked into his house arm-in-arm to be faced by the enraged Nicole. Now, with a feeling of helpless dejection, he could just as easily imagine Nicole rushing at Cassa's face to claw it. He could imagine the faces of his children. The injustice he had done to Cassa when he condemned her to work for the nuns in the hospital. He had known that he was making use of her even while he longed to possess her for himself. He admitted now that it was a form of possession, having her work for him, having her under his command. Had he ever stopped to think, even to see, that Nicole's domination over her sister had daily increased in that time.

He would return to his own house at first light. This time he would make damned sure that Nicole was dislodged for ever out of his family life. Then he would go after Cassa.

CHAPTER FOURTEEN

Mrs Flynn was giving the girls their breakfast in the kitchen when Dermot walked back into his house. There was no sign of his ex-wife. He kissed the girls good morning with a great show of happiness, but Orla looked anxiously up into his face.

"It's all right, Orla. I was up and out early." He turned to Mrs Flynn with his usual friendly smile. "I presume Mrs Tyson's cousins came for her last night. Or did she order a taxi earlier?"

"No, sir. Mrs T. ordered her breakfast to be served in bed – that was a half-hour ago, sir."

"I see," he said. "Thank you."

"I'd like to go up and talk to Mummy," Sandra said hopefully; "I've finished my breakfast." And Orla stood up as well, still trying to catch her daddy's approving eye.

"Run along then," he told them. "I'll be in the study. I have plans, and I hope you will join me, so come down to the study when you are ready."

"But if Mummy wants us to. . ." Sandra began, but Orla chipped in: "It's Daddy's turn after all. We've been with Mummy for the last week in Great-aunt Hilda's house."

That name set off an echo in Dermot's memory of a sixteen-year-old Nicole resenting school in England, but submitting because Sadora was assured that Great-aunt Hilda's wealth would be left to Nicole. He was sure Nicole's expectations still ran high.

"I'll wait in the study. I have some phone calls to make." His voice was pleasantly equable as he watched them running up the stairs. He called out to Mrs Flynn who followed him into his study.

"Yes, sir?"

"I am sorry you have had extra trouble, Mrs Flynn. I like

you to run things in your own way; I have become dependent on you. Thank you."

Mrs Flynn's eyes worshipped him. He didn't have to tell her what was going on, for she probably knew more about his wife than he did himself.

"I intend to take my daughters down to Donnybrook to visit with my mother: that is, unless their mother has some more exciting trip for them." He knew Orla and Sandra loved to visit with their Granny Tyson. "When we are gone, I should wish you to give Mrs Tyson time to arrange her departure, telephone calls and so on. After that, would you lock up, and if you wish to take the day off or have your friend over, feel free to do so. Whatever you wish yourself. If you have occasion to phone me, Mrs Flynn, you know the Donnybrook number."

"Yes, sir." They both turned to see the two girls coming down the stairs, their disappointment evident in their downcast eyes. They stood at the door of the study in pained silence.

"We won't delay, then," their father said. "Perhaps you could pick up your jackets on the way out." In the car he could hear them having a low-toned argument in the back seat, Orla warning her younger sister not to say a word about "things" to Granny.

"But why?" asked Sandra. "I tell Granny everything always."

"Well," insisted Orla, "not today: you ask too many questions, and she would be unhappy."

"Why would that make Granny unhappy?" wondered Sandra.

"I'll tell you when we go home," promised Orla, "and until then just pretend."

Dermot was sad at the thought that the time had come to tell his daughters that he had parted with their mother. He had hoped to have Cassa share their tears; now he felt that they were bound to think that the tragedy was of his making.

He would have to take his own mother, always sympathetic and kind, into his confidence: she would help if she could. Would she wonder how it came about that he was away with Cassa? All so innocent, but how to say that calmly when the very thought of Cassa made his heart turn over. Dermot began to wish he were back in his office, behind his big desk doing the business he was best at, calculating how to make another million. From his office desk, under the portrait of Elvira, he would figure a way to get Cassa back to his side. He had the phone number on her letter, if that was where she was. She had said that her husband gave her the feeling of safety – come to think of it, that was about all the mention she had made of the husband. When she was with me, alone with me, she was safe and so contented.

Mrs Tyson was delighted to see her son walk in through the door. Another son, Thomas, had told her lately that Dermot's golf showed signs of worry; he'd go further and say signs of distress. She reckoned it must be nearly three weeks since Dermot had called. She adored her youngest son, his looks, his brains, and the two wonderful little girls he had produced. An enormous fuss was made, with big hugs and kisses all round. The girls asked to run out into the pub to see their grandad and the "lads" who worked behind the bar. This was always allowed unless the pub was too busy, but it was seldom too busy for the gorgeous grand-daughters to be shown off proudly. The old man used to get their names mixed-up when they were little, but now he had got them "sorted", as he said every time he saw them. The girls loved him, as indeed everyone who knew him did. His was the most popular pub on the south side of Dublin, and had been for many years.

"You'll take a drop of whiskey, son?" his mother asked fondly. She handed a glass and indicated the syphon of soda. "And the three of you will stay for your lunch, if you've nothing better to do."

He took the glass, but he did not put any whiskey in it. Too early in the day for whiskey, and there were the girls to drive home, eventually.

"I'm just back from a week in the west," he said.

"Were you in Galway? I hear it's changed, and I'm glad – we were poor long enough. Did you go out to Clifton?"

"I did," he responded, watching her bright eyes. "I went out in a motor-boat for a trip around the islands."

"In a public motor-boat? But haven't you a big boat for yourself at Erislannan?"

"I wasn't on my own," he said. "I brought a friend, Nicole's sister, Cassa."

It took a moment for this to sink in with all its implications. "And the girls?" she queried. "Were the girls there, too? I bet they loved the motor-boat."

"Cassa and I went, the two of us; she was having a little holiday after a long illness."

"Begin at the beginning, Dermot love."

"I didn't want to break your heart, Mum, with a lot of sad happenings, but you know that Nicole has been in America almost a year, and you probably suspect that we were not getting along."

Mrs Tyson nodded her understanding. In all the years of Dermot's marriage, she could count the number of times Nicole and she had exchanged a friendly call. Family occasions very rarely included that daughter-in-law. One doesn't question these things, and rumour around Donnybrook had it that Nicole did a lot of charitable work with the bishop.

"Six months ago, Nicole and I effected a judicial separation."

Dermot let this be taken in, and then he added, "It cost a great deal, but I was given custody of Orla and Sandra. Nicole may visit with the Gilbey cousins and see the girls. She cannot take them out of the country."

Mrs Tyson appeared shaken. "But isn't it her house you have all lived in since you were married?"

"It was; now it is mine. I bought it outright for the girls' sake. It is their home. When they are of age, they may decide for themselves. Don't fret like that, Mum; we were quite happy up to now. I think they were getting used to their mother's absence. Now, however, she is back from America."

His mother took his hand and stroked it fondly. "Something has gone wrong, son. Isn't Nicole's sister married and living in the north?"

"Yes, Mum, Cassa lives in Carrick-on-Shannon, and I need your sympathy for her. Six months ago, she had her first baby. The baby was born dead. I think she has had a breakdown, and that is why she came down to Dublin for a little holiday. As she said herself: her native place."

Mrs Tyson was quick and compassionate. "And the poor little love was staying in your house when Nicole arrived, was that it?"

"No, Cassa was not staying in my house; I had left her home to her rented apartment when we came back from the west. When I got home, Nicole was waiting for me. Orla and Sandra had told her that I had taken Cassa away for a little holiday."

He could read his mother's face: she didn't know what to make of this turn of events.

"That's not all, Mum. I haven't told Orla and Sandra about the separation. Sandra may be thinking at this very moment that her mother has come home for good. I think Orla may have heard whispers at the Gilbeys. I wish with all my heart that I had prepared them for this before Nicole showed up. Will you help me, now?"

Her kind, loving eyes were a reassurance. "Don't call them in from the shop," she said sadly; "let them come of their own accord and be at their ease about the place. I'll be here with you when you are ready to tell them."

"And you'll help me, Mum? I'm scared of breaking down, and Sandra is such a sensitive little thing."

"They both are. They'll both need your making up to them every minute. Try not to say anything about not loving their mother any more, even if you have parted – that hurts too much. Sit over there in the armchair, son, and settle your mind on what you'll say. I'm going to the kitchen to make sure Nellie and Katie have included three extra for lunch. The lads get their grub in shifts, and we'll wait until their time is up." She was drying her eyes as she went out.

Abstractedly, Dermot Tyson sat gazing out at the traffic on Belmont Road. Strange to be sitting here idly, for his normal days were packed with business affairs, and in this his nature was satisfied. House, wife and children were the other half of his world. In the last six months, he had accepted the attenuation. What had changed? The casual reappearance of his wife, as if there had been no law to stop her? Or, more importantly, the possibility of drawing Cassa back into his daily life? Cassa, Cassa, Cassa; there had never been anyone else. She had been there always, always a beautiful cameo of childish beauty, black-lashed brown eyes, tendril curls tucked into a schoolgirl beret. . .

It was not new to dream of Cassa, but today his mind should be set on his children, the dearest little persons in his world. How best to choose the words that wouldn't hurt? They were still only children, although Orla at fifteen pretended to be quite grown-up. But Sandra? She had an idealistic baby memory of how Mummy had petted her and laughed along with her. He had that memory, too, of Nicole at her most loving, deliciously daring him to her fantastic notions of deviously sensual actions. A driven fantasy, no time for tenderness. That was a long time ago, and since then Nicole had changed, or was it he who had changed? He had grown tired of her, grown older into his middle years, grown out of the lustful driven exertions, and that was many months before everything changed in both of them from the death of Richard Blake. That night his own passion for Cassa had come to full strength, and within a few days Richard Blake's will had been read without a single mention of Nicole. The will had made Cassa accessible to him. She was left all alone in a huge house in the midst of many acres without the means for the up-keep of the place, and he persuaded himself that he was necessary to her in her bereaved poverty – for almost a year: the year of probate. At that same time, in that damned hospital, Cassa became again her sister's victim as she had been before in their childhood. She had run away from Nicole, maybe she had run away from the husband in Carrick-on-Shannon, and now she had run away from him.

If only he had been honest with his children. If only he had told them that their mother would never be coming back, that he had got rid of her out of their life. He could have explained in simple terms, quite lucidly, the meaning of a judicial separation. They might have accepted that without the awkward question of why. He recollected very well the endless whys and wherefores when he and his brothers were kids. But he could not see himself settling the why with the word abortion. His mother had made a little plea not to say that his love of the children's mother had ended, and he could not bear to hurt them deliberately.

"Daddy, Daddy!" A joyful Sandra came rushing in to tell him that "I was allowed to give change, even out of a twenty pound note! And Grandad had shown Orla how to draw a pint of Guinness. She didn't get it right at first but on the fourth time, she did." Then came Orla, her hand proudly in Grandad's hand, her head held high, obviously delighted with her achievement. Mrs Tyson stood at the door, looking at this family group. Dermot had not been pleased with life for a long time, and it had worried her. He was the most ambitious of her sons, and by far the handsomest, and the nicest person ever with the soft heart of a young lad hidden away inside. She had often wondered about the haughty Nicole: were they suited at all? Had he fallen for the wealth of the Blakes? Who could blame him for that after all? His father and herself had had it mighty tough in the early days. At times, Dermot seemed to have grown into the armour of the upper-crust family, the airs of them; and then he would come home on a Sunday full of his old affectionate thoughtfulness, a wonderful son to his parents. Dermot had never discussed the sale of the Blake property, although it was the talk of the whole neighbourhood at the time. Was it almost three years ago?

When lunch was finished, Grandad Tyson went off for his afternoon snooze, and Granny suggested that Orla and Sandra would like to come into the drawing-room for their usual little chat, which was always about their school and their friends. As it was summer holiday now, she would show them snapshots of Auntie Della and her kids and their new hotel. Sandra sat on her daddy's knee, thinking that she, too, would like a little snooze, but that it would be rude to fall asleep in Granny's house, so she would tell Granny something instead.

"Did Daddy tell you, Granny, that Mummy came home from America?"

"Oh, when was that?" Granny asked. "Was that recently?"

Orla took up the story. "She came for our cousin's twenty-first birthday. We had a big party in Great-aunt Hilda's house. She lives in Delgany, but she used to live in England."

"Delgany is a lovely place. I know it well," said Granny. "Is your Mummy out in Delgany with her great-aunt?"

"No, Granny, Mummy is at home in our house. She was having her breakfast when we were coming to see you."

Sandra came wide-awake suddenly. "Will we be going home to Mummy now when we leave Granny? Will we, Daddy?"

Dermot drew in a long, fearful breath. "No, darling, I have an idea she is returning to America. . ."

Sandra had jumped down and run over to her Granny's arms, pressing her face into her soft, blousy bosom. She didn't want to cry, but two big tears were slipping down her hidden cheeks. She didn't want to think, but thoughts were there, and she hoped desperately that Granny would banish them.

"Is that true, Daddy?" Orla asked, and she, too, put her arms around Granny. "Is it true for ever?"

"I should have told you before. I wanted to, but I didn't want to make you sad. I was putting it off because. . . because. . ." His voice broke as he had feared it would, and he couldn't go on against the soft sighing sobs of poor little Sandra. His pleading look was almost too much for his mother, who was all too painfully aware that she had no idea of the full picture. Loving her son as she did, she sought around for the words.

"There, there now, don't go getting upset. You know you are the loveliest girls in the whole world, we all love you the best. Hush up now, pet, don't cry like that, everything can be explained. It'll all come right. . . It happens to us all, folk go away and there's no cure. Orla, lovey, go on over to your daddy. People mean to go on for ever and ever, and sometimes that doesn't work out for them. Give your daddy a hug and help him, that's a good little love." The tears were running down Granny's face, too. Somehow that helped, and Daddy's brimming eyes, too, touched the girls' hearts.

In a trembling, choked-up voice, Sandra asked, "Will we never see our Mummy again?" And Orla's eyes filled with the hope of his fervent denial of "never".

Dermot found a bit of courage somewhere. "Of course you will, darling. She will always be your mother, and she will be back in Ireland, and there will be more parties. It's just the way we fixed things, you know, so there won't be too much change, like school and. . . things. . ." His voice let him down, and he knew he wasn't making sense.

"But she won't be coming in to say goodnight every night, will she? She used to come in to show us her new dresses for dances and dinners, and things. . . and for us to get the scent of her new perfume." Her sweet little face went back into the softness of her grandmother's bosom, and she cried with a heartbreaking abandon.

"Sure, wouldn't it be a grand idea for the two of you to stay here with me and Grandad just for tonight? We'll keep each other company, and Daddy will come for you in the morning. Remember the last time you stayed over, and you were so comfy in Daddy's old bedroom? He can stay, too, if he wants, there's loads of room. Your Auntie Della left a lot of videos, the kind her children like. Of course, her children are all boys, and you can tell me if those videos are just boy-stuff. They always leave their pyjamas here because Della knows I'll keep them safe in the hot press and she won't have to pack them every time she runs the boys up to Dublin. Like yourselves, they love to be left with Grandad in the bar. He tells me they are not nearly so clever as his Orla and Sandra, although they are near and about the same age, and to tell you the truth, they haven't got as nice manners as you two. . ." Her kindly voice went chattering on to fill the emotional gap and give the girls a kind of challenge to get them over the initial shock.

Dermot Tyson had always prized his mother, and now he felt an enormous gratitude, conscious that he would have been lost without her. There would be storms of tears ahead, he was sure of that, but perhaps he would be able to cope now they knew the worst. Would they blame him? He felt a depth of humility and wonder. It was the single aspect of the separation that he had not seriously taken into account, the children's absolute need to know that their mother loved them. He was a victim of his own blindness in more and more ways. Irredeemable? He had a long way to go.

It was a relief for Dermot to be leaving the girls in his mother's care, because Nicole might be still there waiting for another attack. He would be back in the morning, he told them, and they would all do something nice for the day. They could think about it overnight and give him a surprise, but he knew he sounded limp and unconvincing. Their goodnight kisses were not quite cool, but formal, as they turned back to the drawing-room and the videos.

His mother came out to the car, and she reached up to kiss his cheek. "Videos won't cure anything, but they'll distract them for an hour or so. Try not to be too worried, son. I'll tuck them up warm and I'll stay with them until they drop off. I love them, too, just the way we loved you. Take care of yourself!" She waved after the car, but not in her usual way, and in his rear mirror her sadness was evident.

CHAPTER FIFTEEN

To John Gowan the change in Cassa was immediately remarkable. He was glad, of course, but he was puzzled. She accepted without any show of surprise that he had come home so late he did not want to disturb her sleep. In the nights that followed, they went to bed as they had done since the birth of their dead baby, pleasantly silent. Cassa had never initiated their lovemaking. She had always appeared to accept his words of love, and his overtures had seemed to be welcome, but now he found himself adoring her from afar. She appeared more beautiful than before, but infinitely self-contained. He began to wonder if he had ever known her. The tragic barricades of reservation which he had accepted before she went to Dublin were now even more difficult to move aside. The former effusive warmth of his response to an endearment from her, of her casual use of dearest or darling, now froze on his tongue.

They got the conversation of their couple of weeks apart out of the way within the first week. That was easy. She mentioned the beauty of the west of Ireland with enthusiasm and a nice choice of adjectives. He told her he had been over to Colgagh, and while some might call that place very beautiful, he found it wild and windy. She related the trip in the motor-boat, and he said he had had dinner in a good hotel in Sligo and that it was a better dinner than it used to be over there. She recalled for him the pleasant apartment arranged for her by Dermot Tyson. He gave her a tip or two about the plans he could very well be thinking up for summer houses in Colgagh. She said how remarkably kind and thoughtful her sister's husband actually was, not what she had expected, not what she had been led to believe. John Gowan did not find it appropriate to mention his new-found friendship with the young teacher. Cassa talked about her delightful nieces, and John gave her a detailed account of all the extra staff he had taken on for the next eight weeks. She smiled and said that was good, and she clung to anything that was good to keep the image of her sister out of her thoughts, to keep at bay the phrase which scribbled itself across her mind: now Nicole knows.

Cassa walked every day down into the town, admiring Carrick, which was so completely different from any other town, so idyllically positioned with its houses flowing down to the water. She stood on the bridge over the Shannon and whispered hopeful wishes into the flashing river to be carried down its mighty length into the Atlantic, rushing along past the western country where she had known a strange, fulfilled happiness only a few days ago. Somehow the rippling water in the shower at Aylesbury Road had carried her regrets away more easily. Why was that? Perhaps I don't belong here, was her sad conclusion, but I used to feel safe here and almost disregarded by the passing scene. Safe with John and with Melia Tracey and her nieces. Never my nieces, though, and maybe I'll never see Orla and Sandra, ever again. Every day she told herself that she had nothing to fear and nothing to regret, yet when she came back to the house which she must now call home, she saw again the familiar furniture which had been the pride of her mother Sadora in their beloved Firenze. Worse than that, the chairs and tables, pictures and antiquities had all been so boasted of by Nicole; boasted of and coveted. Why, oh why, did I let John persuade me to bring all that stuff here to haunt me? My piano would have been enough to remind me of Papa; it was all I ever thought of as mine. Close to tears, she reflected that months had passed since she had opened it. I played for Frank, and John went off to his office leaving us alone for hours. I played and we talked and I played again. He knew all my secret memories and hopes and fears. I never really talk to John. Not that I don't like him, and

114

indeed I would trust him with my life; it's just that he's my husband, and we take each other for granted. That is what it is, isn't it? That is how married people are, I suppose, with no need for confidences. He used to use love-words, didn't he? And I took them for granted. Now I cannot remember the things he said. All a part of being married, a kind of submission. Yes, I remember now, John said marriage was a way of life.

She had had this guilty thought before, of her failure to observe the vows. Honor and obey were easy. She must begin again now and make sure to love as the marriage vow ordained; love in that sensually gratifying way a man must be loved. John was a nice man, a fine-looking man, and kind and good, and she really had come to like his way of speaking, the forthright way he pronounced whole sentences with hardly a pause.

Without warning, Dermot's face came before her eyes. He was so extraordinarily different from any man she had ever known. Dermot Tyson's eyes were a greeny colour almost like the colours in the river as she leaned down over the bridge as if to get closer and closer.

Cassa concentrated on the slightly upward incline out of the town to her own residence. Deliberately she walked with ease and grace to calm the small turmoil of this urgent necessity to fulfil the vow of loving her husband. Being loyal, being faithful, and enduring the intimacy of the act – above all allowing the good thoughts to dwell on the bad thoughts of facing into another tragedy.

Melia Tracey bustled out into the hall to meet and greet Cassa. "Ah there y' are, there y' are, Mrs Cassa! I was watchin' the sky, wondrin' had you the right coat. The rain is threatnin' all mornin'! Come in, come in. The fire is blazin' in the room and I have the dinner just on the turn. You'll enjoy it: a drop of soup and a nice rack of lamb and the veggies you like. Mr John phoned to say he'd join you for a bit of lunch. Ah willya look at you now, nothin' like the Carrick air to bring the roses back in your cheeks. Now Mrs Cassa, over here! That's right, you'll be comfortable there and take a breather before his lordship arrives. Slip off your shoes, and I'll give your feet a little rub."

She exhausts me, Cassa thought, smiling dutifully. She means so tiresomely for the best, and I'm an ungrateful wretch. "Thank you so much, Melia, you are so good; you must not worry so. I'm grand now, so I am."

"Sure, wasn't I nearly forgettin' to tell you, Mrs Cassa. Glory be to God, I'm losin' me memory. I'll be forgettin' me own name next. Aggie has phone calls written down for you. I'll send her in. Arey'all right now, Mrs Cassa?"

Aggie had a special notebook in which to enter phone messages, and she took a pride in her clear writing and careful recording. Melia Tracey was apt to remark on every suitable occasion that Aggie's notebook could be produced in a court of law. Now she had four messages for the mistress, and speaking with great care, she detailed them. One was from John, looking forward to seeing Cassa at lunch. The next was from Dr Eoin, to say he would like to call over and welcome Cassa home, and hoping her holiday had been great. The third gave a Dublin number which Cassa didn't recognise, and the fourth left another Dublin number.

Aggie was quick to see that Cassa didn't know the numbers. "That last number was a lady's voice, Mrs Cassa, and she sounded very impatient when I had to repeat three times that I was sure you were not at home; that, yes, you had come home from a holiday; that you might be at home later in the day. Twice I said that, Mrs Cassa! Then she musta just dropped the phone, no goodbye or anything!"

Cassa's heart sank. That could only be Nicole.

"And the other number was a man's voice, you know the kind of voice you'd hear on the BBC radio, and very polite,

116

said he would ring again." Aggie held the notebook out for Cassa's inspection. "I'll leave the book beside the phone in the hall, if you like, Mrs Cassa? Will I do that, Mrs Cassa?"

Could that possibly be Dermot phoning?

Cassa came out of a kind of daze. She had never received personal calls here except from John, and then merely to say when he would be home, or if he would be delayed, or to go ahead without him. "Yes, yes, Aggie, that would be great. You are really most efficient, most businesslike. So clever. Thank you so much." Suddenly she stopped, conscious that she was overdoing the thanks. "Yes, indeed!" They both heard the unmistakable purring of the Bentley outside the window. Cassa rose to be ready with a welcome, and Aggie hurried away with her book.

The kiss at lunchtime was restored today, and they were each ready with a gentle hum of conversation to fill any possible gaps. John had made an inner resolution not to participate in the previous prolonged silence, and he had no way of knowing that Cassa was turning over a new leaf. As they collided in their attempts to please each other, they realised this and they smiled it off.

"There is a thing I was going to ask you, darling, if you have the time?"

"Cassa, you know I have loads of time. I'm just waiting to be asked special favours. What did you have in mind?"

Cassa had made a decision when Aggie was telling about the phone calls, but she made a slowness in her voice as if it were a long-thought-about subject: "Do you think you would have time some day soon to take me to whatever dealer you know, to buy a car. . . I mean, I would like to buy a car."

If he was surprised, he didn't say so. "Of course, Cassa. I am sure a car would be handy for you." He gave her a little grin. "I am sure you are tired of the old Bentley!"

She leaned across and patted his hand. "I have driven it so very often, John! I felt pretty good in that little car you

117

hired for me when you thought I had forgotten how to drive. What was the make of that car? A Ford something?"

"It was a bit small, wasn't it? Wouldn't a heavier car suit you better, be more comfortable? They always have a good selection down at Dolan's, and you could test drive any car to see what you would prefer." And he talked on about cars and car dealers in his easy style.

Cassa was very pleased by his unquestioning response, but then that was John, and that was one of the qualities in him which had always made him so nice to be with. Frank had remarked often on that very characteristic during their long summer days in John's cruiser. She noticed that Frank had resumed his place in her memory since she had come back to Carrick-on-Shannon, perhaps because he had loved this place so much. As he had said to her, his brother's house was his home when he was thousands of miles away, the only home he had. Resumed his place? But changed a little, a more peaceful place in the last few days, as if her heart had been released from the vow of silence he had imposed on it.

"So, how would that appeal to you, Cassa? Or would some other day suit you better? You could compare what Dolan's have with what Comerford's are offering – it's a much bigger place, but I have always found Dolan's a fair place to deal, when it comes to guarantees and prices. . ." He had let his words run on, while she had gone silent. "Would Saturday be a good day for us to go down and look at cars? Saturday, Cassa?" Then she woke up, and the deep brown eyes filled with a loving light that cheered him immensely.

She came around the table and pressed her face to his. "You are the best and nicest person. I love that plan, and when you come home this evening we will fill in all the dates and the details on the calendar."

Cassa went upstairs to sit in the bedroom that afternoon. It was a lovely room with the big casement-window looking down over the river. She never tired of that river. Sometimes she came here to read, far away from Melia's radio; today she thought a mixture of thoughts. So, without any protest in this year of 1984, she would have again the freedom of her own car. There was another car out in the garage, but she had never asked for it because that was Frank's car. Melia Tracey would not have approved of the use of Frank's car. Like his room down the corridor, Frank's possessions would always be sacrosanct.

In her own car, she would possess the means of escape if she ever needed to escape from Nicole, who now had her phone number. Her sister now knew that Cassa had been with Dermot for a week in the west. To think of the days with Dermot could set her mind flying like snowflakes, but to consider that Nicole now knew everything would turn the snowflakes into a blizzard. But she must consider: she was sure that that had been Nicole on the phone, and a phone call in Firenze had always been followed by a visit. That Nicole might have gone back to America, that Nicole was a judicially separated wife who walked back into her family and would probably walk out again – all these things should be as nothing to Cassa, but she could not convince herself. She was convinced that, as in their childhood, her sister was on the warpath.

The vision of an enraged and screaming Nicole in this soft, quiet, comfortable household terrified her. The sale of Firenze would fuel Nicole's fury, as would the sight of the furniture in this room and all through this house, and the pictures and the porcelain and the mirrors – everything so beloved of Nicole, and so sacred to the memory of their mother, Sadora Gilbey Blake, and to all the titled Gilbeys. So many times in their childhood in Firenze, and up until the probate of Papa's will, had Nicole strutted around the great drawing-room in Firenze counting her possessions, estimating their value, talking of herself as "the Blake-Gilbey Heiress".

Nicole would have her revenge. The luring of Dermot Tyson was Cassa's final lamentable act. The innocence of the small holiday would have been reconstructed as a three-week honeymoon of unmitigated lascivious pleasure.

I have my husband, John, though, Cassa thought, and with his help she cannot harm me now. I have not been fair to John. I must have him on my side. I will begin this very night and show him what a loving wife I can be. Her heart quailed at the thought of forcing herself on a good man for such a selfish motive. She repeated aloud the vows she had taken at the altar: to love, honor and obey. They had been through the motions before... before... before... and then the horror of the birth swept over her once more. It was an image she could not endure nor speak or think about.

Now she fought against trembling tears as she heard footsteps on the landing and a knock on her door. It was Aggie: "There is a phone call for you, Mrs Cassa. He asked if you were at home, and I said you are. The same as this morning, I'd say."

For a moment, Cassa was tempted to plead a headache. "Right, Aggie, I'll be down in a minute."

To have the phone beside her bed in the Aylesbury apartment had been heavenly, so why not here? She had asked for a car, why not a telephone extension? What would John think of that? From the second flight of stairs, she observed that the kitchen door was ajar and the radio much lowered.

"I am sorry for the slight delay. In this house there are two flights of stairs down to the telephone in the entrance hall. This is Cassa now. . ."

"Sweet girl, I get the message; I am to be satisfied with your discreet replies."

How could she not have known that she was longing for the sound of his voice, the familiarity of the accent? She had to steady her hand on the receiver. "Yes," she said.

"Dearest girl, I am so glad you are safe and sound. I waited for a call to put me out of. . . worrying myself sick. I realise that is difficult, is it?"

"Yes," she said.

"Do you regret our time together, dearest?"

"No," she said.

"You know I love you, Cassa."

She paused and then, "Me, too," she said.

"Thank you, dearest, I needed to hear you say that. Thank you. Could I have stopped you from. . . running away?" His voice was so tender.

"Not then," the two small words conveyed to him two heartbeats.

"She has not gone back to America, Cassa." It was a warning note now.

"I know," she told him.

"The children had shown her your letters, the letter-heads with your address and your phone number. They were so proud of telling her about Auntie Cassa, and so delighted when she wrote it all down. They thought you would be coming back and, there would be a great reunion, a family celebration."

"I guessed," she said.

"That means she has phoned. Has she, Cassa?"

Her answering tone had become a shadow, and he knew that tears were not far away. "Yes, today."

"Dearest girl, this is all my fault. Will you come back down here? I could protect you here. I am completely to blame; I had never dreamed. . ."

"No," she said with an effort. "No on both counts." It hurt that the great big man of substance and power and handsome looks could be brought down to a helpless voice on a phone. She forced out a kind of plea, "Your office phone tomorrow?" and she put the phone down.

As she went up the stairs, she heard the radio coming to

life. She smiled wryly. The simplicity of the curiosity in the kitchen made her feel vulnerable, wondering again did she belong here. In the bedroom, she stood at the window as she had stood in the endless months of her unwelcomed pregnancy in prophetic fear. And after the tiny death, she had clung to this view of the river with the summer cruisers in their holiday mood. Had she been waiting forlornly for time to pass, for forgetfulness to take over? The one place of safe-keeping in her marriage to John had vanished into disappearing time. Now she remembered that last night when they had driven through Dublin city and she had chosen to see John as the one place of safety in her whole life when she should have been alive to him as a future husband. He was her escape that night; she was sure that the time of bondage was over, and he was her refuge. But only recently in another place, a loved family place, a vision of time standing still had opened out like a flower for her to pluck and hold to her bosom: a translucent few days of fleeting time.

Then the black shadow of Nicole came again. At this very moment, Cassa needed to gather all her resources to put herself back in a safe way of life with her husband, to prove herself in the exact kind of togetherness he had aimed for in their early nights of marriage. It is absolutely necessary now that when Nicole comes he will believe that I have been a true and faithful wife. Nicole had always exacted vengeance. Why else would she seek her sister out, far from the only man who knew both sides of both sisters?

Night came at last with all Cassa's resolutions prepared, as a woman in love with her husband would prepare. The mirror approved her choice of attire, her hair was glinting from the brisk brushing, and she used the perfume which Dermot had noticed. She would receive John in the bedroom, and they would go down the stairs together to share an aperitif. She would take his arm in the hall, and she would smile at him with the most loving smile, sincerely conjured up to impress on him her further intention.

Aggie came up the stairs with a telephone message and was quite taken aback by Cassa's appearance. Her eyes stared in wonder, and she stuttered for a few seconds, and then the message came out clear: "Mr John said to go ahead: he was delayed, he will be late." Still staring, she fumbled as she closed the door.

It was long after midnight when Cassa went to bed. In a strange way, John's absence seemed significant. Had instinct warned him off? Had this reconciliation come too late? It must have been after two o'clock when she heard his footstep on the corridor, and the door of Frank's room opening and closing.

CHAPTER SIXTEEN

Cassa had to conceal a smile. As if they were guests in a small hotel, she and John met in their dining-room on the dot of nine o'clock, almost bumping into Melia and her loaded tray, causing her to exclaim, "Glory be to God, Mr John, will ye look where you're goin'!" Then she was muttering apologies. "It's my old knee, it's at me this mornin' – must be the change in the weather."

Cassa and John steered around the old woman, murmuring good mornings and both looking to be amiable. After all her usual comments on the food and the weather, Melia took herself back to her kitchen without the final instructions about enjoying their good hot breakfast. This rare last-minute silence hung in the air.

"Melia is a little off form this morning," suggested Cassa.

"I know what's biting her," John said. "She objects to having another bedroom to turn out. It was late and I didn't want to wake you, Cassa."

"That's very sweet of you, darling, but I wouldn't have minded. Don't worry about Melia. She said yesterday she is always looking for spare work for Tessie."

John seemed glad of a subject for comment. "Would you like Melia to let Tessie go home? I'm sure they could use her at home with the big family they have."

"Tessie is only out of school, and I could think of a better way for her than going home to be a little slave."

"Oh, like what?" enquired John. "Melia might have something to say if poor little Tessie got big ideas!"

"Would you mind if I bring up the subject with Auntie Melia? There are several suggestions I should like to make. Tessie is a bright little girl, who takes a great interest in the conservatory. Horticulture, John, what do you think?" In an obscure way, Cassa was aware that she was trying to map out her own future in this household.

John grinned. "Fire ahead, Cassa. You are the one who knows how to be diplomatic with Melia Tracey. Keep your ears covered. You can tell me all about it this evening."

Cassa had more to say, but it was clear that he had an office waiting and he must be away. It used not to be like this, she thought. In the beginning he used to indulge me. Melia Tracey often said, "He has all the time in the world for you, Mrs Cassa!" Now Melia was back in the dining-room, gathering up, putting away, fluttering over and back, and she had a deliberately preoccupied look on her face as if to imply that Cassa should make enquiries. It had never been easy for Cassa to deal with Melia, who had made it clear from the beginning that Mr John was the Master, with Melia Tracey Second-in-Command. Cassa's personal experience with a housekeeper was based on Sadora's Rules, and one of them was "Never make free". John had his own set of rules which amounted to "Give Melia her own way. She has been around me for the past twenty years." In her first year, Cassa was expecting, and in the second year she was mourning, unfit and averse to asserting authority. On this morning, Cassa had come to breakfast with a new rule: "Make a fresh start." She was intent on making the phone call to Dermot Tyson, and she was hoping for a bit of privacy in the hall.

Cassa asked Melia if there was anything she could do.

Melia looked surprised, as if to say, "Well, that's a good one!" And Cassa maintained her smile while Melia pondered.

"The two bedrooms on the first floor, Mrs Cassa: I was going to have a few words with Mr John. It came into me mind that yourself might decide – not that I would dream of putting words into your head, and of course if it was going to go on as it is, it might be a good idea. . ."

When put to it, Cassa could be as forceful as Sadora. "Perhaps you are telling me that you are not in favour of the late Father Frank's bedroom being casually used?"

Now Melia bridled. "The late indeed. . . may God preserve his immortal soul, may the saints befriend him in Heaven. When I get ideas, Mrs Cassa, Mr John always says, 'You go ahead, Melia. You know the run of the place.'"

"Perhaps you would like to tell me what these ideas are."

Melia didn't hesitate. "About Father Frank's room and all his bits and pieces he left in my charge for me to look after until his next visit, that's what I mean to say, ma'am."

"Certainly, Melia, I appreciate that. Should my husband come in very late, you would prefer that he use a different bedroom?"

Now Melia was confused by the tone of voice. "It's all right by me once in a while, but the other bedrooms. . . if the situation is permanent. . ."

"I should imagine that the use of that bedroom will only be once in a while, during the busy season when the office is working late."

"Well, I never saw it happening before." By her nature, Melia Tracey was a candid person. "Almost every night when yourself was on the holiday, Mr John was out until two and three in the morning – he'll kill himself with work, so he will."

"I certainly hope not," Cassa said in a kinder tone. "If you are in favour of opening up the other bedrooms, Melia, then I personally think that is a great idea. Is there any way in which I could assist you?"

Mollified but still puzzled, to judge by the look on her face, Melia bustled off. "Today is the day. All else is done, taken care of on Monday, Tuesday and Wednesday. Aggie and Tessie have nothing else to do on a Thursday, and I'd be pleased if they had more to do."

Cassa was stung by what was unsaid: Melia's nieces had been brought in because a baby was expected. Cassa should feel specifically guilty, that was conveyed in a backward glance. Actually she was relieved and glad that the bedroom of the dead priest remain sacrosanct. That was how things should be. Later in the morning, Melia and the two girls moved up to the first floor. Cassa nervously hoped they would be gone out of the proximity of the telephone for some time; there were two bedrooms, two bathrooms and a box-room all to be made fresh and usable. With luck, the noise they made and their ongoing chat would cover Cassa's voice.

It would never have occurred to Cassa to remember that she was the mistress here, to banish the staff and demand privacy. Typically, she was prepared to be put through to Mr Tyson by several secretaries, but Dermot answered immediately, and his voice sounded deeply moved. "Sweet girl, are you all right? Assure me that you are all right, please, Cassa."

"So far, so good." But her voice quavered, and she hurried to add, "Just apprehensive."

"Cassa, surely you can depend on your husband to protect you? I ask that, but I feel a total responsibility, and if I could descend from the sky and gather you up from danger, I would. I want you to be sure of that, darling girl. Tell me, what of John? Do you tell him of your fears?"

"Suddenly I am not sure." She took hold of her voice to make it stronger. "Last night I made a resolution to really keep the marriage vows."

"Did you ever break them, Cassa?" His voice was stern.

"No, but I forgot to take the duty of loving in a serious and committed way. Do you understand?"

"Yes," he said with authority. "Yes, and I can guess why. There is a danger, and you don't want to go through it again. I would not let that happen to you, Cassa. I do understand, and I am ready and waiting for you. I would guard and cherish you and worship you for ever, my darling. . ."

"Please, Dermot," she begged, "the concept of infidelity is not an easy thing, I mean, not easy to. . ."

"Listen to me, Cassa. I know what you are saying and I know your purity of thought. At this moment, the only thing worth considering is to protect you from Nicole. Perhaps I do know her even better than you do. I have been told of phone calls she made in my house. It has left me very shaken. I think she will find you and attempt to wreck your marriage. She knows so well how to shake anyone's confidence."

Quickly Cassa said, "On Saturday I am going to buy a car. My own car."

"My sweet girl, now I know how frightened you are. When Nicole turns up at your house, and I am sure she intends to, do not go anywhere with her, no matter what blandishments she offers. Promise me? Take down Della's phone number in Donegal." Cassa wrote it down in Aggie's phone book, always so importantly placed beside the phone with a selection of biros.

"I am taking the girls to Donegal for a holiday in Della's place, in Port Salon. This is an annual event for them, and they love it. We will travel up on Saturday morning, and I will stay until Wednesday. If you think we could meet in Carrick-on-Shannon on Wednesday, phone me with that news. I love you, dearest. Trust me, please trust me."

There was a commotion on the stairs above Cassa's head. "I understand everything," she said softly. "I must go now." And she put down the phone.

She had left her jacket on the hall chair; she gathered it up and went swiftly out the hall door for her daily walk. It would be comforting to go over each word he had said, to stamp the firmness of his voice into her waiting thoughts. That she must act in a fugitive manner because she felt unfaithful was not good. Cassa determined to walk off the bad feeling with all the energy she could command. She told herself that she was childish, still feeling the effect of Nicole's aura as she had as far back as she could remember.

CHAPTER SEVENTEEN

He had said he would come, and Hazel was waiting by her opened door underneath the perfumed woodbine. It was after seven o'clock, and the sun was still high in the sky, turning all the empty fields to gold. She was amused by the urgency of his phone call at lunchtime: he had sounded like a man out of his depth! In the last week, he had been all action; tonight he might get to the words, perhaps to some commitment. A weekend in Paris would be nice. A trip abroad would be great after the weeks of exam papers, thankfully almost wrapped up now. Perhaps the weekend after next. It was easy to fob off Tom Frame, who never questioned anything. Somewhere exotic? She rather fancied Paris, a super hotel and a bedroom filled with flowers: camellias and mimosa, flowers she had never seen and fragrances she had never known. Parisian flowers would be *fin de siècle* romantic, and the cambric nightie interwoven with Chantilly lace ivy leaves would be just the job in that sweet-scented bedroom.

When the Bentley turned into the boreen leading under the big house to her flat, she was ready to fly into his arms and love him with vivacious endearments as if they had been apart for months. John did not resist. Endearments and compliments and suggestions were exactly what he wanted, if only to get rid of the empty feeling that he was not needed by his wife.

Cassa was as lovely as he remembered, as sweetly courteous, as charming as a wife could be, but she had become politely withdrawn. She had not rushed into his arms, and her slight kiss was perfunctory. John was perhaps half-aware that Hazel had set a new standard, less than half-aware that neither had he overwhelmed Cassa on her return. Both had gone to their separate beds. He could not imagine Cassa in skimpy silk, sitting on their bed, panting for him at two in the morning.

Taking Hazel into his arms now, as eagerly as she was taking him, he forgot that his main business here tonight was to break off the affair. First things first was John's instinctive impulse, and his wife Cassa had slipped away from his mind before the sun had set over Lough Key.

From their first meeting, Hazel had summed up the entire incidental experience of John Gowan's love life. Regattas on the river in Carrick-on-Shannon were the opportunities for local young men to enjoy the sights, and the more deep-dyed sights came from some other town, usually north of the border – and safer that way. In Carrick-on-Shannon, a man could get the reputation for being what they called a Lothario – or, with less class, a common necker. John Gowan had enjoyed the hectic river nights until he grew out of them, and grew into the upper ranges of the business community where a man watches his back. Apparently, Hazel guessed, he had married a beautiful woman who had never roamed the streets at night, metaphorically speaking. Hazel was a small bit disappointed that he knew nothing and realised that initiating could be a slow process. The first hungry kisses gave her a fast learner. It was never a matter of love, or a making-of-love; there was no such pretence. They were there for pleasure, but neither did they neglect the compliments. Hazel knew the power of her beauty, and it was a new delight for John to have a woman fawn on his masculinity.

"How did I ever get the idea that you were a homely little thing?" murmured John.

"Oh, but I am," her tongue whispered close to his ear. "Wasn't that part of my charm for you, my pet, all that talk about my mother and my family? It softened your heart and gave me an entry. You like entries, don't you?"

Their murmuring whispers gave satisfaction to their

mutual impulses. They were two of a kind, and chance had told them so. Instantly, they had recognised pursuit in each other beneath the cover-up of the ribbing quips.

"I heard you did your thesis on seduction," John ventured, "or was that your doctorate?"

"When they give you your degree, you have to pass an oral, did you know that?"

"I don't believe you; you'd never pass an oral with me! You'll be telling me next that they expected a demonstration?"

"They did, but tonight is your turn – full marks if you hit the high note." She had a secret kind of kissing which silenced and thrilled and communicated a scourging of desires into far places, so remote it seemed as if desire had not reverberated there in a lifetime. That must have been the case; there was scarcely a breath of sound in their intercourse.

Time actually passes, but who counts the hours?

"Have we left it too late to go out for dinner?" John questioned apologetically.

"Makes me hungry, too." Hazel was smiling in pleasured contentment. To go out for dinner would give her a prospect of introducing the possibility of Paris.

They had been back a few times to the same restaurant; they were now calling it their "Gnashers". The food had improved, and the wine was very good.

John Gowan was not a man for beating around the bush. He lifted his glass to Hazel. "How am I ever going to do without you? You're a great woman."

"Are you?" Her white smile was wonderfully pretty and open and so honest.

"'Fraid so." His tone was regretful. "My wife is home, settling down again."

"My darling John, I am so happy for you." Now she raised her glass. "May I wish you all the happiest years still to come."

131

Somewhat surprised, he said, "You don't have to be so cheerful about it. I thought you would miss me."

"You know I will, John. We have had the most marvellous time together, and I'll miss you every moment of the day. I'll have nothing to look forward to. Nothing."

"I wish it had lasted another couple of weeks," he said, totally unaware of his disloyalty.

Bloody juvenile, thought Hazel, but it's not over yet. "I am going to be so miserable without you, dearest John, that I am going to give myself a tiny little trip – somewhere . . . anywhere – just for a chance to dry my tears." Her eyelashes fluttered down, hiding from him the sadness of her words.

John Gowan was genuinely upset. "Hazel, please don't! I didn't mean . . . that is to say, I was not . . . you mustn't think . . . the thing is. . . you see. . ."

Hazel came around to his side of the table, and taking his hand in hers, she said gently, "I know, John, I know. You must do the right thing. Don't worry about me. In time, I'll be able to put you out of my mind and begin to think again about Tom's concern with getting married. . ."

Unexpectedly, a stab of jealousy shot through him. "That's not going to be soon, is it?"

She looked down at his hand and caressed it with her fingertips. "When I come back from my little trip, I should set a date."

"Won't our friend Tom think it odd for you to go on a trip without him?"

"I won't be telling Tom – this is going to be my own time for getting away and remembering. Tom would say something stupid like 'Can you afford it?' This weekend, Tom is going fishing with his angling club. Nothing about 'afford'!"

The very words "angling club" had always had bad memories for John, bringing back the awful picture of his crazy mother mourning for his drowned father. He shoved the

132

picture away and put his arm around the girl by his side. "Tell me what you have in mind for this trip, Hazel."

She was very careful, and soft-spoken. "Whatever I can best afford, John. I will look into the travel agent's in the town. Is this our very last dinner together?"

"No," he said with a rough note in his voice, "surely I owe you a lot for all you have given me. I mean it, Hazel. I'm not talking about money, but that, too. You have been generous, and I know I was not exactly in your class – you are more than I deserve. Let me give you a little in return. Why should you go alone, and why should you have to afford a bit of a weekend just because of me. I am not sure if I am saying the correct thing, but you know, Hazel, that I . . . I mean to say, I promise. . ."

What half-measure he had in mind was never uttered. Hazel rushed in deliciously exuberant: "You are an absolute darling, John, just the very best friend I ever had. Shall we go back to my place for an hour and, if you change your mind, you can tell me then?" And, she said to herself, we'll kiss your promise into bed. After Paris? Well, who knows what to expect after Paris.

It was even later than usual when the Bentley drew into the yard. He was surprised to see the lights were brightly lit on the first floor. Melia Tracey had arrived in the world years before the electricity pylons, and she remained suspicious. In her view, if the government insisted on electricity, then the public shouldn't have to pay an exorbitant price for it. A floor of the house lit up at three in the morning to clash with the dawn of a new day would never be Melia's work.

The first floor was laid out, as it were, for inspection: bedrooms, bathrooms, corridor – all bore the evidence of a thorough spring-cleaning and were comfortably ready for occupation, the bedclothes invitingly turned back. In one, his robe and pyjamas were neatly folded on a chair.

He went up to the next floor, and switched on the lights. Frank's old bedroom had been stripped: the bed was bare of any covering, and several pictures were lying face to the wall on the floor.

John Gowan's wounded pride raged into a contest with unacknowledged guilt forbidding him to open the door of what was, or had once been, his own bedroom. He turned out all the lights. He went down the two flights of stairs, going out as carefully as he had come in, and got back into his beloved Bentley and drove out of the yard. An honest man in all his business dealings, his private life was his own affair. Right now, rage predominated. His wife had issued an unmistakable ultimatum. No thought for him in all the months he had patiently waited for her to come back to him. Had she any idea of what he had endured? Did she know what men are made of? Effin' stone? No word of any sort – just a flamin' ultimatum! It did not occur to him for a single minute that he was taking the offensive, that his wife had not accused him of anything, much less of adultery – such a word had never entered his mental vocabulary.

The rising sun had turned the Shannon into a river of gold when John Gowan pulled into the Bridge Cove and saw his own cruiser, *La Vie en Rose*, safely moored in his own jetty. Your own possessions, he reflected, can restore your confidence. You can strip off, have a hot shower instead of a sleep, change into nonchalant summer clothes, and with renewed energy, enjoy a breakfast from the nicely stocked fridge. Perhaps consider a day's fishing further down the confluence, in a bypass unknown to tourists.

There was this "trip" to wherever. His heart didn't beat faster at the thought of it, but it would be one way to wind up the business with Hazel. He looked around for the Jameson and took the bottle and glass to the shady side of the deck. Good whiskey was the right stuff for figuring out the way to go about putting a good face on this trip. Secrecy

134

was revolting but necessary. They must leave Carrick separately, going in different directions, or some acquaintance would be sure to spot them rolling away in the Bentley. His friendship with the young teacher would be denounced as "an affair" in the town. Melia Tracey was a devoted denouncer of affairs in Carrick, regaling every detail and warning her nieces that when the cat's away, the mice can play. Melia had made her own of every catchphrase under the sun, that was what Cassa said. Ah, Cassa.

That name seemed to be a signal for another injection of Jameson's wisdom. Melia Tracey claimed she could read minds. No doubt but that she had interpreted, for her innocent nieces, his wife's outrageous ultimatum.

Well, Melia, after this weekend, the mouse won't play any more. Get this weekend trip over, and the cat will move back in. . . He lay back in the warm sun and gave his thoughts over to a much-needed snooze.

CHAPTER EIGHTEEN

When John Gowan had cleaned up, locked up and bid a fond farewell to *La Vie en Rose*, it was two o'clock on a Friday afternoon, a beautiful day of brilliant sunshine. Into the Bentley and up to his office. He would delegate anything of his usual weekend duties to Joan, make a phone call to Hazel and collect a few necessary items from home. They were well accustomed to his having to take off for a weekend during the busy season; if there weren't already a tourist problem, he could invent one. The important thing was to get this Hazel "trip" over and done with. Return of favours, recompense, call it anything at all, probably include a piece of good jewellery. Do that with some diplomacy and make sure to leave her with a good taste in her mouth. No reprisals. Settle back into normal married life which, come to think of it, had seemed a bit more promising since Cassa had had the holiday. A wife would be entitled to get a bit narked at a week of late hours. . . not that he was trying to prove any entitlement, but she had been cold as ice for long enough. Cold, callous and dismissive. Don't get worked up, he told himself. It's over now.

In his office, he rang Hazel. "Your car okay?"

"Absolutely," she told him.

"Meet me in The Beechgrove in Shop Street in Drogheda, between six and seven this evening. Do you know The Beechgrove?"

"Sure. For what, John?"

"Whatever you say, until Monday. Okay?" He was in no doubt she'd think of somewhere; no doubt she had already something worked out. It would probably mean driving to Dublin or Cork or wherever. Belfast would be an easier drive from Carrick, but Belfast was a town you couldn't be certain of, a place full of problems likely to boil over – he could do without that under these circumstances. So, meet in Drogheda and take it from there, to wherever she had in mind, and on Monday it would be over and finished. For secretive schemes, he realised, he hadn't much taste.

When he drove into the yard, he saw Cassa in the conservatory with Tessie. Cassa saw him, waved cheerily and came out to greet him with a fond kiss on his cheek. "We were beginning to worry about you, John. Are you all right?"

"I'm fine," he said. "I stayed on the cruiser last night. It was such a beautiful night."

"Oh, I do wish I had been with you. I was only thinking last night that we should make sure to go aboard while this weather lasts. Perhaps for the weekend, darling?"

She was wearing a smock for her gardening, and she looked young and very lovely. She took his arm to lead him into the conservatory, telling him in her gentle way about her ideas for the plants. It would be so easy to fall under her spell again, to trust her with his life as he had done two years ago, to make love to her in the unaccomplished way he had made love before. He held his nerve.

"Not this weekend. I have to make a trip south; something has come up and I'll be away over the few days. . . Cassa! What's the matter?"

She was clutching his arm, and the lovely colour had gone out of her face. She was suddenly tottering and pleading with him: "It's about my. . . my sis. . . Nic. . ."

"What are you saying? I can't make out your words. Begin again and go slowly. Are you feeling sick, Cassa?"

Tessie had taken off across the yard, evidently frightened, crying "Auntie Melia! Auntie Melia!" And Melia came rushing out, followed by Aggie, and pushed John to one side – men who stayed out all night without as much as a phone call got no respect from Melia Tracey. With the two nieces helping her, they escorted Cassa into the house and into the sitting-room. John was bewildered, but he recognised that

137

Melia made the most of an occasion. He could hear her quacking her anxieties and issuing instructions. He bypassed the sitting-room and took the stairs two at a time; there were a few things he would need to slip into a travel-bag for a rapid exit. Last year the hot sun in the conservatory had a bad effect on his wife, but last year wasn't Cassa carrying their child? Concerned, he turned to go downstairs and heard his wife coming up the stairs; she was coming slowly as if to alert but not to disturb him, and her thoughtfulness touched him.

Opening wide the bedroom door, he put out his hand to her. "Was it the hot sun; was that what it was?"

She took her armchair by the mantel and made a great effort to smile at him. He hoped she wouldn't start to cry; the crying sessions after the death had unmanned him, and he was almost glad when the long silence fell. Tears he couldn't abide. He took a deep breath.

"I am sorry about having to go away for a day or two," he said.

"Do you have to go? Has it got to be this weekend. Would next week do, John?"

"It has to be this weekend. Why, what's up?" He sounded harsh, and her lips quivered. It wasn't like him and he knew it. "I could make all the arrangements for next week – we could take a real break, Cassa."

Her lower lip was drawn in for control, and then she said, "Don't you remember we were going to look for, or to see about, my new car?" Obviously he had forgotten. "You were going to bring me to. . ."

"Oh, is that all?" Now he sounded impatient. A glance at his watch had told him the time: Hazel would have left home and set out for Drogheda. "I'll take you to the dealers on Monday, wouldn't that do? You could be waiting a couple of weeks anyway. They don't sell across the counter, you know." It was a poor attempt at joviality. Why should he feel guilty: she had gone off to Dublin when she felt like it. But he did feel guilty when he saw her face. After all, he knew Cassa was an angel. "Excuse me while I get my shaving stuff in the bathroom."

When he came back, she had gone. He took his bag and went downstairs, intending to give her a light-hearted good-bye. She was nowhere to be seen. Time was getting on. Cursing inwardly, he drove off. Some miles out on the road and feeling remorseful, it occurred to him that she hadn't gone downstairs at all. She must have gone into Frank's bedroom. Maybe he should have brought that up, the unspoken ulti-matum. But, as if he had been there and witnessed the spring-cleaning, he knew now it was down to Melia Tracey. It was exactly the sort of treatment Melia would mete out, like a mother with a naughty son. If he hadn't got himself into this mess, none of that would have happened.

When she heard the Bentley revving out of the yard, Cassa went back into her own bedroom. Listlessly, she tidied up a few things he had left scattered.

If she had blurted out her instinctive fear that her sister intended to descend on Carrick-on-Shannon and present herself on this doorstep, what would John have said? That Nicole would be very welcome? That he would be delighted to meet the sister at last? What way could Cassa have explained to her husband that their married days in his dear Carrick-on-Shannon had been only an intermission in time; that the day of punishment was at hand; that she had always known her sister would come to exact a return of all the money and all the treasures of their parents' household.

As far as Cassa was concerned, Nicole could have it all, every last item, every pound. But that would never be enough. Cassa should have chosen the role of spinster, should have stayed in Firenze, let the old house wither to the ground in the course of ageing years and starved to death because she had never learned to work the system of earning money.

Why had she taken a path out of Firenze and up to this safe house? Hadn't she always known that Nicole would find her, and, if that was the only way, her sister would beat her to death. She recalled Nicole's threat of this final beating when she was four and it was Nicole's eighth birthday: "Tampering with my things." What had she "tampered with" that day? Or what had she done wrong to warrant any of the threats since then? Until now. Cassa knew now why she was going to be made pay: she had stolen the legacy and, worse still, she had tampered with the ex-husband, the fantastically handsome husband who had thrown his wonderful wife out of his domain.

Cassa walked slowly over to the casement-window to take a last look out at the busy river, where dozens of multi-colour flagged cruisers were sailing in the sunshine. Two years ago, she had come to this place for that very intermission now coming to an end, for the intervening time it would give her to be with Father Frank. That was why she had come. And they had had their time, their own precious time, the vivid cruising days of loving Frank, unforgettable and lost for ever. She had admitted it to herself, long before this: the expectant hope of his return from Peru was there always and ardently. Marriage to John could be shuffled off. John was the shadowy stand-in for the man she adored. Frank had vanished into eternity within an earthquake, thousands of miles away across the world. Nothing that her sister Nicole would do to her now could alter the certainty that Frank and Cassa would sail for ever in the summer waters of the Shannon.

She closed the window and shook herself free from sentimentality, for that was all it was. Another day perhaps, in some other place, she would indulge those dreams. She hoped she had learned something in Dublin about being decisive – she sincerely hoped she had. She went downstairs into the hall and picked up the phone. In Aggie's phone book was recorded the name of the car-hire firm in the town.

"You may remember me," she enquired, "Mrs John Gowan? We had a car out on hire a few weeks ago."

"Certainly I remember you, Mrs Gowan. A Ford two litre."

"Do you have that available today?"

"Yes, we have, Mrs Gowan. I can see it over in the show window, all shined up and ready to drive."

"Would you be able to deliver it up to the house? It is in. . ."

"I know the place, Mrs Gowan. From time to time we service the Bentley. What time would you like it – I'll draw up the contract now if you like? For the weekend, is it?"

"Let's say for a month beginning today. In my own name. As soon as you can. Please make sure the tank is full, and oil and water, and two sets of keys. The cheque will be waiting. Is there anything else about tax or. . .?"

Pleased to be of assistance, the garage owner reassured her. "As it happens, Mrs Gowan, before John hired it for you, he put it on his own insurance and we have it on our premium – it's taxed to the end of the year. Do you need two sets of keys?"

"My father always advised it." There was pride in her voice.

Aggie, having a vested interest in the phone, had been earwigging. "Are you all right, Mrs Cassa? Do you require help?"

Cassa could see Melia's alert face a little behind Aggie's head. As Melia herself would say, in for a penny, in for a pound: "Aggie, I am expecting the garage man to come with a car which I shall be hiring, and I shall probably take it for a spin when it comes."

Without giving her time for further enquiry, Cassa sailed up the stairs to her room. To herself in the mirror, she said,

141

"You are coming along, Cassa Blake, and it's time to depend on yourself – you haven't much choice!"

She changed into slacks and her smartest jacket. She never used much make-up, but just to prove something to herself, she tried out a little extra today. Yes, why not? Today she would have a car all her own, which was something to celebrate, to cheer her up.

When the car came and she had put her signature on the contract, she took a small pleasure in the freedom of making out the cheque. She asked the man to go over the gears with her in case she had forgotten since she had driven it before. It was familiar and easy. She turned the car in the yard and drove out, up the incline and away from the town road. When she had driven this car a few weeks ago, John had kept her in and around the town so she would be prepared for Dublin traffic, he said. That was thoughtful of him, and he was a thoughtful person as a rule.

Now she closed her mind completely on John. She would drive out into the country, where she remembered seeing a cosy-looking hotel on the Sligo road. There she would drop in for afternoon tea, and there she would feel free to make her phone call to Della's hotel in Donegal. It would be a message for Dermot, only a message, but the thought that someone, somewhere, wanted her to be in touch was an exhilaration in itself.

She found she was taking a quiet joy in the very act of driving, in the necessary concentration. There were many cars on the road, many strange licence-plates – in July the tourist season was midway through. She liked the quiet air of prosperity about the new houses, mostly bungalows with colourful gardens and with signs for bed and breakfast.

With a new-found sense of shame, she remembered that the tourist season of last year had been viewed from her bedroom window, inertly, without the slightest interest. Poor John, he must have been so disappointed in her. And the tourist season she had so recently witnessed in Galway? All she saw was Dermot Tyson's handsome face, and all she heard was his dear familiar accent inciting her to fall in love with him. And had she?

She found the small hotel. It was late in the afternoon for tea, but the manageress seemed to know Cassa's face and made her comfortable by a window. When the time came for Cassa to pay the bill, she asked if she might use a phone, perhaps not the public one beside the reception desk. "I might be delayed in getting on to the person for whom I have some news," she explained to the manageress.

"Certainly," answered the lady. "This is a slack time of the day in the office. This way, madam."

"I am most impressed by your hotel," Cassa said, trying not to sound patronising, like Sadora in her heyday. "I should very much like to take your brochures – I get a lot of visitors asking for accommodation."

"Thank you, madam. I'll get the brochures at reception. I thought I knew your face: are you Mrs Gowan, John Gowan's wife?"

If Cassa had planned to make a quiet phone call incognito, she had learned something today. Her father always said that everyone in Dublin knows everyone – everyone in the country, more like! The manageress was pulling out the chair and settling Cassa comfortably at the table and the phone, and Cassa was murmuring a rather confused thanks. "We all recognise the great work your husband has done for our tourism, Mrs Gowan. He works all the year round. We all appreciate that, we do indeed. He's a wonderful man for the tourism."

"It keeps him busy," Cassa smiled. "He's off south today on the same track – I'm doing a little exploring on my own."

There was more, but at last the manageress left and Cassa breathed a long sigh of relief. She dialled the number of Della's hotel.

"Tyson's Hotel, Port Salon. May I help you?"

"Cassa Blake here, may I. . .?"

"Cassa! It's great to hear from you. This is Della. There's a guy waiting for your call all day. I'll put you through to him."

Cassa's troubled world righted itself on its axis and came to a heart-stopping thud.

"Sweet girl, are you all right? Where are you? Can I come to you, can you come to me? Dearest Cassa, dearest, dearest, let me hear your voice, tell me that you are safe."

"Dermot, I have been rehearsing what I want to say, but I think I am very shaky, so may I get it all out in one piece?"

"Take a deep breath, pet, and tell me every detail. But are you all right?"

"I am not injured in any way. I left home late this afternoon, and up to then there was no sign of Nicole. . . No, don't say anything, Dermot; let me finish. . . I am ringing from a small hotel, The Culvert on the Sligo road, west of Carrick about an hour's drive. I have a car on hire today and for a month. There hasn't been time to buy a car. My husband has gone away on a business trip. That's about it, Dermot."

"When will he be back from his trip?" His voice was full of anxiety.

Cassa was not sure. "Monday, perhaps."

"Are you going to stay where you are until John is home again? Why don't I join you there? I've been frantically worried since the moment she got hold of your address. I must protect you, darling. It's always been my fault where Nicole is concerned, now more than ever. She has no right, but there is never right or reason in the things she does. I could be with you in a few hours – why not, Cassa?"

"No, no, no, Dermot. Not here! Everybody here knows John Gowan. Not here, not anywhere. I have made up my mind to face this on my own."

He was shocked. He felt with all his instincts that his ex-wife could exact a terrible penalty; he remembered all too well the threats she had made when she realised she had been completely disinherited. She had searched almost insanely for her sister Cassa then. Nicole had taken herself to America when he had left her, but he had known very well that America was a temporary place. Nobody had banished her, and she had not banished herself. He should have known when he got the letter looking for Cassa's address that Nicole was laying out her purpose of revenge. She hadn't needed the Galway revelation; it was just one more flaming arrow aimed at Cassa's guilty heart.

"You cannot face Nicole on your own" Dermot said. "Cassa, it is my fault, my responsibility from the beginning."

But Cassa had taken a firm grip on the courage she had never found before. "No, Dermot, it was never your fault. You weren't there when I was four, and six, and eight, when she was determined to teach me all those lessons I have never learned. I will beat you to death, she always said. And quite truly, she inflicted many, many cruel punishments on me for many years. I should have told on her, but she was my mother's favourite, and my father needed me to be brave and good – he said that every day."

"Cassa, Cassa, listen to me. Stay where. . ."

"It's over, Dermot, now she has caught up on me. She hated me to touch anything she believed was hers. Tampering, she called it. I tampered with you, yes, I know I did. I wanted to – and, dear man, I loved every moment of the tampering. It was as innocent as all the other things my sister accused me of, but it was tampering because you were once hers. Now she has good reason to get me, as she so often threatened. Good reason."

"She has no reason, darling; reason was never her strong point. I am coming straightaway. . ."

"And so is Nicole. I feel her coming presence. If she is

already in Carrick-on-Shannon, Melia Tracey will be showing her around the place where I live, a house full of the
priceless stuff Nicole gloated over in Firenze. No, Dermot,
don't – please – don't say another word. I have not told my
fears to my husband: I have said nothing at all. He would
not credit that I am in dread of my own sister. Maybe I
should have told him. I think I tried once, but a kind of
inbred loyalty kept me back, and I was always thinking that
perhaps the worst will never happen. Now I think it will.
And, Dermot, please don't step in now to save me, or I will
go on living in fear of her for the rest of my days. It is over.
I am putting down the phone."

Her voice had held up almost to the end. She had surely
never made so long a speech in her life. Mostly Cassa's
words were hesitant and gentle. Dermot looked at the
phone, empty of her voice, still in his hand. Her dead father
would have been proud of her: she had sounded so brave
and good and pitifully inexperienced.

He went out of the office to find Della. "That was Cassa
from a hotel on the Sligo road, The Culvert. Do you know
it? Could you book me in there for tonight? I'll keep in
touch with her, and with you, from there. Depending on
what happens, I could be back here tomorrow. Before we
left Dublin, I told Orla and Sandra I might have to disap-
pear for a day or two. Okay with you, Della?"

She put her arm around him; they had always been closely affectionate and very proud of each other.

"Everything will be just as if you were here, don't worry,"
she said. "Here's the Bord Fáilte map: all the hotels are
marked for easy finding. And good luck! Take care of
yourself."

CHAPTER NINETEEN

In the last miles across country to Drogheda, John Gowan made up his mind he might as well enjoy this few days with Hazel. He was immensely attracted to the girl, and she had been good for him. She had taken his mind off what was beginning to look like a failed marriage, yet maybe even now about to be shored up if his wife so pleased. . . Well, perhaps after he got this weekend put to bed, so to speak, and he grinned sheepishly. He had felt a bit sorry for himself – a man needed the odd boost. Since the day of the dead-born baby, in all the tragic tears and in the midst of Melia Tracey's loud lamentations, no one had thought of offering him a helping hand. His wife appeared to accept a kind of heart-broken responsibility, and all Eoin Magner could say was that Cassa would come round in time. How much time? Practically a year, and until the day he had driven her down to Dublin, she had never shared a smile with him. . . much less shared a few hours of hotly loving copulation.

It was not a word he had been overly familiar with before, but Hazel used it a lot. "Let's copulate – just for fun!" And it was fun, a warm comfortable release of energy. He found himself revelling in the phrases Hazel thought up for the amorous caresses she bestowed on him. He knew very well that he was somewhat inexperienced; he had never had the time really, what with building up the business, and he accepted her adoration as his due – that was the way it was with romantic lovers. Hazel had intimated that he should never expect in marriage what he enjoyed in free love; in free love, she said, he could abandon all restraint; free love wasn't the same as everyday living with three meals on the table and the light out at bedtime.

Hazel, prettier than ever, was waiting for him in The Beechgrove. Her welcoming smile was beautiful – she had the knack of expressing candidly deep affection in her glance.

"Lovely to see you, John. I was spinning out this," and she indicated the glass on her table. "Will you join me?" He sat down, admiring her.

"Not just now," he said, "later."

"Are we off somewhere?"

"Well, we're not staying here," he glanced around. "What had you in mind?"

She had an appealing way of arching her dark eyebrows, "I was in hopes that you had a surprise planned for us. For myself, I'd like to go to Paris. I know there's a night flight from Dublin – and there are seats."

This was typical of Hazel, he thought, and he had to laugh. "Isn't it strange that you didn't ring me up and remind me to bring my passport?"

"I would have, but I remembered one night when you emptied out your wallet on my bed, and your passport was there along with your driving licence and a lot of other necessary papers. It's there still, isn't it?"

"Paris," John said. "Why not? We should make Dublin in an hour, and no doubt you know the name of a handy hotel in the city of Gay Paree?"

Hazel's face was ecstatic. "You could have Aer Lingus book us into the hotel."

"They'll do that?" He feigned surprised at such efficiency; it was as if Hazel flew off to foreign cities every weekend.

"And, John, we could ask them to put flowers in the room for us."

"That, too," he affirmed robustly. "Whole gardens of flowers!"

He was entering into the spirit of the trip exactly as she hoped he would. Hazel was not prepared to admit it – she kept hiding it, kept warning herself that a weekend was a weekend – but she had fallen in love all over again. Madly.

Passionately. Vulnerably. And again with a married man. She hadn't wanted to, it was not what she had in mind.

Paris was not new to John. The Tourist Board Management Committee had held the sales group meetings over there and in other continental cities in the past ten years. Since last year, many women in management came along, and occasionally there were wives. Last year he had thought of mentioning Paris to Cassa, but last year she had had no interest in anything he had suggested in the line of a holiday. Her grief covered her in silence. Thinking of his wife made him reluctant to leave the country. Dublin would have done fine for this trip, or Limerick, or Cork, or Kilkenny – a town he was very fond of. One sideways glance at Hazel's pretty face and he said no more.

"Lots of times," she told him, "I have read that Paris is for lovers."

"'Young' lovers is what I heard."

"John Gowan, you are the youngest lover I ever had."

"And there have been dozens, I suppose? Don't start counting, or I'll throw you out of the car at Balbriggan."

"Whatever about dozens, dearest John, you are the youngest and the nicest and easily the best-looking, and I don't have to tell you, I love you ahead of all the others." She made this announcement knowing it was beyond belief for the solid man driving his Bentley, but telling him she loved him in her own fashion. "I bet all the women who work for you are mad about you."

He laughed aloud at this. "Especially my secretary, Joan? I've had a hard time not falling in love with Joan. She's four foot seven inches and weighs sixteen stone. She can run the whole business single-handed; she is (as Melia Tracey says) 'A wondher to Jaysus!' but Joan never told me she cared about me."

At the airport, John Gowan found that Hazel had done a fair bit of preplanning. They were very nicely booked into the executive class, which was so much to her taste that he suspected this was her first time. Making out the cheque, he noticed that the hotel was expecting them, that a taxi would be waiting. His eyes were twinkling with amusement. "I am being very well catered for," he said; "even the perfect secretary, Joan, couldn't have done as well." Yes, he thought, Joan could run the place, and that was just as well at this moment when he should be there getting in hand the publicity in preparation for the Shannon Boat Rally at the August weekend, the big event in the cruising year. That's where he should be right now: in his office, not flying off anywhere.

When they had been comfortably seated by the airhostess, he turned to the girl by his side, giving her an untimed and very promising kiss, his hands touching intimately against the silkiness of her blouse. "Pretty, pretty," he whispered.

"I love the way you kiss," she whispered back. *"Encore, s'il vous plait."*

John needed to sit there, to realise that the rush was over; not concentrating on traffic, he could let the plane take over while his thoughts returned to the rally.

Hazel's thoughts took time to assemble. She would have preferred a week to get ready; the sudden command to be in Drogheda within the hour had jarred. Her actual knowledge of this man was limited to his sexual appetite, and that had taken an amount of stoking to bring it up to her standard. His desire for an ongoing affair must be established within the next forty-eight hours – not only his desire but the absolute possibility. In any town like Carrick-on-Shannon, where your neighbours were always related by marriage to your first cousin-twice-removed, the absolutes were set out in stone. She had fallen for this man, and although she might never get him past his wife's legal apron strings, there were ways to be indispensable. The strategy of implanting compulsive lust had already begun; Hazel knew

150

very well what a man must be expecting when he takes his young lover to Paris for a hidden weekend. He must be given more, unforgettably more, of the delights he had tasted in Hazel's bed. She looked at his pleasant face: his eyes were closed, he was taking a little rest. He had told her his age would be forty-five in this year of 1985, and to her twenty-eight years the difference was considerable, but in those years he had amassed his wealth, and to Hazel that was all the difference worth talking about. She had loved the lazy flicking out of the chequebook, with no raised eyebrows as to the amount of money. No queries at all. She had grown tired of Tom Frame's questioning of every non-affordable, non-necessary item in their days. Tom had his place in her life. A little later on and she would make it a worthy place, but in the meanwhile she adored the unaffordable, and she meant to have it. The strategy might be slightly sinful, but it was a risk that had to be taken.

Their room in the Parisian hotel was all a romantic woman could have wished, and there were flowers: freesias ornately set among trailing green leaves in exotic eastern bowls. The bed was so exquisite, a four-poster with satin draperies. A bit over the top, was John's thought. It was evident Hazel was utterly charmed, although she was the one who had booked and expected the top de luxe.

"Dearest John, do you think that Napoleon and his empress might very well have spent a night here, making-love in between battles?" She crossed the big room and stood within his arms, gazing up at him with adoring eyes.

"I think it calls for champagne, Hazel. Is your French equal to ordering supper sent up?"

Hazel was equal to everything the trip would offer. Eating their French supper and drinking each other's health in champagne left her free to display herself in all her joyful youth. John Gowan, secure in the belief that he was paying a debt to this pretty girl, felt that he could push the boat out as far as it would go. When Hazel's trip was over he would resume his normal life with his wife and Melia Tracey and the buxom Joan, and his beloved business with its very important Shannon Rally.

After a night in the four-poster bed, and a day of Parisian delights, during which they had chosen a gold bracelet, in which at her request the jeweller had inscribed "§ Hazel 1985 §", John found it flattering to walk the streets of this romantic city with so delightfully pretty and so young a girl clinging to his arm. In the supreme comfort of what Hazel described as their Napoleonic four-poster, there was another night of uninhibited delights such as he had not previously known. Unleashed passion gave a man a new concept of his own powerful virility, and he liked that.

Towards dawn, John Gowan was not quite so sanguine about life in the slow lane in Carrick-on-Shannon. When the time came to leave the luxurious bedroom, he amazed himself by asking, "Do we have to go home today?"

Hazel, it seemed to him, was a rock of sense. "You know we do, dearest John. Don't spoil our wonderful few days by starting to make phone calls to your office, and to your home. I know you should, but please let's say goodbye at Dublin airport."

"Why not in Drogheda, where you left your car? I'll want to be sure you are all right for the road, Hazel."

"I may stay over in Dublin for a couple of days. You have the Bentley at the airport, so you can move off straightaway, John."

"Why Dublin?" In some part of his mind, he had stored the notion that in their last hour (and he supposed it had to be their last hour) driving up from Dublin to Drogheda, he intended get up the moral courage to say the words which were essential to gloss over the trip, and he would make sure the words were final. In his Bentley, easygoing talk came easily to John Gowan.

"Why Dublin?" he repeated, and to his further surprise he added, "What's in Dublin?"

Hazel chalked up a silent victory. He was going to miss her.

"There's nothing in Dublin, just that it would give me time to become accustomed to being without you, my dearest. Driving off in the same direction, your Bentley swiftly miles ahead of my little car, I'd be thinking of traffic when I would want to be dreaming over the days in Paris."

And the nights, he thought. "Come over to me," he said, and he took her in his arms. He was deeply moved by her sad, almost childlike, attitude. He knew, now he knew, it would have been a sight better to have left her in her garden flat under that fragrant woodbine. But was there anything to stop him calling in there occasionally, just to say hello? The ice-cold manners of his wife made a fellow go peculiar, and sometimes now he found it difficult to imagine Cassa responding to him ever again. But she had responded in the beginning: they had had a child, they had a son. Briefly, he had been allowed to be a husband and a father. Briefly.

He held a very different woman in his arms now, a woman who knew enchanting ways to woo a man. He had drawn Hazel more closely up to his own height, and she was kissing him slowly, delicately, on his mouth, his eyes, his neck. Her lustrous black hair, not yet tied back for the day, was falling all about his hands, driving wild his desire to lift her up and take her in the big French bed.

"Once more, little girl, once more," and she murmured to him as her hair fell across the pillows, "Once more, and not ever again, dearest John." Never forgetting strategy, fantasy and fornication were woven into Hazel's wishing-web.

CHAPTER TWENTY

When Cassa drove into the yard, she was relieved to see no other car parked there. If her sister had arrived – uninvited, naturally – there would be a large, impressive limousine. Nicole had never been known to travel in a bus or a train; she had gone from a bicycle to a posh sports car. Cassa well remembered the fuss their father had made of that expense – it went on for a month.

Melia and the nieces were out of the back door as soon as she stepped out of the car. She presumed they were there to welcome her back, but they had news on their minds as they ushered her in. Aggie had been very busy on the phone: there had been as many as four calls, and Melia was anxious to assure Mrs Cassa that Aggie had written all these in her telephone book. Little Tessie, who told the world in Carrick-on-Shannon that Mrs Cassa was definitely more beautiful than a film star, had obviously been alerted to some form of alarm, and was nodding her head anxiously. Cassa felt it was appropriate to show equal concern.

"You are so kind and thoughtful, all of you. How would I ever get on without you? Thank you all very much. Perhaps we could share a cup of tea in the kitchen, and then Aggie would read from the telephone book?"

Cassa could uneasily imagine four irate phone calls from Nicole, each one angrier than the first. Wherever you were in the country, when she picked up her phone, you had to be at the other end of the line. It was ever thus. Four unaccepted phone calls would put her in a towering rage. Cassa would be punished. Could Melia protect Cassa? Nobody could now. The unanswered phone calls were only one of Cassa's sins.

"Mrs Cassa, you don't usually put sugar in your tea," Melia said. "Are you feelin' all right?"

Cassa made an effort to smile brightly. "Yes, Melia, grand.

The sugar is nice, at times. Aggie, would you like to read from your book?"

It wasn't necessary, but Aggie stood up to her full height, showing all her teeth in a vast grin, and then she opened the book: "The first call came just after Barney and Joe delivered the car and you drove out. In the region of three o'clock, a little after. I could almost have called you back, if you were walkin', that is, but you were gone up the hill, as you were drivin'." Aggie paused dramatically, giving Cassa time to interrupt, but it was her Aunt Melia who rushed in.

"The mistress doesn't want to be here all night. No need to make such a production of it." The fact that Auntie Melia loved productions was merely incidental, and Aggie knew that. Cassa concealed her own smile and leaned forward to encourage Aggie, who now consulted her book.

"The first call – that is, in the region of three o'clock – was from a lady, a lady's voice. Not an accent from around here, and not the Dublin accent; could be English. She got it hard to believe that Mrs Gowan was not at home, and harder still to believe that me, who was answerin' the phone, hadn't an idea where you were, nor when you would be here to answer the phone. She questioned me about six times, I have it written here. At the end, I said to her that she could leave a phone number. Or a name. That was when she rang off, without a by-yer-leave nor thank you."

That had to be Nicole. "Were there more calls, Aggie?"

"Well now, Mrs Cassa, if I hadn't it all written down here, you would be hard put to believe it, and that's a fact. Auntie Melia will tell you, I was in great doubts to believe me ears, seein' as it was yerself she was askin' for, and seein' as I had me best voice goin' for the phone. It isn't as if I was bein' cheeky or anythin'. . ."

Now it was Melia's turn: "Ye can take it, Mrs Cassa, Aggie was what you would call betwixt and between. She has great patience, has Aggie. . ."

However, Aggie wanted to keep the floor. "Three times in all that happened, Mrs Cassa. I have it all here, in detail. Three times, the identical phone call, only worse the third time, which was at seven o'clock!"

"Worse, Aggie?" enquired Cassa gently.

"Angrier and angrier, Mrs Cassa. I was on the point of calling Auntie Melia when the woman banged off!" The lady had become a woman.

"I am so sorry you had a bad experience with a phone call meant for me," Cassa said. "Did you say another call, a fourth call, Aggie?"

"The other call was all right." Aggie consulted her book again. "It was for you and Mr John. He said Mr John would know him. The father superior of Father Frank's order, he said he was, and he would be obliged if you and Mr John would get in touch with him as soon as possible. He was calling from their monastery in Dublin. He said Mr John had been there and would know it, and he repeated the number three times. I am sure I have it properly down in my book, for I repeated it back to him twice. He was very polite and spoke ordinary. He said to write down: 'as soon as possible'."

"Aggie, you are wonderful, and so conscientious. Thank you for all the trouble and the great writing in your telephone book. You are so dependable. You must excuse me now, I think I am ready for bed. Goodnight, Melia and Aggie and Tessie."

There had been several calls from the superior of Frank's order in the past eight months, since the earthquake in Frank's Peru – her heart soaring in wild hope at the first phone call and beating painfully until her clenched fingers felt her wedding ring. There would be more phone calls from Frank's order with no more meaning than the first one. John would deal with the call when he came home.

As for themselves, they had not been able to share Frank's going. In the same way, they had not been able to

156

share the baby's death. Cassa felt total responsibility for both deaths. That day when Frank came down to the cruiser to say goodbye, she should have been strong; she should have thrust herself on him. It must have been possible to break down his will with the force of loving him. He and she had spent three long months together, hour after hour in idyllic harmony, happy beyond words to give and expect nothing in return. Her marriage to his brother had forfeited her right to remember their glorious summer, that day they had stood watching the sunset over Lough Boderg hand in hand, his fingers twined into her fingers. When Frank went he took all of life with him.

And yet, passing by Frank's old room every night on her way to bed, she was never sure, never perfectly sure that he was not still there. Tonight, after the phone calls, she wished he could be there so she could confide in him her fears about Nicole, of which John knew nothing. Cassa knew that when she entered her own bedroom, foreboding would close in on her as it had long ago in Firenze, when they were young and she had done some stupid thing to send Nicole into a raging temper. Or when she was working under Nicole's management in San Salvatore Hospital and Nicole would come with her own key to the door bringing a humiliating message from the one she called her lord and master. Cassa felt little confidence in her own recent friendship with Lord Dermot, lovely while it lasted but no help now.

She stood in her favourite place by the window, looking out on the flowing river. The coming of Nicole, and there was no doubt in her mind about that, seemed to Cassa like a sentence of death. She thought about the power of prayer, and for an hour or so she concentrated her thoughts until she saw herself as childish. If everything went wrong, could she blame her guardian angel? Then began the questions: what way could she plan to escape from her sister? Would John come home tomorrow so she could creep around in his shadow? Would it be feasible to walk out on her sister, get into her car and drive off? But where to? She recalled the night she ran away from Firenze to find a refuge in Carrick-on-Shannon. Running away was catching up on her again, the myth of safety from a vengeful Nicole. It was fatalistic to think there was no escape, but she knew there was none because now she recognised her guilt. She had played the role of a thief exactly as Nicole had said when she stole a coloured hair-ribbon from Nicole's treasured collection. She was ten and Nicole was fourteen. To be pinched with a pliers wouldn't be enough now. To be again reduced to poverty, even to beggary, would be the ultimate cost of getting Nicole to leave her alone for ever.

She had been close enough to beggary, but in those days she had had Firenze to shelter her. Dearest, darling Firenze. Oh God, oh God, what madness made her sell Firenze? Cassa admitted to herself that the sale of Firenze had given her a wonderful comfort, never known before, including the possession of a chequebook. She had scarcely used it, but it was always hiding in her handbag. Her agitated thoughts stopped right there: wouldn't the chequebook be the very first thing that her sister would demand? And all the documents in Mr Boyce's office. Nicole would find out that Cassa had gone to that solicitor in Dublin to secure a safe position for herself. There was nothing safe for Cassa.

At last she managed to dismiss the self-pity, undressing and slipping reluctantly into bed. She thought of John off at some sales conference. If he were here at this moment. . . Thinking of him, she remembered her resolutions – she would curl up close and he would turn to her. This time they would kiss; this time they would share. There might never be another chance. Strange that none of the phone calls had been from John; he always called if he happened to be away. Sleepily, she missed his warm, comfortable presence in her bed.

CHAPTER TWENTY-ONE

Perhaps today would be the dreaded day. Don't mention to Melia that you hardly slept, that your hands are too shaky to put on lipstick, that you don't know whether to dress in a gardening guise as if all that mattered in the world was attention to the conservatory. Cassa hesitated over the idea that she should dress very sensibly, ready for flight. From her window she saw the river cruisers already afloat under a cloudless blue sky. She knew that over breakfast Melia would comment on the sensible clothes, while giving out her daily weather forecast, advising instead "a nice summer frock, or the flowery skirt that looks so well on you". Melia would rehearse the Queen of England for her day ahead: it was Melia's way, and Cassa was almost used to it by now. The gardening outfit and the shaky look – watch out or you'll fall on the curve of the stairs; hold on to the banister.

Breakfast was always the same, including the forecast, not only for the weather but for each duty that lay ahead for Melia and the nieces. Each day in the week had its own set of duties.

"You've lost the appetite, Mrs Cassa? You hardly touched it." Melia said this every morning while continuing to pile up Cassa's plate. No point in a protest: for Melia to present a meagre meal would never happen.

"It was delicious, Melia. You cook so well." Cassa tried to vary the thank-you words. Then she added airily, "Would it be all right with you if I borrow Tessie for a few hours in the greenhouse? We didn't quite get finished the other day."

Melia was a born begrudger. "I have the silver on me mind. Teresa'd do better learnin' how to clean silver properly – you'd think her hands had the palsy. But, given the day that's in it, a bit on the hot side, she can go for an hour or two. She'll be needed in the kitchen at midday."

Spending time in the conservatory brought Cassa back to Firenze. Sadora had been a great gardener, with half a dozen underlings to assist her. When Cassa was a little girl, their conservatory was the envy of all their friends, featured in the magazines of the time and opened to a select group once a year.

"I heard there is a great garden centre in Virginia, across the Leitrim border in Cavan." Cassa felt she should encourage little Tessie, a shy and inarticulate seventeen year old. "Now that I am using a car, we could go across to Virginia and order loads of seedlings and cuttings for next year. You'd like to go there, wouldn't you, Tessie?"

With a turn of her head, Tessie indicated the kitchen, "Would she let me?"

Cassa realised she wasn't sure. "Of course, your aunt would let you. She knows that we intend to have this place absolutely glowing with colour, with every kind of hothouse bloom that could be imagined."

Aggie came strolling across the yard, her phone book in her hands. "It was the same voice as the other day, was that yesterday? The voice I said was a BBC kind of a voice. For you, Mrs Cassa: I wrote it down."

Today was going to be a day to try the patience of a saint, to quote the usual Melia. "Yes, Aggie, do you want me to go to the phone?"

"Oh no, Mrs Cassa. He expressly said not to call you, 'expressly' is what he said, but he was on this number if you wanted to speak to him."

"And then he rang off?" Cassa enquired sweetly.

"Yes, ma'am. Then he rang off, but I thought it was funny."

"Funny, Aggie?"

"Well, funny because it looks like a local number to me."

"Something to do with the hired car," Cassa said vaguely. "Tessie, could you climb up and lift down the small bag of cactus compound on that shelf. We have neglected these special little pots lately, haven't we?"

I wonder where he is, thought Cassa, and there was a small bit of comfort in the thought, but only a small bit. If Dermot is near by and not in far Donegal, he must know something. That only added to her own apprehension while she was standing here pretending to poor little Tessie that she knew everything there was to know about the miserable cactus plants. She steadied her hand to hold the trowel into the bag and put a small deposit of the compost in each little pot. Waiting was the worst part, the temptation to run away the same as always. Even when she was thirteen, she used to run away from Nicole and hide in the deep woods beyond Firenze.

At midday Melia signalled for Tessie to get back to the kitchen, and directly after that Aggie came out to report a phone call. "That was the lady with the puffed-up way of talkin'." Aggie was enjoying her role. "She said she definitely did not want to speak with you; she wanted to know if you are in."

"And what did you say, Aggie?"

"Well, of course I said you were here, Mrs Cassa. Sure couldn't I see you through the glass door at the end of the hall?"

Cassa had to clear her throat. "Did the lady leave a message?"

"She just hung up, Mrs Cassa. The line went dead. Auntie Melia said to tell you that your lunch is ready when you are. It's a salad, she said."

Cassa followed Aggie into the house. In the cloakroom she washed her hands with a certain ceremony, thinking of the Gospel story of Pilate. Then she took up the salad so nicely laid out on a tray and returned to the conservatory. Melia's face, through the kitchen window, disapproved, but as Melia told Tessie frequently, "There are times you have to stand on your own two feet."

The town hall clock had struck the half hour when the

161

plum-coloured Rolls was driven into the yard, and the three females came in one rush out through the kitchen door, their eyes (as Melia would say later) out on sticks. A very tall heavy-set man came around the big car to open the door for the lady, who stepped out. "Thank you, Clive!" she said in an affected voice.

To see Nicole for the very first time was to be struck dumb, smitten, bowled over, enraptured, captivated, fascinated. She was an accomplished blonde beauty; her hair and her skin and her teeth possessed a collective sheen of brilliance. At an unacknowledged forty years of age, she had a figure and legs of lissome elegance.

"You remember Clive, don't you, Cassa?" In the depths of the polite question was the recognition of Cassa's remembrance. Clive Kemp was no secret, for he had been in Nicole's circle since distant childhood, and Cassa almost curtsied to find him still installed at every crossroads.

"Welcome to Carrick-on-Shannon," she said. "Would you like to come into the house?"

Clive appeared to be impressed. "Is that the Shannon, Cassa? Is that your boat by the jetty? Quite a sight, all the craft sailing by your place. Very colourful – it's like flags of everywhere!"

"They probably are," Cassa replied in the very gentle voice which she knew had always irritated her sister. "Tourists, from everywhere. Would you like to come into the house? Perhaps a drink? Perhaps we could rustle up some lunch?" There wouldn't be many chances to be uppity with Nicole, so Cassa pushed a little further. "Yes, Clive, that's my own little cruiser, although we have several more, all much bigger." Her voice remained calm, but her body was trembling. Don't be frightened of Nicole, she thought, she can't hurt you now you are going to give her everything, everything, everything. It's in my power to give everything that was given to me, and after that I'll never have to face her again.

They were walking towards the house, and the three women in the doorway were backing awkwardly towards the kitchen, still gawking at Nicole in her elegant attire and the enormous moustachioed Clive, who were (as Melia would later repeat) "a sight for the gods".

"Your staff, I presume?" Nicole condescended to enquire.

"Well, we have a man for the yard," said Cassa courageously. "Mrs Tracey and her nieces, Aggie and Tessie. May I introduce my sister, Mrs Tyson, and Mr Kemp." Melia's face reflected the fact that Cassa had never had family visitors in the two years since she had come to Carrick-on-Shannon – and what visitors! Melia came as near to a goggle-eyed bow as was decent.

Cassa led the visitors into the sitting-room. "Do sit where you will be comfortable," and she indicated Sadora's couch with the heirloom cushions while she opened Papa's drinks cabinet. Clive Kemp had chosen to settle his huge frame into what had always been Richard Blake's favourite armchair. He appeared to be looking around with curiosity.

"What would you like to drink, Clive?" Cassa enquired politely.

"I say, Cassa, this room is quite a showpiece. It's like Adams on the Green! It's like something I've seen somewhere. Oh, yes, whiskey would be fine and a splash of something, thanks."

Nicole shook her head at him. "Of course, you've seen it all before, you silly man – it's my parents' furniture from my old home. Weren't you the crafty little one, sister, to hold on to the most valuable stuff, even the piano!"

"It was my husband's idea," Cassa said, "and the piano is the piano Papa bought for me on my twelfth birthday." Here in her own drawing-room in her husband's home, Cassa's voice held firm. "And your drink, Nicole?"

"Thank you, a snifter of brandy. I'm missing some of our pictures from the front drawing-room – were they sold?"

"No," Cassa handed her a double snifter, "there are pictures on the staircase, and in several other rooms."

"The big portrait would look well over that old-fashioned fireplace instead of that mirror."

Clive Kemp wasn't too happy to have been ticked off. "I remember that portrait in the drawing-room in Firenze – one of your ancestors, a very sexy lady showing off her expansive boozalum."

Nicole shook her head at him. "That is Elvira, a titled lady married to General Richard Denton Blake, who is famous in history books; he served the Queen in India. Queen Victoria, Clive. And where, may I ask, have you hung Elvira?" When Cassa hesitated, Nicole added stridently, "You haven't sold the picture of our wonderful great-great-grandmother? Answer me, Cassa! Our great-great-grandmother's portrait, a famous portrait! Sold?"

"I never liked it. I gave it away." Her words came out in a cowering whisper. Cassa half-expected Nicole to throw the brandy glass into her face.

"That was one of the most valuable treasures in Firenze. You knew that: Mama constantly referred to that picture. It was a big item on the insurance. That you didn't like it was not a reason to give it away! I've said it before, Cassa, you are an idiot! You never grew up! You're a fool!"

Just then there was a tapping on the door. "Come in," Cassa said shakily.

Melia had changed into a smart white apron, and her fluffy white hair was drawn back with a bandeau. "Mrs Cassa, we've set the table in the dining-room if the guests would like refreshments. There's a nice salad and the ham I cooked for the weekend turned out very nice, not a bit of fat, and the soup is ready in the small tureen – your favourite, Mrs Cassa. Ye can have your choice of desserts: the summer pudding or the homemade toffee ice cream that Mr John is so mad about. . ." Nicole had risen from the sofa.

"Yes, miss, was there somethin'?"

Nicole was speaking, again with her duchess accent: "We won't bother. . ."

But Clive had risen mightily out of the armchair. "It sounds absolutely fabulous, and I, for one, am positively starving, and your homemade food is bound to be away ahead of the local hotel where we stayed last night. The breakfast is still lodging."

"Clive! Very well, Cassa, we'll share your lunch with you as it appears to be prepared."

There is a cloakroom in the hall, Clive," Cassa told him. To her sister, she said, "On the first landing, just the same as in Firenze long ago, there is a bathroom. I'll be in the dining-room across the hall."

The lunch was very good; Clive Kemp certainly seemed to think so. Cassa's memory of long ago threw up a snap-shot of Sadora commenting on his insatiable appetite, wondering if her cousin Miranda Gilbey ever fed him at all. As Melia Tracey told the visitors, on one of her many trips in and out, "The clean plate is the proof, full justice done."

Clive wasn't short on conversation. He had read all the brochures in the hotel, and he was full of information about cruising on the Shannon. He wasn't going to leave this place until he had hired a cruiser and spent a few days aboard. He was, of course, a sailor, and the Gilbeys always had a yacht at Dún Laoghaire. "I am looking to you to put me into this sport for a few days – you will, won't you?" he besought Cassa. "Give me all the gen."

"That is really my husband's department," Cassa replied in her gentlest voice. "He'll be home tomorrow, I am sure. Why not wait, and he'll see to all the details?"

"What details?" put in Nicole aggressively. "Trust Cassa to make a big deal of it. Why couldn't Clive have a try-out on that little thing in your garden?"

For once, Cassa was glad to have a quick retort. "It's big

business, Nicole. Life insurance and all that. Besides, you have to book in advance and be instructed."

Clive Kemp was courteous in his thanks, a little crestfallen and perhaps a little surprised at Nicole's voice when she stood up and said she was ready to go and they would be back tomorrow.

There was something of the small boy about the big man, as he excused himself and said he would see them out at the car. He rapidly disappeared into the cloakroom. In the yard, Nicole faced around to Cassa.

"You told a lie about the portrait of Elvira. You knew damned well how valuable it was, didn't you? You sold it."

"I gave it away," Cassa replied. "Your daughters will inherit Elvira."

Clive came towering up, affable and pleased after his visit to the cloakroom. Beyond a look of hatred out of her sister's wonderful blue eyes, there was nothing more. Nicole got into the Rolls and it was driven out and away.

To Melia Tracey, watching from the kitchen window and relaying the scene to Aggie and Tessie, it was a strange parting, not as much as a kindly handshake between three relations, which was strange indeed between two sisters – no little farewell kiss. But there was no doubt in Melia's mind that Nicole was the most gorgeous female she had ever laid eyes on. And her rich voice! And her clothes!

Within an hour, Cassa came down the stairs. She had changed into a summery outfit, and she was carrying an overnight bag.

"Melia, I have a few things to do in the town. I shall be meeting my sister there. Don't be surprised if I stay over, hardly had time to talk. Look out for me in the morning. You were so good with that marvellous lunch. I was sorry you had extra trouble. Thank all of you very much. Why not take a couple of hours to rest up?" Melia was on the point of uttering flowery compliments about the beautiful couple, but Cassa promised a big chat all about her sister tomorrow.

Feeling anything but cheerful, Cassa managed a happy wave as she drove out of the yard and headed in the direction of the Sligo road.

She had checked up on the phone number written in Aggie's telephone book by ringing it and being told she was on to The Culvert. She would phone Dermot from the first public phone, and if he were still there, she would join him. If he were not, she would stay anywhere she could. In the hope of his waiting for her, she drove very carefully.

Dermot Tyson had explained in his professional manner to The Culvert manageress that his sister Della in her Port Salon hotel had entrusted him with some requests for John Gowan, all to do with cruising down the Shannon. He himself was en route to Dublin (and Dermot passed her his business card). It seemed that John was away at a conference, and Mrs Gowan was coming along in his place. They would probably stay overnight – that is, if the manageress could book a room for Mrs Gowan?

"I have met Mrs Gowan lately," said the manageress. "She called in for tea."

"Of course," he said; "that is the very reason we are meeting here. Mrs Gowan is most impressed with The Culvert. Did I mention that she and I are in-laws?"

So, as it happened, Mr Tyson was reading *The Irish Times* when Mrs Gowan walked to the reception desk. He greeted her courteously and offered to take her bag and show her to her room. The girl at the desk gazed after them, lost in admiration.

On the other side of the bedroom door, Cassa collapsed into Dermot's arms. He had noted the strain in her eyes, and he lifted her up and carried her to the bed, supporting her head on to the pillows as she fought back the tears.

He was as upset as she was. The situation was plain to him, but words did not come easily; he felt it was best simply to share her distress. He understood that Cassa's tears were for her own failure to earn her sister's acceptance, leading her to run away again. Her sister's husband would never have been Cassa's idea of a safe haven, he knew that, but there was no one else – no husband of her own just then, no family, no friends. He held her affectionately as he would hold his own tearful little Sandra, scarcely allowing his hands to move, and the only comforting whisper that came to him was the age-old, "There there. There there."

In a while, she calmed down and brushed away the tears. "Dermot, lie down beside me," she murmured.

"Not here, dear girl; the staff walk into bedrooms in hotels. Come, we will sit by the table and we will talk." He lifted her up gently and settled her into a bedroom chair by a small table. "I will ring down for tea." Cassa made an effort to look more at ease, running her fingers through her hair and wiping her face with Dermot's proffered handkerchief. "You are always lovely to look at," he told her comfortingly, "always and always."

When the girl brought the tea, he asked her what time dinner was served.

"It begins at seven-fifteen, sir."

"Then please book a nice table for two for eight o'clock," he said. "That all right with you, Cassa?"

After the tea, Cassa was relaxed enough to tell him that nothing disastrous had happened during Nicole's visit. "It was the absolute nothingness of it that got right into me when I was driving down here. Every mile of the road I felt less and less of a person. I had psyched myself up with all the resolutions of all I was going to offer her, and all I was able to give them was lunch!"

"Were the Gilbey cousins with her?"

"No, I wish they had been! It was that odious Clive Kemp.

He's been knocking around as long as I can remember."

"I know," Dermot said quietly. "What were you going to offer her, Cassa? Did she ask for something?"

"I thought I told you, dearest Dermot: everything. Didn't I say that to you on the phone? She can have everything that was left to me."

"I'm afraid that is out of the question, my dear Cassa."

"But I own all that was left to me by my father, and Nicole was left nothing. You know she will never forgive me, Dermot. She will haunt me until she is satisfied. The possessive way she glared around at the furniture today! She turned over my mother's cushions in her hands – I could see Sadora giving them to her; Sadora would want her to have the cushions. She was always telling us the cushions came with Sadora into Firenze from her famous uncle who was an officer in the French army in the East somewhere, and a lot of other things very sacred to Mama, and a lot of Gilbey money which Nicole always said was what kept Firenze going when Papa was so extravagant: race meetings and travelling and all that." It was the verge of tears again.

Dermot took her hands firmly in his. "No more tears, darling. I've been around since Nicole was sixteen, and I know, better than anyone, what she got from your estate. I think you know, but I'll repeat it, that Nicole's marriage dowry was sixty thousand pounds, and in 1970 that was a huge amount of money. My background was a local pub, and the immensity of that dowry blinded me – and the house which was a wedding present to Nicole, not to both of us, but to Nicole. You were seventeen then, Cassa; you didn't know me, but you were the one I wanted to marry. That surprises you, my little love, but Nicole always knew; and that is another reason why she has made it hard for you. The dowry bought me over, easily, because I could not think of marriage without money, and at that time a rich marriage set a man up in Dublin. Your father suspected me, and rightly so. I was full of a young man's greed, and on that night the very mention of your name was forbidden."

Cassa was listening to every word, and she was thinking that perhaps it was true, maybe she had never grown up until this day. All of his experience was part of her life, and she had never experienced any of it.

"Have you heard enough, sweet girl?"

"Not nearly enough, Dermot. Please tell me as much as you can."

"Perhaps it will help you, Cassa, to separate yourself from Nicole, and to judge how best to safeguard your own interests in her regard."

"Dermot, all I want is to stop being afraid of her next move. She will always be my sister, and yet I want to be rid of her."

"I wanted that, too, Cassa; and I thought, as you are thinking, that I could buy her out. On our separation, I bought the house from her at her price, which was two hundred and fifty thousand pounds. I gave her treble that sum in separation money and eight hundred thousand for sole custody. Whatever her lawyers asked, I let them have. She fought your father's will through two courts, and we were still married then, so I paid the legal fees."

Cassa couldn't begin to take in the addition of such sums of money. She made several attempts to speak. "Is it the pictures and the furniture, then? It was John's idea to hold on to all that stuff and bring it to Carrick-on-Shannon; I thought I'd like only the piano."

"And do you play it, Cassa? I often listened to your playing on the nights I called to Firenze to leave Nicole home, in the months before the marriage. When she went in through the hall door, I'd drive a few yards down the avenue, get out of the car and listen to your music until I'd see your father's shadow crossing the room to put out the light. Do you still play?"

Cassa bent her head to kiss his fingers; she had never dreamt of this man's tenderness reaching back into those days when her father sat with the dogs at his knee and expressed a critical fondness for Mozart.

"Will there ever be a chance that I'll hear you playing again?" he asked.

What she heard in the question was his wish that she come and live in his house. The great brown eyes were not refusing him. "I never play now. I must start to practise," she told him.

"Must I wait until you're perfect?" And then he added, "No matter what you feel about generosity to your sister, give her nothing. She would sell the lot!"

"Are you sure?" Cassa asked. "Sell the things she gloats over?"

"It is not a secret that Nicole put your mother's jewellery up for auction in America. The Gilbey cousins were full of that news – they couldn't wait to get home to give interviews in the newspapers. She didn't dare sell your mother's things while your father was still alive. I had your solicitor talk to her solicitor about the fact that none of the jewellery had come to you. I felt sure you would have liked something. You never heard? No, I don't suppose you did. The auctioneers had seldom seen the like in San Francisco. There were items going back four hundred years – close enough to some throne or crown, and Nicole had the documentation. She was always very secretive about all that stuff; she had separate insurance the same as Sadora had – they both knew a lot about insurance."

Cassa remembered. "We share our own secrets," Nicole boasted constantly about her private chats with their mother, and Cassa was made jealous and desolate. "Was there something for Orla and Sandra, something from their grandmother, Sadora?" she asked Dermot.

"No," he said shortly, as if the fact had hurt, "nothing of a family nature."

171

"I am so sorry." Her voice was so sincerely sorry, the expression in her brown eyes so full of sympathy that Dermot was reminded of the twelve-year-old little girl he had rescued out of the traffic at Donnybrook church. "Do you really know, sweetheart, that I have been in love with you for more than twenty years?"

Now Cassa was smiling, whole-heartedly smiling, and thinking that there is nothing a woman likes more in the world than to be told she is loved, and that by the handsomest man she has ever known. They both stood and moved into each other's arms. She was beginning to know his type of kiss: now it was the edge of the volcano, guarding her against the full eruption of his need. This was a kiss of preference, and he knew the exact perfect emphasis to draw a sweet return. He was not yet sure with Cassa, but there just might be a protracting promise. Even if far into the future.

"May we meet in the dining-room? In ten minutes? And, Cassa, please don't lie down on that bed. I don't want to come back and find you fast asleep again."

CHAPTER TWENTY-TWO

Absorbed in each other's presence and not too concerned with the food, they drew out the dinner time until long after ten o'clock. He was an easy conversationalist, and she liked his choice of interesting topics far removed from her present plight. For his part, it was not a task to amuse her.

"What about a brandy to finish the night, Cassa?"

"I'll come with you to the bar," she smiled at him, "and I'll have a mineral. I am going to leave here quite early tomorrow and head for home. You know very well that I was going to run away, don't you?"

"Was I only the first stop on the way, sweet girl? Was that all I am? Your first stopover."

"Yes, Dermot, but more than the first stop, the first fountain to slake my dried-up resources. I feel as if I have stood at the same high fence as long as I have been alive. The fence was still there when I fell in love, when I got married, when I ran away. The abject inability to cope with my sister's hold over me has made me a worthless person."

"You said that before, Cassa, and I am telling you never to say it again. Your poor view of your own character reduces to ashes what other people think of you."

She lifted her dark glance full on to his face in the same sensual manifestation of Elvira's rapturous gaze. Very softly, she said, "What other people think of me is utterly precious, and I value their thinking with all my worthless heart. . . yes, Dermot, allow me that word. Look at me running for help to one man and my worthless heart tied up in vows to another man. . . love, honour and obey."

Dermot wanted to make a passionate declaration. It was wiser to let her words pass now, and think of them later.

When they were going up the stairs together, he asked if he might come to her room.

"Did you think I could do without your goodnight kiss? Yes, dearest, come when you are ready for bed." With another woman, that was a royal invitation. With Cassa, revealed as she was in that Elvira look, he still could not be sure. If he failed to come to her room, she would very probably just drift off to sleep. Dermot knew he would not take that chance. He gave her the time it took for him to undress and shower, and time enough for her to change her mind, to turn the key in the door or put the chair against it.

Her door was slightly ajar; he closed it and stood inside.

"Am I welcome, Cassa? "he asked.

"You are welcome, dearest, but not with the hundred thousand welcomes!"

He understood, as she knew he would. She tucked the quilt against her side, making room for him on the bed. "We are here for one last little talk," she said. "I depend on you to give me more of the courage you gave me earlier today."

Very steadily, he said, "I am going to be there in your house in the morning when Nicole comes." Her face showed her astonishment.

"That is why I am here, Cassa. That's the reason I came from Donegal. You are not going to be alone. I am coming with you. . . please don't say no. . . please hear me out. Please, Cassa. From the very beginning – all right then, from the time I was calling to the house and getting engaged to Nicole, from the first night I saw the portrait of Elvira, I loved you, I wanted you. And, sweet girl, if you could only know how I admire you, your simplicity, your lack of bitterness. Since the beginning, because of my stupidity and Nicole's jealousy, your sad unhappiness has been my fault and my responsibility. I realised fully and tragically where I had gone wrong when, like a humble slave, you reported to my office for employment, and worst of all when you sent an invitation to your wedding. Oh, please

174

don't shake your head like that; this is the truth. Believe me, dear Cassa, I must make up for the past."

The tender tone of his words was almost too much to bear. She turned towards him, her face offering to be kissed, but he drew away.

"If I kiss you, I'll be lost," he whispered. "I cannot take advantage, you have never known the way. . . no, Cassa, no. . . not now, not here."

He walked well away from the bed, making a pretence to examine the bedroom pictures of country landscapes. She watched him for a moment, then she followed him and stood so close that he must embrace her.

"I'm sorry, Dermot. I seem to have become addicted to your special kissing." The funny face she made broke the tension, and they both laughed, almost with relief.

"You won't always get away with that kind of flattery," he told her, lifting her up and back into bed. "We will meet in the morning at breakfast, and we will finalise our plans. Carrick-on-Shannon about eleven o'clock? Yes, my darling, I mean it. I am going to see this out right to the finish." From the door, he sent a kiss across his fingers, and he was gone.

It is recorded in a diary of that time: they both slept the sleep of the blest, happily gratified in the security of at least being under the one roof. In a diary given, here and there, to a little reflection on Sadora's Rules, a little remorse for thoughtless behaviour, a little purpose of self-amendment, there is not a word nor a hint of the sin of infidelity. Strange, that!

CHAPTER TWENTY-THREE

On that Monday morning in July, the dawn flight from Paris landed safely in Dublin Airport at eight-fifteen. At ten o'clock, the Bentley delivered two disembarked and very contented passengers to The Beechgrove in the town of Drogheda. John Gowan had determined on a few placating words with Hazel in the hour's drive between Dublin and Drogheda, and he managed to persuade her to give up her idea of staying in Dublin. He wanted to close the chapter, as it were, sign off and go home. Listening to Melia Tracey's words of wisdom during the past twenty years, the handy phrases were very useful. He spoke kindly about the straight and narrow, and the toeing of the line, and the getting back in step, not to mention covering the tracks and mentioning nothing to anybody.

He covered his own self-consciousness with a bit of light-hearted raillery, and Hazel laughed aloud. "You sound like my father," she said, "but I get the message."

John let it go at that; he was contented to have the trip over and to be back in sync with his wristwatch and the oncoming schedule of the boat rally. Hazel was contented with the trip itself, which foretold hope for a future liaison, and John had turned out to be quite a guy, more in line with her wealthy lover of ten years ago. It was sweet and acceptable to be judged so pretty, so young and so innocently unused as if he were her first. Hazel was aware that John was learning new tricks, and she was amused by his macho cover-up. More than a little in love with him, she was immensely pleased with her trophy of the very expensive gold bracelet. She was graphically demonstrating her pleasure with the bracelet as John was signalling the car on to the main Dublin-Belfast road. He wondered what she was going on about, waving one hand in the air.

Then he was ahead in the traffic. In tune with the Bentley, his mind moved into top gear, leaving Hazel and Gay Paree out of the mainstream. Time now to concentrate on the Shannon Boat Rally, the big event of the year, the big wage earner. This would be the twenty-fifth year of the rally, and there would be a full week of boating, as many as four or five events on every day. On the last day, Saturday, the prize-giving and closing dinner would be in the luxurious Bush Hotel, which always provided a memorable meal. Last year, he had been fairly knocked about when Cassa could not, or would not, come to the dinner. There was a lot of comment: a local girl would be forgiven, excuses made, but a woman from Dublin was bound to be different. In her absence, he had drunk too much and got himself fairly plastered. That hadn't helped with the earful he got from Melia Tracey – on Cassa's behalf, he supposed, but his wife had said nothing at all about his bad behaviour. Actually, he mused, she may have kept up her silence whether or which. That silence! It had withered him.

He got his mind back on estimating the thirty-five competitions and the events suitable for all tastes. The cruisers were his special pride, but the big firms in the business were all catering for the barges this year also. In Uncle Tim's time, there had been many Shannon barges, and the ones that now came for the rally added to the colourful aspect of the competitions. And that reminded him: he had enjoined Joan to be extra careful about third-party insurance. He'd get on to her later today about that and about insurance for the water-sports competitions. And tell her not to overlook the arrangements for the children's talent contest, and especially the Young Mariner competition – that one drew great following. The sailing cruisers now should merit their own class, he would see to that, and in this coming week there would be the necessity to have special classes for hire boats, and overseas visitors. Joan had invested in phrasebooks for the enthusiasts who knew no English; a few specific phrases would have been mighty useful last year!

Coming up the last mile into Carrick-on-Shannon with the mighty river in full view, John Gowan's thoughts were racing in all directions with plans and propositions for the rally. It was like this every year: July went by in a flash until the last week, that was the important one. The last week was counted in days, each day making rally history not only on the Shannon river, but on his own Lough Key, and in Dromod and Drumsna, and of course in Athlone. The Westmeath cruisers carried off many of the prizes, more than the Carrick clubs. In fact, the mariners from Athlone really fancied their chances every year. They brought the crowds, though. You couldn't doubt them – you could bet on them!

Rather than pass his own house and go directly to the office, John Gowan drove into the yard, and he was very surprised to see a Rolls Royce parked in the centre space. Not only that, but the affluent owners of the Rolls were standing out in conversation with Melia Tracey, whose head was characteristically thrown back in exclamatory mode, and the two nieces were obviously in a flutter at the kitchen door. "Effin' tourists" was John's summing-up. They're looking for a safe place to park and Melia is ordering them out of her sacred premises. When John pulled up, she flew over to his car. With Melia on the defensive, you got the full story into your face.

"It's all very well when visitors comes back the second time to say, you know us we were here the other day, but when the mistress and the master is gone away, you can't expect to walk into the house as if you owned it and be waited on hand and foot and expect to be inspectin' all the things which is not for you to say what's what and walkin' around like the sanitary inspector to see if the place is workin' right or is it under water when the river has overflowed. . ."

He had seldom seen Melia Tracey so worked up, and to calm her down, he heard himself expostulating while the rich-looking couple looked on in evident disdain, which set John against them immediately, whoever they were.

"Hold on, hold on, Melia! No, stop for a minute! Give them a chance to ask what they want. No! Wait a minute, it's a valuable car and if they are looking for parking. . ."

Melia Tracey wasn't hearing him, and her voice got louder and less coherent. "They've asked what they want, Mr John! They want to walk inside as if they owned the place, and the woman was bold enough to say to that man there that she was considerin' the mirror which is hangin' over the mantelpiece in the dining-room. Mrs Cassa's mirror! Mrs Cassa's mirror! She was here yesterday and the man as well. She's supposed to be Mrs Cassa's sister, and what's more, Mr John, seein' is believin' and I saw no sign of sister in Mrs Cassa's greetin' nor their partin' neither, and what's more to the point. . ." and she heaved her shoulders up ready to take in more wind, ". . . in my view. . ."

John seldom got angry with Melia Tracey: she had been a staunch supporter since the tough times when he had taken over his grandfather's house and set up the business with Uncle Tim's money. There were, however, times when anyone would want to throttle her, and this was one of the times.

"Mrs Tracey!" he shouted, stopping her in mid-flow. "Will you please be silent for five minutes and give me time to sort out what is going on." He stepped nearer to the couple. "Would you please introduce yourselves to me? I am John Gowan, the owner of this yard and this house."

"And handsome with it." The woman turned, and her patronising comment was instantly forgotten in the beauty of her luminous smile. "I am Nicole Tyson, Cassa's sister, and this is my friend, Clive Kemp. Clive drove me up from Dublin to visit my sister. We have been admiring the cruisers on the river. Are they all yours?"

"A lot of them," John said, "but not all." He was taken aback. He had simply assumed that Cassa was inside in the

179

house, but evidently she was not. She had never talked at length about her sister, although she had said lately that her sister had split up with the husband. He could hear Melia somewhere behind him muttering angrily, and behind her again was Aggie making frantic efforts to get someone's attention. He was thinking that he should have been here at home and not where he was. But who could know where he was? He turned back to Melia: "Mrs Tracey, has Mrs Cassa gone down town? Shopping? Gone to mass?"

Melia glared at him. "It's Monday," she hissed, "not Sunday." She put her hand on his arm. "Move over here, over here, come on!"

Mrs Tyson and her friend strolled across the yard and down to the river, no doubt expecting John Gowan to follow.

Melia dug her fingers into John's arm; she was still hissing. "You be warned by me, Mr John. I don't trust them, and neither should you. They were pokin' about here yesterday – they're up to somethin'. And in my view, Mrs Cassa was frightened of them, and she hired a car and drove off, and she hasn't been seen since. She did warn me she could stay overnight, but it was a lie, or an excuse because it was stayin' with her sister was what she said, and Mrs Cassa is still gone and them two are back. And no sign of Mrs Cassa!"

John's guilt caved in on his head, and he roared at Melia: "What d'you mean, no sign of Cassa? What car? When? Yesterday? What time yesterday? She said she was staying with her sister? In the town? Why didn't the sister say? I'll ask her."

And he turned, but Melia grabbed him tighter. "And betray Mrs Cassa in a lie, is it? I don't trust them." She lowered her voice. "If they've done any harm to Mrs Cassa, I'll. . . there's that feckin' phone again. The bloody thing hasn't stopped ringin' all day!"

"It could be Cassa." John rushed to the back door, but the dutiful Aggie got there before him.

She handed him the phone. "It's the same again," she told him, "I always recognise a voice: the superior of the order, about the tenth time since yesterday!"

With weary reluctance, John said, "John Gowan here, Father Chaparas," and he sat down heavily. Sometimes this excitable priest could go on and on, and never anything new. Missioners in Lima were still compiling all possible data about the earthquake in Peru: how many churches, how many missionary priests, how many hundreds of people, how many schools full of children. Eight months ago, but it seemed like years. John shifted the phone to the other side of his head and prepared to listen. Chaparas' broken English needed concentration.

"John, is it you? That is good, Cassa is not the one to hear. This news may be very good, may be bad – are you listening? In the village of Frank, it was Sonaquera, in the highest peaks, on the borders of Bolivia. I was there when I was a young priest: very high, very remote. Worst part for hundreds of miles, the earth always shaking, always, and then came the terrible roar with miles of mud slides, who knows how many miles – you listen me now? In earthquake all peoples were not buried. The mountainside carried three villages down into the valleys and up and over, up and over, you hear me? Up and over it happens in earthquake, over a distant mountain range of other much further Andes, much more distant, far, far, all sliding and rolling and – do you hear me, I am reading this part to you? Yes? Many, many were, they have said, buried before the shifting earth came to the end. But not all! Not all! Those peoples, some hundreds, were then among strangers, you know? You understand? Different dialects, and peoples who arrive there out of the earthquake were not wanted, not welcomed, many injured left to die, all tribes moving on, the earthquake people were to them ghosts from another world, and the tribes, they are still primitive in that place, the tribes were

181

terrified. You hear me, John? No sharing of their food with poor shoddy ghosts, clothes all in tattered pieces and poor food, and not much, too little, water to share with strangers." The priest paused, and John had to break in, his forehead sweating with sheer anxiety.

"For God's sake, Father Chaparas, are you trying to tell me something? Are you going to tell me something about my brother Frank?" John's voice broke, tears and sweat running down his face. "Have you seen him? Have you? Please! Please! For the love of God, tell me!"

The Spanish priest, too, was deeply moved. Frank Gowan had been in the seminary when Chaparas was master of novices; he it was who had urged Frank to the foreign missions. Chaparas was a heavy old man now, a superior when Frank was a magnificent fellow in his forties, the full flowering of his priesthood yet to come. "No! No! I have not seen him here in the Mother House. No! He is not here. All we have of him is a few moments of communication with newspaper men . . . reporters? Yes, that is it. It was a brief report, and a picture, and from Lima they send to us the paper and the picture of a crowd of the ones left there, and it is Frank in the picture, of that I am sure. A few lines in a Lima daily paper. There were three archaeologists caught also in the moving earthquake, and there was attempt of airlifting them. Reporters write in the paper that they will go back for other peoples. They go back when airlift is to be able to be going, I do not know when they go. . . they do not know when. . . the weather too depends. Airplanes in the peaks of the Andes not much, not daily air service, no never, but they have trains but with earthquake, the trains not much for a year now. You hear me? I am looking at the newspaper, and it is your brother, I know him all his life since a teens boy. Yes, I am sure. It is him."

"We've got to get him out of there!" John shouted into the phone. "We've got to get to him. If those newsmen got there, we can. I'll get back to you later, and I'll count you in, Father. You have the language, like Frank. We'll all go. My wife is not here now, but I'll get back to you. I have to believe it's good news, it has to be. Thank you, thank you, I'll get back to you." The priest was still talking, but John had to find out urgently where Cassa was. In the same instant that he rushed into the yard, two cars drew in and two people stepped out: Cassa and a man he had seen somewhere before.

John never noticed the consternation, surprise and confusion in the yard. He took Cassa's arm and almost precipitated her back into the house, into the hall and in front of the telephone. Where she had been was never asked. As she was rushed past Melia and the girls, the back door was securely shut and bolted. Whoever was standing in the yard could stand there as far as Melia was concerned: she and the nieces were all ears to hear what Mr John was shouting about.

"Cassa, Cassa, Cassa: Frank has been found after all these months! Father Chaparas was on the phone. Frank was seen alive by news reporters! It was in their newspapers, and there was a picture with Frank in it – Chaparas is certain it is Frank! A newspaper photo! Sit down, sit down. Here, Cassa, hold my hand. Don't faint on me. Melia Tracey – oh there you are – make coffee. Get some brandy – have some yourself. They think Frank is going to be restored to us; that was the order on the phone. I'll go to Dublin; I'll have to get a visa. I'll book flights to Lima: there's no time to be lost. For God's sake, Aggie, what are you trying to say? Well, you go out to the yard, Aggie, and tell those people to go home. What? Whoever they are. Yes, now. Immediately. Tell them to move their cars and find another place; and tell them I am too busy to talk about the cruisers – they'll get all the information at Bord Fáilte in the town. Shift them, Aggie: you've moved tourists on before."

It was a job Aggie enjoyed, and indeed she was very good at it. As Melia was fond of saying, "Some of those tourists come for a week and think they own the place," but when Aggie went into action, they didn't know what hit them.

Between the coffee and the brandy and John's exhilaration, when Cassa finally drew breath, the Rolls and the Merc were long gone. She had time to reflect that if the respective drivers had been given an explanation for their ejection from the Gowan yard, it would have been an adequate one. Absolutely adequate: a man long lost and given up for dead had been seen in a far part of the earth, and he would be found. There would be feasting and rejoicing, and in the whole wide world nothing else was of the slightest importance. Cassa's every emotion was drawn back into the summer of cruising down the Shannon with Father Frank. She was careful to draw a conscientious net around any other straying thoughts. More than that, she allowed the once familiar longing for Frank to reinvade her spirit, causing her tender concern for John's rocketting hopes. That was how it had been for her and Frank and for John in those idyllic sunny days, when only the slightest filament of desire divided her love for the two brothers.

CHAPTER TWENTY-FOUR

With a shouted injunction to move off before she called the Guards, Aggie slammed the back door in their faces. It was a gesture noisy enough to put the dazzling Nicole into a furious temper, but she held it back. She preferred to appear at her best because her ex-husband was staring at her with undoubted admiration, and her surge of reciprocation was undeniable. Dermot Tyson's physical perfection had never lost its power to invade her senses with desire, giving her always the urge to bring him into a state of subjection. She dismissed the recollection of his contemptuous resistance. That was then, this could be now. Of course, the evident admiration might not be based totally on her beauty.

The amiable Clive Kemp took his apprehensive bulk down to the water's edge, at a safe distance from the rejected husband.

"You never give up, do you?" Dermot said. "You are still in deep mourning for the Blake antiques."

"At least I am not running after another man's wife. You always had an obsession with my sister. You are well aware that she is a crafty little bitch; what has she got that you want now? Money, of course – your god! The way you got me. Cassa won't part; you're wasting your time."

Nicole followed Tyson as he walked towards his car. "Wait, Dermot, I want to ask you something. What's going on inside the house?"

"I haven't the faintest idea. I presume that Mr Gowan was bringing his wife back into order. Some men do it that way." He was at the car.

"Dermot, just please me one last time. . . what's going on with Cassa? With you and Cassa?"

"You want me to be honest with you, Nicole?"

She nodded eagerly. "Please, Dermot, she is my sister, after all!"

"Who'd ever suspect it? There is nothing going on, nothing. Cassa was sick all last year, and she came to Dublin for a short holiday, and now she is home again."

He was into his car and starting to turn in the big yard; then he was gone out on to the road and away. It would be a fairly long journey to Donegal, but Orla and Sandra would give him a wonderful welcome. As they always did. He loved that. He remembered what Cassa had said about the "nothingness" of an encounter with Nicole. There was never a contribution, never a supplement; Nicole queried and punished. The children's faces had been so miserably disappointed when they had raced up the stairs full of loving hope for a day out with Mummy. Had she given them anything in return for their childish faith. . . and yet they had renewed their expectations that she would be at home waiting for them. He had to believe that children were resilient. He was the parent who must make up the difference. Cassa might never be available – a stupid word to think of Cassa, but what other word was there now? Something urgent and undeniable had taken place in the Gowan household.

Left behind in the yard, Nicole let her half-restrained temper slip. In the Rolls, she held her hand on the horn and kept it blaring until a puzzled Clive got behind the wheel and dared to glower at her.

"Don't mind that," she cut off his mumblings. "Let's get out of here!"

CHAPTER TWENTY-FIVE

John hadn't wanted Cassa to make the trip to Peru. After all the shocks and tragedy of the past year, he felt that she was too fragile for such an arduous journey. But Cassa was adamant. If there were any chance that her beloved Frank would be found alive, she must be there, too, to welcome him back.

In the hurried days and nights of frantically urgent preparations for this unexpected and undreamt of journey to South America, her husband might have sought the distraction of comfort in Cassa's feminine warmth. There had been times when her arms holding him to her bosom had given him a special joy in living. She became conscious that her support was felt unnecessary at this time of fearful anxiety. Physical apartness was all he asked, his disjointed energy focused on finding his brother. Like a demoted actress, she missed her old role, reflecting upon the rare, mysterious quintessence of loving to be found in the dregs of an old desire.

Endless hours of flying above the clouds followed. Unable to settle into sleep, unable to pass time by eating or reading or watching films, and unable to formulate the news awaiting them at the end of the journey, Cassa came at last to the wide-awake dream always there when she drew back the casement in her bedroom. Frank as she imagined him: the sheer resplendence of the man against the sky, his sapphire-blue eyes, his half-foreign accent. Then his unwanted words: "For us there can only be a silence of the heart." Marriage to his brother had not banished the dream, nor had it gone away with the baby who was to come and who was to be named Frank. Out beyond the casement, across the yard and far up the Shannon she had gone to share her tears with a dream. Tears of grief for an unfulfilled love and tears of shame for the lawful husband who had never been part of the dream. Afterwards, the weary months of silent unshed tears in her belief that Frank had come for the child in the moment of his birth.

This belief must never be spoken aloud, or everyone would say she had lost her reason. It would be best for a calm and passive future to get rid of this notion, and Cassa had tried to free her mind. "Taken the baby to heaven," that was what Melia Tracey had said. "Straight up to the throne of Almighty God." But when a weeping Cassa had implored to be told who took the baby there, Melia had answered, "The guardian angel, of course!" With all her heart, she wished she shared the simplicity of Melia's lifelong faith. In Firenze, her parents had taken for granted the customs of their religion. Faith was skin-deep in Firenze. If there had been a live baby to share with a live husband, would she have relinquished the dream?

Thoughts sped away swiftly in yet another interruption, and there were many interruptions to shorten the flight, for which she was grateful: John stirring restlessly in the seat beside her, Father Chaparas snoring to the roof in his heavy sleep, the hostess with yet another offer of food or drink. Sometime soon the hostess would be coming with hot towels, signalling that the long flight was coming to an end. Cassa closed her eyes resolutely, collecting her thoughts, getting herself ready for the best that could happen at the airport of Lima, building a fortress in her mind against the worst.

At last the plane began the descent, circling for an hour as if to give the three hundred passengers time to view the city of Lima below. Chaparas had told them that Lima was a very large industrial city, trading in textiles and chemicals and glass. He had said not to expect a wonderful scenic place, and from the window beside them they saw enormous palls of smoke enveloping all the skyscrapers.

"Why did I expect mountains?" John asked harshly, his face set in grim lines. "Where are the forests and the sea?"

"You will see them when we get outside the city, a couple hours," the priest told him. "Is different outside, many factories here."

Getting through the airport itself was tedious and took more hours, but there was a car waiting for them, and eventually they were on their way to Father Chaparas' monastery. The traffic was in gridlock in all the streets.

"I thought," Cassa said in an effort to break the silence, "that I would see a Spanish city like Barcelona – the name 'Lima' suggested that."

Father Chaparas was at some pains to defend Lima, having spent many hard years on the mission here. "I have all the history of this city," he said. "When the *conquistadores* build the city for a capital city of Peru, they build it on the Spanish style; some paintings still there are, and it was very fine. That began in the year 1535. Pizarro brought the Spanish builders, he come from Bilbao, my mother's grandfather also from Bilbao. Pizarro with a small army of his followers, he conquer Peru for Spain. Pizarro is a *conquistador*. He laid waste the Inca lands, that history of the Incas goes to the 1200s. Lima great city for Spain, but it was destroyed by an earthquake that wipe out of this Lima was in 1746. It was one hundred year for rebuild, and never the same plan of Pizarro; the Lima what you see now is the rebuild, and much commerce come in a hundred year. And more in a hundred year after that: industries, cement works. The city is not now Pizarro's city; he was a true Spaniard."

John and Cassa exchanged a glance; the pride in Chaparas' voice was unmistakable. The priest was old and he must be very tired from the journey, but he had mettle. Life in the mission fields would build a degree of toughness in a man's character, and Cassa thought again of Frank: less now of Frank in the sunset at Lough Boderg, and more of Father

Frank the missioner, labouring among this strange race, hundreds of them glimpsed as they strained at the innumerable traffic halts. South American people, she thought. He talked of them so much, all the time; they never left his mind. His people in Sonaquera. Was he trying to stop me from falling in love with him? Was he preparing me to let him go? And here I am now, filled up with the joy of seeing him again. I wonder does he remember his ceremonial embrace each evening, the fleeting kiss on my hair and on my mouth? I wonder.

When the car turned off the road and into the long sandy avenue leading to the monastery, the atmosphere of the many buildings became distinctively Spanish. Instinctively John and Cassa felt for the handclasp of hope and reassurance. There could be news here. There could be at the very least a word of communication, three days since the last phone call which said nothing. Father Chaparas roused himself when the car pulled over.

"*Bienvenidos! Bienvenidos,* John and Cassa, to the Monastery of San Juan." A troupe of white-robed friars came out from the arched doorway, all smiling their welcome. Many introductions were made, the luggage was picked up by willing hands, and the visitors were escorted into the spacious entrance and up a wide staircase to their cells. Evidently it was not the custom to cater for a married couple. Each cell had a flat, narrow bed, a table and a chair, and an open cupboard to hang up clothes. It looked as if Cassa would have to negotiate her own way for any toilet arrangements she might require. Now they avoided each other's eyes as John muttered grimly about booking into a hotel.

There was instant relief when the superior explained in tolerable English that as there were no monks in cells on this level of the monastery, the couple would have the water closet all to themselves. There was a subdued wave of amused laughter when the white-robed men saw the faces of the two visitors. Cassa had respect for male humour, and she nodded politely. John's face was a thunderstorm, as the monks backed off down the stairs. He steered Cassa into his cell and let his temper fly.

"What the hell are they on about? Whose idea was it to come out here? We passed several hotels on the way! Did Chaparas tell you about this arrangement? Not a word said when we arrived! Why don't they give us the latest news? Why? What was that tall guy shouting back when they were on the stairs? I don't see anything to smile about, Cassa. Don't they realise the serious business we are here for? Do they think we are effin' tourists on a camping holiday?"

Cassa stretched herself on the narrow bed. "Lie down beside me," she invited.

"I wouldn't fit on that thing," he muttered, but he pulled over the chair and sat down. "Well?"

"We are here for one night, only one night. Tomorrow we will be flying to a town that is a bit nearer to the earthquake disaster."

"How do you know that, Cassa?"

"Because," she said patiently, "while you were up to your ears making all the complicated travel and visa arrangements, I listened and made a note of all Chaparas' plans. He lived here for years and he knows the languages. Wait now, John, we have to remember that the order has to find our Frank, but not only our Frank. They have three other priests lost out there, and they don't know where, only that they may be alive."

"And when we get to the other town, what happens then?" John always took time to change direction. Cassa could only guess: she thought that they would be taking one day at a time. John had spared no expense to get here, and before they came away she had heard him say to his office on the phone that he would expect to be well back before

191

the end of the month, which wasn't much more than two weeks away. The Shannon Boat Rally would still have been on his mind.

"The monks were saying that we have jet lag and we should rest for a few hours," Cassa told him. "That's what Father Chaparas said."

"What were they shouting on the stairs?" John still resented their amusement.

"That they have their dinner at seven o'clock. It was an invitation."

"Do you know how to speak Spanish?" he asked.

"Only the conversational phrases that Frank taught me. I am going to look for the bathroom."

"Okay," he said wearily, "my turn next." He was a little surprised at her calm: why didn't she fall to pieces after that hell of a journey? Why didn't she burst out in exasperation? He used to know what way the wind blew, but now he had lost his bearings.

In the morning, John made suggestions about hiring a car, a heavy-duty, four-wheel-drive vehicle, a super-jeep. The monks were convulsed with laughter, and enquired how much time did he think he had on his hands? The plane would cover thousands of miles from Lima, and their nearest point of departure from the plane would necessitate a journey on foot into the higher peaks of the Andes. John had no need to worry about that, they told him, for the monks had all the equipment, and they were hardened climbers. To look at him, they said, John appeared to be a very strong man, and Frank had often related to them what a great boatman he was, never given to fatigue.

It was very quickly established that Cassa was going nowhere. It was not a place for a white woman, although they had heard of a white woman in the Andes exploring, a traveller writing a book.

Cassa was bitterly disappointed, but she could not protest.

She knew she looked frail. John did not protest on her behalf either. Frank was his own brother, and that was that.

Of course, of course, if there were the slightest suspicion of a meeting with Frank, even a sighting, Cassa would be the first to know. They would radio every day, everywhere the reception was good, often twice a day depending on weather zones; at night was often best. Father Superior would see to it that Cassa had access to a radio. There would not be such a facility in any hotel in Lima.

The superior, Father Damascene, assured her that there were many expeditions out searching for Frank and the three missioners in similar circumstances. Contact would be made, she could be sure of that. Buried and resurrected: yes, even in Peru that was not a new story. The piercingly direct way Father Damascene said those words as he gazed at her evoked the story of Easter Sunday when Mary Magdalen found the tomb of Christ empty and the Crucifixion already a mere memory.

Cassa, shivering unbearably, went out into the brilliant sunshine. There they found a grotto where she could pretend to be praying as she wiped away her tears. How much did Father Damascene know about her and her relationship with Father Frank? Had he been Frank's confessor? Had Frank carried the guilt for her confession of loving him? What had seemed an untutored innocence in her may have been an iniquity to a celibate priest. Each evening at sunset she had gone into his embrace: it had become their ceremonial moment. . . except for the evening of that glorious sunset over Lough Boderg. Was there a guilty surge of untoward passion? A sensual exultation that had never come into her marriage with John? Suddenly she remembered an evening on *La Vie en Rose,* John telling her how Melia Tracey had said that Father Frank was fasting and praying in preparation for his departure. That was after Lough Boderg – the day after?

Cassa looked up at the statue in the grotto. It was a female statue, but not the Blessed Virgin despite the furled blue garment; she wore a metal tiara with her name, Santa Rita. Perhaps a Spanish saint, and perhaps I should pray to her for guidance. I seem to have made a lot of attempts to pray in the recent past, and not succeeded at all. She wished she were back in the days when mass on Sundays was all the prayer you needed for the week.

John found Cassa at the grotto. It was obvious she was distressed. He presumed that her tears were tears of disappointment because she was being left out of the group going to search for Frank. John had always known that no matter how fond his brother was of Cassa during that long summer holiday, Frank would return to his priesthood. There had never been any doubt of that in John's mind. Although he was fully aware the priestly vocation had been forced on his brother, John knew instinctively that Frank's mould had set, long since.

"Inside," John said, "they are saying there's no time to lose. Apparently, the weather can change without any warning, and the weather is the important thing. Looks as if we will be shoving off after dinner, about nine o'clock tonight."

"Do you think I should get them to book a return flight for me?"she asked.

"Couldn't you wait for me to get back?"

"What would I do all day here?" Cassa enquired gently.

"I suppose you could help," he said.

Cassa stared at him without answering.

CHAPTER TWENTY-SIX

"It is a present, a gift," said Father Damascene to Cassa, who was standing under the arched door. "You will find it useful on your walks." He held up a rosary beads in silvery filigree. "This is made by native people, here in our workshop."

Cassa hesitated, and he softened his voice: *"Un regalo para la dama solitaria."*

She was unsure of this priest, but she took the rosary in her hands. *"Gracias, Padre Damascene, par el bello regalo. Gracias."*

From the table in the entrance hall he held up a white parasol. *"Un paraguas? Quemadura de sol! El sol es caliente."*

"Thank you," she said gently. "I will be careful to avoid sunburn – as you say, the sun is hot." On these words, she opened the parasol and walked slowly away into the garden. Some sixth sense in this priest, she thought, had told him that Frank had made great fun of teasing her in Spanish. A sixth sense? Or had Frank talked to Father Damascene about their excursions into the far waterways of Carnadoe? Surely not. Surely all that had passed between them two years ago had been hidden from everyone. Her husband John had never questioned her, nor had it ever occurred to her to mention Frank's name in any form of confidence to anyone. Cassa's heart admonished her: he had come to her at a time when she needed a friend. This missionary priest, Father Frank Gowan, had found her and befriended her in the dismal days in San Salvatore. She had not sought out a priest to destroy him. But why had she come thousands of miles in the mad hope of seeing him again?

At the grotto of Santa Rita, she sat under the shade of the parasol and took up the rosary beads. Although the heat of the sun made her eyes close, she kept on to the end. The nuns in Loreto had been devoted to the rosary, and she remembered how she and Louise had often tried to "mitch off" the prayers. Louise couldn't stand the Litany of the Saints, which went on for ever. "Tower of Ivory, camel soap," she'd hiss, and Cassa would collapse in a fit of giggles. Ah, Louise! Even now I cannot bear to think of you.

Cautiously, Cassa made her way along the sandy paths, avoiding the thorny roots, going slowly and admiring the strange cactus shrubs – anything to fill in the time until she could enquire about radio messages. In the hall, the monk on duty held up a card on which was printed: FATHER CHAPARAS SPEAK YOU. Then he struck on a gong six times, holding up that number on his fingers and pointing to the name. Cassa understood to wait in the hall for the old priest. When he came, he had some news from a radio call: their men had completed the flight. There was no news of their missioners. They had hired a truck and set out, and they would radio in the night.

Father Chaparas was sympathetic. "You very sad?" he asked Cassa.

She hesitated for a moment, and then she answered, "I should not have come. I am useless here, and I feel I should go home."

His answer told her that her departure would be a relief to the community, not that they found her a burden; but simply they were at a loss. "Ah yes, Cassa, Damascene was of the opinion you would find the days long and empty, with your husband not here. Do you propose to look for a plane back to your home? There are several airlines, several routes, to the east or to the west. The airline we come on is always heavily booked – they like to make full the plane: three passengers good, a single one wait sometimes two weeks to book for the seat."

Yes, Cassa thought, I got that message. Damascene would like me to be gone before Frank comes safely back to base.

"Would you be able, Father, to hire a taxi for me to go to the airport to see about arranging a flight?"

"No problem," he said. "I will speak with Damascene after the *siesta*."

"Ah yes, of course, the *siesta*. That, too, for me," Cassa told him. "It will use up the time. *Gracias, Padre*." She walked up the wide stairs, carefully putting one foot in front of the other, her head held high. Once into her cell, she burrowed her face into the narrow bed and gave way to a passion of tears. She had not cried like that since the time after Papa's death when the utter loneliness of her big house had enclosed her. Their mother, Sadora, had a philosophy about rejection, that it's the one thing that brings on self-pity. Firenze and Sadora's Rules were inextricably mixed up in Cassa's mind.

The Rules usually worked, and Cassa got rid of her self-pity under the shower in the monks' water closet. Then the brisk brushing of her hair. When the dinner gong struck its single stroke, she was able to present herself in the monks' refectory in so demure a fashion that not one of the monks would ever have suspected this sedate lady of a deeply resentful streak.

The meal was fish again, some unfamiliar variety, not pink or white but a saffron colour. Smoked over a fire, Cassa guessed. The rice was covered in a red sauce, perhaps tomatoes. Dessert was an ample slice of sweet melon.

When the monks had chanted the grace after meals Father Damascene indicated his study to Cassa, and she followed him in. He left the door wide open, and he did not invite her to sit down.

You'd have been quite safe with me, Cassa thought irreverently.

"You enquire for a visit to the airport? Would thirty minutes after eight o'clock be suitable for you?"

"Tomorrow morning?" enquired Cassa.

"No, tonight. Tomorrow no one is free. Brother Anton is off duty tonight. If tonight is suitable for you, he will drive. The airport is open at night, twenty-four hours. Your mind is, how you say, made up?"

"At half past eight, I will be waiting in the entrance hall for Brother Anton," she said.

"*Muy bien*." Father Damascene walked her to the door and shut it firmly behind her.

The massive carved grandfather clock in the hall was striking eight o'clock, which gave her time to wash and change. She must make sure to pack all the documents in her bag, so many of them, not only her passport. It was probably as difficult to leave this country as to get into it. And the travellers' cheques, never forgetting her own precious chequebook, and of course plenty of Peruvian coinage. Chaparas had distributed coins to beggars the day they arrived.

Brother Anton was not chatty by nature, or he distrusted his amount of English. When he found a space in the enormous car park, he made it clear that Cassa could find the booking offices as best she could, on her own. That took a lot of walking. Her inability to communicate was frustrating and time consuming. Luckily, some of the clerks (all male, she noticed) were happy to practise various languages, and finally she made her needs known in rusty French and with the help of the documents. It was almost a miracle when, at last, having submitted all her bona fides half a dozen times, she found herself in possession of a first class ticket to Paris on an Air France plane in a few days' time. She who had wept with joy for coming to Lima now clutched her bag with the marvellous ticket and almost danced. Paris was one step from Carrick-on-Shannon where home was, and Melia Tracey and the heavenly nieces.

Then Cassa spotted the line of telephones. Why not phone home? The instructions were in many languages, and it took time and patience to get the charges reversed, but she did not want to be cut off. As clear as if only inches away, there was Aggie's unmistakable soft Leitrim accent in what was known to the household as her phone voice. Then Melia joined in, and every little detail about John and Frank was told over and over. Melia had been studying the stars, and the tea leaves, and she was convinced that her beloved Father Frank had never died at all. Hadn't she said that at the time? Didn't she do up his room against his return? When, when, when? Melia and the girls took it for granted that when Cassa arrived home in a week's time, they all knew who'd be arm in arm with Mr John and side by side with herself. They had Cassa quite convinced. If only. . .

"Melia," asked Cassa, "what time of the day is it in Carrick?"

"Sure, what time of the day would it be only gettin' up to midday?"

Cassa saw the clocks all around the concourse: midnight in Lima.

"And you'll all be having lunch, so I'd better ring off." Cassa didn't want to ring off at all. "I'll see you all soon!"

"With the help of God and His Blessed Mother," yelled Melia into the phone. "Oh, wait a minnit, Mrs Cassa, Aggie wants to say something – can you talk to her longer?"

Cassa was only too delighted; she was in no hurry to rejoin Brother Anton.

"Go on, Aggie, I'm listening, and I can hear very clearly."

Aggie was back on with her best voice. "It's not about a phone call, Mrs Cassa; it's about a visitor we had, and Aunt Melia made me write it down in the phone book. Will I read it out to you?"

"Go ahead, Aggie."

"It happened two days after you were gone off with Mr John with all the rushin' and all the way it was in a hurry. Well, the man who was here the day the phone call about Father Frank called. He drove right into the yard, and he had two lovely young girls with him, two beautiful young ones with, as Auntie Melia remarked, very good manners for what's goin' nowadays. I have the names here, Mr Dermot Tyson, and Orla and Sandra. They were passing on their way to Dublin from Donegal where they had their holidays. He was a brother-in-law once removed (I have that written here, although I never heard of it before, but Aunt Melia says it's common enough among the upper classes), and he was enquiring for yourself, Mrs Cassa. He made his enquiries through Auntie Melia. She told me to write this down, that she was so taken with him that she invited them to come in for tea and maybe the young ladies would like to wash up (which in your absence she never does, she says to tell you). The gentleman wasn't going to, but the girls said they'd love to see Auntie Cassa's house. Auntie Melia was charmed with him, and she said under the circumstances (that is, him being the brother-in-law once removed), she sat him down and told him the whole story about the earthquake and Father Frank wandering around out in the wilderness and his brother Mr John and the order's priest and yourself all gone to rescue him – that is, him who was mourned for dead. Auntie Melia told me to add on here: 'a gentleman every inch, and there's not one born every day'. And to add to that, we enjoyed his visit, and his daughters."

They said their goodbyes all over again, with all the holy saints joined in. Cassa walked away from the phone. She did not think Brother Anton would observe, but she made an effort to straighten her face clear and free from the smiles and the tears. Giving all the coins to the beggars in the car park made her even happier.

CHAPTER TWENTY-SEVEN

In the morning, Cassa took the filigree rosary to the grotto. Santa Rita was still there, her tiara in place, her blue robe undisturbed. That was the comforting thing about statues: in your childhood and in your womanhood, they remained exactly the same. Was Rita a virgin saint who had never known the loneliness of loving a man? I'll never know, Cassa thought; the day after the day after tomorrow, I'll be far away from here on a little island where we have Saint Brigid who was a friend of Saint Patrick, and that seems to be enough for us. Or is that just my ignorance? What nationality of a saint were you, Rita? Cassa gripped the rosary beads and made an effort to concentrate on the prayers, but the thought of a little island persisted in taking over: a little island in the Atlantic Ocean with no monstrous mountains like those ferocious Andes towering against the skyline, always threatening disasters and deaths. The mountains of home were green and mossy, and not one of them had ever turned upside-down in a ghastly earthquake. Tomorrow morning would be her last morning to come to this grotto with its fearful view of those mountains.

Yet it was to these mountains she had rushed, her heart held high with a wonderful expectation.

Tomorrow night, Brother Anton would drive her to the airport. Was it ungrateful of her to be glad? Profoundly glad.

In the arched entrance to the monastery, it was the duty of a brother to set the sign of a new day, no doubt to remind the holy men that each one of them was another day nearer to death. Cassa had noticed that as a monk passed the sign, he made the sign of the cross. Today she too made the sign, reflecting that although she didn't know much Spanish, today was undoubtedly the middle of July and the year was 1985. Then she saw that Father Damascene was signalling from his office.

He seemed sightly more gracious than usual, with his Spanish greetings and remarks about the weather. Still standing at his door, he told her he was waiting for people from the National Geographic Society. He pronounced this very carefully, perhaps in case Cassa had never heard of such a society. She said nothing, simply nodded.

"They should be here at midday," he said. "You *comprende*: they went in search to explore? Men they photographed were prisoners: many men, women and children also – how you say? – 'displaced' by the earthquake. After the photographs, they were taken back to jail. Many were criminals, robbing and worse after the earthquake, thieves and murderers in handcuff and blindfold."

He led the way into his office where Father Chaparas and several other monks were studying magazines. Cassa recognised the unmistakable *National Geographic*. She sat down and looked at the pictures, but they conveyed nothing more than bunches of ragged men heavily bearded. The monks around the table were staring at Cassa as if she would supply an answer. But to what? No one had mentioned any radio calls from her husband.

"Father Damascene," Cassa asked gently, "what are you expecting to arrive here at midday?"

"Expecting? No! Hoping, yes! *Siempre esperanza*. These men with no papers, no passports, are claiming to belong. Some already restored to their families, some looking for sanctuary that is not theirs. No papers, no identification, *comprende*? Much was lost from families in the earthquake. Criminals who have stolen the contacts of other prisoners. You *comprende*, identities? Is a big 'write-up' for papers and for magazines. And television and radio. *National Geographic* very honest – reputable – will bring men here who claim they are our brethren, our brothers!" He drew

202

himself up proudly: "And we will judge who they are. We will know!"

Cassa's heart was beating so painfully it must surely break. She stood up quickly, slipping out through the open door, and fled up the stairs. With her back to the cell door, she made an effort to bring her thoughts to order. The way the monks had stared at her meant they had been told that Frank might be among the bearded men who were claiming to belong. They knew, of course they knew, that she was here in this monastery waiting for the return of Frank. Why otherwise had she come? They knew his brother John could have come alone; the very way they had stared at her was an accusation. A few words had leapt off the pages of the magazine, and one of them was the word "torture". A Frank who had been tortured, a Frank who was blindly seeking a place to take him in, a disoriented Frank? Cassa recalled his lovely face: his sapphire-blue eyes, his strong straight nose offset by his lean dark cheeks. . . and then his close-cut wavy hair; she had often longed to run her fingers through his hair, to know by touch the silky, silvery feel of it. She had so many longings in that summer, simply to kiss his mouth as he lay with closed eyes in the heat of the sun, to pretend that she had thought he was asleep. And the constant longing to press her body closely into the outline of his body when he took her into his arms for their evening farewell. Closer, my darling, closer, closer. Each evening at sunset, all those chances to break the tranquillity of his silence. But she had never dared. With Frank respect came first. How was she so sure of that, since she had never dared to overturn that respect?

And now? If one of those dishevelled men in the magazine should turn to her and say, "Cassa, don't you remember me?" By midday she would know, surely she would know, if the earthquake had taken Frank. And if it had not?

Cassa pulled her chair across the cell to the narrow window. From here, she could see the sandy avenue as it came down off the hard road and entered the grounds of the monastery. It was pleasant enough to look at the ancient trees flowering against the intense greenery of the bamboo. If your mind were at ease, with nothing to perturb the steady beat of your pulse, maybe this was a place you could forget unlawful desire. But no, Cassa thought, those terrifying mountains in the background would for ever threaten disaster. She pictured a caravanserai of trucks and cars and busloads of cameramen such as she had glimpsed in the *National Geographic*. They had to come this way: the avenue was the only way in to the monks' stronghold of cloisters and chapels and workshops. She had observed that this monastery was a closely guarded, secret place. She would not go down to join the staring monks, but would wait here at this window. She looked for the filigree rosary beads. It would help the waiting to pray, but today prayer deserted her. Reason and thought deserted her. The waiting seemed for ever.

After midday the traffic began. Instantly there appeared a cordon of the white-clad monks and brothers, many of them, more than Cassa had seen around the monastery. They must have come in support, and it was evident their command was "so far and no further". In a confusion of stopping and starting and shouting and backing off, finally all the traffic came to a halt, and men began to get out of the cars and vans and buses. From Cassa's window it was not easy to distinguish men from men; and as they were all roaring at each other in Spanish, it was impossible for her to know what exactly was going on.

Cassa was tempted to dash down the stairs and see for herself if her most beloved person were out there in the loud mob milling under her window. In the same breath as she moved to the door, she realised that if he were down there at the arched doorway, Frank had no way of knowing that she was here. Damascene would not reveal her presence: from the beginning she had sensed an enemy in him. And understandably so, of course: that was what Damascene was there for, to protect his priests. Cassa went back to the window.

It took a long time of negotiations and cameras and signing of papers and shouting and pushing before men started getting into the cars. Loading of equipment took longer, and eventually Cassa got the impression that the cordon of monks was reassembling around four men who would be permitted to stay in the monastery. She stole very quietly out of her cell to peer down the staircase, the better to see these men. Sadly, she was no wiser. The monks, led by Damascene, ushered the four men through the entrance hall with no show of a delaying welcome. They were there and they were gone. Two of the men were short, even stubby. The other two were similar in height and build, both tall and broad shouldered, both bearded and in rags.

When all was quiet, with no movement anywhere, Cassa knew it must be *siesta* time. The sun would be at its fiercest, but she had had enough of the bare cell. Rita's grotto would be preferable. She took the parasol and the filigree rosary and descended the stairs without a sound. Santa Rita was still safely in her resting place, surrounded by cactus plants; she was someone to talk to, and Cassa needed to talk.

Whatever is going on in the monastery, she concluded, addressing her thoughts to the saint, I was never going to be told. If there were radio calls from my husband John, or radio calls to him if today's news events were of any consequence, I still wasn't going to be told. I don't think I ever remember myself feeling that I am an important person, so what's different today? But surely someone should have told me what's going on? But then nobody ever thought of consulting me. I must never have had an opinion to boast about. I feel things, though, even if I never said them. Sadora is never very far away, things she impressed on us. I remember about self-pity. Beware of self-pity, it is the most corroding emotion, was what she said. So I had better get over that. Had you a mother, Rita? I loved my father best. I don't remember loving my mother, only fearing her.

Cassa felt she had come to a poor pass, making conversation with a statue. She was glad this would be the last time. Her own little island was waiting for her a plane flight away. Tomorrow! Tomorrow! She put up the parasol, took out the rosary beads, and she made a mighty effort to pray for grace, grace to behave rationally – that was another of Sadora's injunctions. Yes, that was the word, injunctions.

In this strange country, it was easy to follow the path of the sun. Once it tipped below the horizon, darkness came swiftly then, as if a closing curtain had descended. Very soon it would be dinner-time in the monks' refectory. Cassa wondered if there would be a strange face at the table. She would shower and dress and perfume in tremulous anticipation. Could behaving rationally wait for another day?

There seemed to be more antiphons and responses than were usual in Father Damascene's intoning of grace before meals; he seemed to be encouraging some sort of uplift of the spirit, and to be standing taller. Cassa looked at the face of each monk as they filed into their places. Many of them were hunched over with the years, a few young with open, unaware faces. As each monk passed Damascene's high carved chair, he raised his eyelids in respect to his superior. There was no pair of sapphire-blue eyes, and Cassa exhaled with relief and regret, her indrawn breath followed with extreme caution for fear of Damascene's suspicious eyes.

When the meagre meal ended with another series of chants, the monks went to the big chapel for their evening prayers. Cassa had gone one night to listen, finding their chanting dolorously musical. Tonight she left the refectory and headed for the stairs. Tomorrow night, Brother Anton would take her to the airport. It was in her mind to pack her things neatly and leave the cell in good order. Perhaps tidy up John's cell. For all she hadn't been told, maybe John was on his way back to the monastery. There was something different. Maybe John would know; maybe he had been told by radio. Maybe, maybe, maybe.

"*Señora Gowan!*" It was Damascene's domineering voice. "*Venga aquí.*"

He was standing at the door of his study as Cassa walked slowly across the hall; somehow the look of him raised no bright tremor of hope. She followed him into the room, the door left wide open as usual. He said a whole sentence in Spanish, and to Cassa's questioning eyes he translated it.

"The lamb who was lost has returned to the shepherd. *Comprende?* Our prayers are answered, our prayers are heard in Heaven, and our beloved son is come again to the pasture."

No lightning flashed in Cassa's mind. "My husband?" she asked a little fearfully.

Damascene may have been expecting a swooning Salome, for he looked taken aback, disappointed. In his sternest voice, he said, "Your husband's brother, our dear son Frank, has been returned to our safe keeping."

Perhaps Cassa could have shouted aloud for joy, but not in front of this priest, who was adamantly repossessing the treasure which surely should be hers and only hers – repossessing before she could reveal her long-lost claim on the one miraculously given back. An instinct of pure pride took hold of Cassa's voice. "That is good, Father Damascene, I am very glad for you."

"That is not, how you say, the reaction of a kind woman: our son has been returned from the dead. *Comprende?* He is back with us, in our care. You do not ask for his health? We have given the news to his brother on radio, and he expressed, how you say, overjoy. Your husband, John, will, we hope and expect, be back in this house tomorrow in the evening, after sunset, they say."

"Is that all?" Cassa asked.

"No, not all. Your husband say on radio you are to speak with his brother. Not my idea, *comprende?* In the morning, I will say to Frank, our dear son, that you, his brother's wife, is here in our monastery. If he will wish for talk, then it will be so. Is not what I wish for, *comprende?*"

Cassa longed to answer, to let out a flood of words, to say love and joy and gratitude, to waltz around the room, to sing with sheer delight. She fixed her eyes on the triumphant face of this priest, and if she could show disdain she hoped he saw it. She turned to walk away, projecting her voice as icily as possible: "I will be saying my rosary in the grotto of Santa Rita at eleven o'clock tomorrow morning."

Then she took the stairs two at a time. She wanted to be out of sight of this priest equally as much as he wanted her out of his sight. She was surprised at herself, at the vehemence of her thinking. Cassa had always supposed that other people knew best, especially men. It must have been far back in her childhood she first got the notion that it was more courteous to just tag along, not to push yourself into someone else's limelight. Safer, too, because her sister Nicole was never far away, always ready to tell Cassa what a fool she was. Nicole had their mother's authority to say so: "Keep an eye on Cassa; she is such a little silly. Such a child."

It was a long night in the cell. There was an hour of sleep followed by hours of being very much awake, listening to the rustle of the trees. There was a necessary making of resolutions, the resolutions she had made about loving and honouring and obeying, and the resolution about being a faithful, constant woman to the man who had made her his wife. That must matter; that must be made to matter. Do not think of Frank's evening embrace; do not, do not. Just keep thinking of all your good resolutions, so many of them that it was like putting gravel through a strainer and hoping to see a few stones come out; but the gravel turned to dust as the night wore on.

CHAPTER TWENTY-EIGHT

Frank was waiting for her at Santa Rita's grotto at eleven o'clock. His face was perhaps thinner, but his deep-set eyes were as intensely blue. In the full white robes of his order, he presented a commanding presence. He held out his arms to her, and, hardly daring to breathe, she went right back into his so-familiar embrace. He kissed her hair and her eyes and lingered a moment on her mouth. Then he held her at arms' length exactly as he had always done. Her heart soared in joyful expectation.

"Cassa, Cassa, how do you get to look more beautiful than I thought I remembered? When Damascene told me this morning that you were here, here in the monastery, I was expecting to see a buxom matronly lady – the last thing I heard, you were going to have a baby! The baby must be a year old now – a boy or a girl?"

She should have realised that he knew nothing that had happened since the earthquake. She should have realised. And Cassa was not good at long explanatory speeches. She began, but the right words would not come; perhaps she might break down in tears with the very effort. Who would have filled in the interval for him? Hardly Damascene, who might know nothing anyway. Cassa tried again: "Melia Tracey has continued to write letters to your name at the order, but of course everyone else knew that you never got letters because you were dead in the earthquake." Cassa looked up at him. "Melia believed she was making offerings to her patron saint!"

Frank laughed softly. "And now she will be entitled to justify her foresight to the neighbours all over Carrick-on-Shannon. Don't mind Melia Tracey. Talk about yourself; tell me everything just as you used to."

"It's too long a story. Don't let's spoil your first day back in the real world with sad stories." Cassa was exultantly happy to gaze on his dear face and be received back into his arms. "Frank, it's absolutely wonderful to see you, and you look so well. Were you one of the men I saw last evening?"

"I must have been!" he laughed. "The brethren ganged up on us, and we've been steam-bathed, turkish-bathed, shampooed and shaved and de-liced, and then they began all over again. I had got quite used to the horrible smell of myself. Talking of which, you are as fragrant as an angel along with being so very beautiful; how do you manage that?"

This was the teasing Frank she remembered. "At tremendous expense." Unsteadily, she smiled, hoping it was her best smile.

They had always assumed they knew all about each other; now she wondered suddenly was she sure of that. She could not speak about the dead baby, and she never had. Nor could she ask him about his being in prison for months. He never liked questions about himself. If there were anything to tell, he would tell. And when would that be? In the years ahead when he and she. . .

"We have a time allowed to us," he said, reading her mind as he had done all through that summer on Lough Key. "Damascene has given us an ordained space of time. It may not stretch to an hour."

"An hour to settle all our future?" she asked in wonder.

His deep voice expressed concern for her: "That was settled when I left Ireland two years ago, Cassa. This is my place, and now more than before. Cassa, Cassa, the things I have seen. The people in the mountains are back in the earliest times. The mission is needed more than I had ever known. From the day I entered on the apostolic life, I was committed. I became a solitary, a bohemian. I walked out of my youth, and there is no going back. I tell you it does not take six years of absence to make you a stranger to your own brother. You write letters, you receive them; you ask questions of those you knew, and they think they are answering you. The years are fleeting, and a day comes when you forget the voices, and you hear only echoes."

Cassa wanted to tell him that it was not years ago since Lough Key and she had not forgotten him, not for even half a day. She began, but he seemed launched on an explanation, as if she must be told once and for all how glorious a vocation was his. Respect compelled her silence.

"In another six years and another, responsibilities weigh on you. You begin to look for a return, as if you had invested your own selfhood. And the missioner dwells among men who have all the failings of childhood but who lack its charms. You have begun to love those forgotten people with a power of devotion that no ingratitude from them can repel."

Perhaps the recollection of passing time brought his attention back to the woman standing humbly by his side. "Ah Cassa, Cassa, you are exactly the same as I remember, the little listener totally absorbed in my endless disquisitions. Was I haranguing you, poor child?"

Cassa made another effort to smile brightly. "As Melia Tracey would say, you may have a method in your madness! I needed to be told those things. Thank you, Frank."

"Come, Cassa, we have a few more minutes. I see that Damascene has sent out the cavalry." There were now two white-clad figures strolling up and down on the sandy avenue. Frank drew her gently into the curve of the grotto. "Sit beside me on this bench and assure me that you are a happy and contented wife to my brother. I am uncouth. I should have started with that question, shouldn't I?"

"Questions don't matter any more," Cassa said softly. "Now it would not make any difference." All the words of desire and of tender love she had cherished for him were like the leaves of these ancient trees, rustling only in the

211

night when the breeze stirred. In the heat of the day, there was the silence he had enjoined on her.

"Is it forbidden to hold your hands in mine?" she whispered.

"Hold my hands and let us talk in another language for our last moment. We fell in love. Yes, I know, both of us. The temptation was wonderful, beyond belief wonderful. Love of a woman is not comparable to any other joy. I have met men who looked back on their earliest years rejoicing in the love of their mother for them. I had no such memory of my mother. You showed me the abundance of a woman's love."

He tightened his grip on her hands until it almost hurt.

"I could not have left you, Cassa, if John had not been there to look after you. I knew you would be safe with John. I knew all about your fears, your aloneness, your grasping sister. I saw your life for myself in San Salvatore; poor little Cassa, you needed a friend. I knew John could deal with all the problems, and he had everything whereas I had nothing. Cassa, all I know for a livelihood is my apostolic work. What could a man like that offer a woman like you?"

He was not asking a question, but Cassa was rushing into trying out the words to tell him he had no need to have anything: money or position would never matter, because she had sold Firenze and she could give. . .

He got to his feet, a tall man prepared to speak. Perhaps, she thought fearfully, to have the last word. As he stood there so tall and fine-looking against the brilliant greenery, Cassa saw him as a crusading saint in a stained-glass window of dazzling colours, his banner held aloft against all temptation, going forth to defend the truth. In the glittering sunshine, the whiteness of his robe was like plated armour of shining steel. Then he came down to earth, moved a little nearer and spoke in the tender tones she had yearned to hear since that long-ago day on Lough Boderg.

"I think of you always, Cassa When my thoughts are of you,

and I cannot banish them with prayer or with work, there is an old verse which has to help, and sometimes it does:

'The heart's heart whose immured plot
Hath keys yourself keep not;
Its keys are at the cincture hung of God. . .'

"Dearest Cassa, sweet Cassa, look up at me. No tears now. Please, Cassa, no tears. You have proved that you can make a life, for John and for a child. I give thanks to Our Heavenly Father for that. Look up at me, Cassa. . . you live constantly in the deepest recesses of my heart. You are locked away, and I can never, never enter there and let you go. I know that you have understood. On the day I took my solemn vows, I dropped that innermost key back into eternity."

The two white-robed figures who had been parading the sandy path now stood beside the grotto. The time was up.

Without a backward glance, the three monks walked away. Cassa thought they are walking a man back into custody, into incarceration, into prison. Not so! They were stepping it out: the sand was swirling under their feet, and there was a jaunty lift in their step. She watched until they were gone around the last curve of the path. It seemed then the world stopped quite still for an empty desolate pause. . . perhaps to give Cassa time to take in how very little she had ever understood.

CHAPTER TWENTY-NINE

Father Damascene was waiting for her under the arched doorway, and he signalled his office. Cassa stood in the vast hall; every movement now was irresolute, but the cell at the top of the stairs was at least a refuge for the final few hours.

"*Venga aquí, comprende?* I speak with you, *señora.*" Cassa took another step towards the stairs. She didn't like this priest, and she had seen the leery look of triumph on his face. Yet another step and her hand out to take hold of the banister.

Damascene made his voice much louder. "A radio call from your husband: he wishes that you will remain until his return. It will be midnight."

With her back turned to him, Cassa said, "I have an arrangement with Brother Anton to take me to the airport at three o'clock. You can forbid that, of course, but my husband will understand the difficulty of booking plane tickets. He will be grateful that one of us got away."

Damascene held an ace card. "Your husband's wishes are, he says on radio, you will together have further interviews with his brother."

"They can do that alone," said Cassa, continuing up the stairs, trying hard to feel proudly isolated. Maybe Brother Anton might be allowed to come and take her to the airport, or maybe not, but nothing on earth could force her to meet Frank again. She sat in the cell and waited. A word she had never used came out of the air: sit here and grapple with your feelings. Grapple? Grapple? Where to begin? No, better not to begin now. With a bit of luck, she would be out of this monastery and sitting in a plane for many hours. Maybe then she could grapple.

As slowly as possible, Cassa spun out the hours with

showering and brushing and delving into the make-up case. Hopefully, she placed her two pieces of luggage outside the door. Almost prayerfully, she put her handbag and jacket at the ready. Then, at last, she heard the knock on her door. There was Brother Anton of the lugubrious visage, the luggage in his grip. She knew she was going to be sitting in the airport for hours, but if this was the time insisted upon for her departure, let it be so. She glanced back at the cell, which was all in neat order. Everything in her handbag had been carefully checked twice. Drained of emotion, she felt like a parcel posted in error and now being redirected to its proper destination.

There was no sign of any monk come out to say goodbye.

"Los padres?" she enquired. *"Retirarse?"*

"Retiro anual."

He was never talkative, but she persisted.

"Adonde? Lejos de aquí?"

"Si, señora. Monasterio Cajamarca."

"Tambien Padre Damascene, Hermano Anton?"

"No, él no, señora."

When he opened the door of the car for her, he closed his face like a bird of prey with a bony beak. She should not have questioned him in her faulty Spanish. He would deliver her to the airport, but dare she open her mouth again. . . She was not sure if she had got it right. It seemed that Damascene had dealt swiftly with the sheep who had returned to the pasture. He had packed them off to a distant monastery for their annual retreat. How would that affect John's return tonight? For a moment, Cassa smiled. She could imagine Melia Tracey's answer to that one: "I hope Mr John washed the floor with him." It was the first normal thought Cassa had had for days.

In the airport, Cassa was again amazed at the chaos. There seemed to be hundreds of young couples queuing up for flights, all good-looking with dark skin and wonderful

215

eyes. Every young couple had a family of children – five or six or seven – who all fought obstreperously with each other. No matter what the young parents handed a kid to keep it quiet, the other kids grabbed it, and the parents pleaded with them to give it back. Cassa wondered where were they all going – it was like an emigration.

This airport was not a place where you could sit and mourn. You couldn't even stand to think. You simply joined your queue. It took Cassa all the available time to make sure she was at the right check-in and to hold on to her place and her luggage against all the pushing and screeching. It took an age to find her departure lounge, to get there after a long walk, to find a seat and watch the clock. Sit! Just sit and wait. Don't lose this seat. Forget you are hungry and thirsty.

How strange not to remember making this air journey in reverse a matter of days ago. Her husband and Father Chaparas must have carried her through the crowds; they must have made all the arrangements, must have mercifully wiped out the hours of waiting, as they ministered to her every need. But John wasn't that kind of man, was he? Not a professional diplomat in the courtesy game, more cavalier.

When at last she was given her comfortable first-class seat in the plane, she was showered with attention. It had been the only seat available on the night she had booked, and it was good. Her hostess told her that the first "hop" was to Hawaii, where there was an hour-long stopover; the second was to Singapore, where they would change to a different airline, stopping over for a few hours. At Bahrain, Air France would take over again; then it was Rome; and after Rome, Paris.

"It sounds like a very long journey," Cassa remarked.

The hostess looked surprised. "From Lima to Paris? Yes, madam. It is a long journey. The Pacific is the biggest ocean. We cross the Date Line. We drop and pick up on the way.

Not many tonight are going the whole distance. Perhaps about forty hours, depending. Usually more hours."

Cassa looked into her own memory in amazement. Why had she no recollection of those hours? The abyss of that headlong flight to find Frank was a dark cavern at the precipice edge of every thought. She made a mighty effort to keep her mind firmly in the immediate moments, to enjoy the flight. Wasn't that what people said at airports? "Enjoy the flight!"

The food was tasty, delicate, and after Hawaii, Cassa napped peacefully. In Singapore the plane was emptied out. Their names would be called when the departure was almost due, and all passengers must respond and be escorted to their places in the Singapore Pacific aircraft. Failure to do so would necessitate calling in the airport police.

Singapore, she thought, was the most beautiful and efficient airport in the entire world. She had no difficulty in phoning Carrick-on-Shannon, hearing Aggie's important voice and giving her the details of the arrival in Paris. Then Cassa felt she could relax for a couple of hours and become distracted from her thoughts. She could not but enjoy the pleasure of walking up and down by the avenues of spraying fountains, the flowers in full perfumed growth, the boutiques of colourful silken fabrics. The muted background music must have been composed for this wonderful spacious area. She was almost sorry when she heard her name being called: Cassandra Blake Gowan – she had forgotten for the moment that Blake was on her passport. A different plane, a different hostess, but still the utmost luxury of first class.

"It's a strange thing," Cassa said to the new hostess, "but I cannot remember ever seeing Singapore airport before."

"Perhaps you did not, madam. But the plane is always evacuated of passengers in Singapore. There are other direct flights from Europe avoiding Singapore, from New

York to Vancouver to Ecuador. Over the North Pole is favoured by certain airlines, madam."

That must be it, Cassa decided. We went some other way. She still remembered nothing beyond an instinct of anticipation, but even that was being gradually eroded. Enjoy the flight, she repeated to herself, enjoy the flight; but each hour she became more tired and restless sitting still.

From the air, Rome was instantly familiar. She recalled educational trips with her mother, resented by a resisting, rebellious Nicole. "Not the Vatican Museum again!" Long time ago. Cassa was very tired now, and she hadn't the energy to think out what she would do in Paris. Enquire at the Aer Lingus desk for the next flight to Dublin? Of course, she would have to have booked her seat in advance. It might be tomorrow. Another dreary night. She closed her eyes wearily on the idea of looking for a taxi and finding a hotel. But that was the sensible thing. First, of course, she would ring Carrick-on-Shannon. The sound of Aggie's voice on the phone would cheer her up, and Melia's comments now that she knew for certain that her patron saint was in the land of the living, seen and verified by an eye-witness. . . Cassa's eyes filled with tears. Stop thinking about him. Stop! Stop!

CHAPTER THIRTY

By the time Cassa had got her luggage off the carousel and struggled out to the arrivals area, she hadn't a breath left. She looked for somewhere to sit down and figure out the next move.

"Permitte que j'assiste la belle femme avec les baggages!" A warm Dublin voice, a laughing voice, a voice that reminded Cassa of Papa. She dropped the luggage, and he lifted her up into his arms. It's what you do in an airport, isn't it, she thought, and all around her people were doing the same thing, kissing and hugging as if they hadn't met for years. It was worth forty-eight hours of travel, a hundred hours, to arrive like this. All around there was so much noise of voices greeting each other in many tongues, it was impossible to whisper and silly to shout. Cassa found herself returning kisses and clinging to this so welcome, so handsome man. She was using phrases of love she had never used before.

"Dermot, Dermot, put me down!"

"You need a couple of cognacs, my darling." Which was exactly what her father would have said, so exactly that she was back in Dermot's arms for a grateful kiss. With one of his arms supporting her and the other arm engaged in carrying her bags, they joined with the crowds making for the exit. No one but Dermot Tyson could summon up a taxi in seething Paris at midnight. Just like that, as if by magic! Maybe it was his tall stature, his looks; maybe it was his air of affluence. In the taxi, Cassa laid her head against his coat, smiling up at him.

"What a wonderful welcome," she murmured. "Wherever did you learn your French."

Bending his head to kiss her lips was fully acceptable, and tired though she was, she recognised this kiss: it was the edge-of-the-volcano kiss. "Where are we going? Hotel?"

"I have an apartment in the New Center. Would you accept a room for the night, Cassa?"

She hugged his arm. "And tomorrow, you will tell me what I am beginning to suspect. Phone calls with Melia Tracey?"

"Tomorrow will be time enough, sweet girl. I will make a full confession when you have had a night's sleep. Now, Cassa, don't fall asleep on me, an old habit of yours. We're nearly there." His voice was protective and soothing.

"This is the second time you have put me up in an apartment, Dermot," she smiled at him in the lift.

"And you are an ungrateful little wretch," he smiled back. "The last time you walked out on me."

At the door of the luxurious apartment, Cassa looked around. "Am I your only visitor? No Sandra? No Orla?"

"Put your mind at rest, Cassa. Your sister, Nicole, is not here. The girls are back in Donegal, still on holiday. Look, this is your room. Do you like it?"

"It's exquisite, as if it were designed for a woman."

"It was," he said, "but not for my ex-wife. She has never been in this apartment, and she knows nothing about it. Not the address, nothing. I remember that timid face, Cassa: you are expecting Nicole to materialise out of those curtains!"

The safest thing to do was to go into his arms and let him reassure her. And that helped, until he drew away. "Little temptress," he teased. "Come, I promised you a brandy, and then we'll discuss supper. Or will we? I can see that awful flight has been an ordeal. Why don't I tuck you into bed and put out the light and postpone the supper until breakfast. It's too late to unpack, darling. We have all tomorrow to unpack."

Cassa was so tired, he helped her to remove her suit and blouse.

"And more?" he asked. "You are almost asleep, Cassa."

"I can manage the rest later," she whispered; "thank you all the same."

With gentle care, he lifted her into bed, and in a few seconds she was asleep.

That famous Edwardian tactic of a man taking advantage of a woman did not enter her dreams. Very early in the morning, she woke up. She was quite alone, and the only sound she heard was the far-off muted sound of traffic. Confused wisps of thought came and went; a rejected woman? A woman who would have been unfaithful to her husband if she had been given the chance in Lima? Did she actually have visions of a white-robed monk capturing her like a sheik of Araby? And how did it come about that a happily married woman was sleeping in another man's flat? Dermot was the nicest man in the world, but what was she doing here? Why didn't she insist on a hotel? Shouldn't she have argued with Dermot? Something about propriety? Sleepily, Cassa couldn't get quite as far as questioning the moral grounds for her present position in someone else's bed. She turned over comfortably and went to sleep again.

Dermot was drawing back the curtains, and the room was filled with sunshine. Cassa sat up suddenly, forgetting she had no nightdress; her bra straps had slipped down.

"I could get used to that picture," Dermot said. "You are almost as gorgeous as Elvira. Now then, be a proper little miss and dive for cover. I've brought tea – Parisian coffee is used for mixing paint. Good girl, Cassa; you'll feel better after a cup of tea."

She drank the tea obediently while she lined up the questions: the hows and whys. Dermot watched her in cautious admiration. At this moment Cassa was all his, but obviously she was in full flight from the last event. It was his intention to weigh her down, so she must give up her propensity for running away. He would not exactly chain her to his side, but enjoy her full confidence and trust in him. He could wait a little longer.

"Shall I give you my side of the story first?" he asked.

"That would be great, Dermot, but may I get dressed before we talk, please?"

"Of course you may, darling girl. I have set the shower for you, and I'll wait in the salon. A breakfast then? You must be hungry."

Cassa was smiling when she joined Dermot in the salon. "I have never been in so absolutely beautiful a bathroom," she told him, "never, ever! I could have pottered around in there all day. I had finally got used to the monks' water closet in the monastery: stone walls, no heat, no mirror and no place to put anything down."

"But friendly monks standing by?" he queried, and Cassa chuckled.

"No monks on that level of their monastery," she said, "and I never saw a friendly monk. Contemptuous, severe, austere, obedient above all. The superior made it clear that he begrudged my presence."

"Not even one friendly monk?" he asked.

"The way you ask that question tells me that you have been in deep conversation with Melia Tracey."

"One friendly monk?" he persisted.

"I'll be honest with you, Dermot: I suspect myself of having had obscure hopes of one friendly priest. The hopes foundered."

"Were you in love with him?" Dermot asked.

Cassa thought about that for a moment. "What is it, being in love? Is it a lot of happy memories from a day in the sun? Is it a response to an inner need, a response given by a person who remains uninvolved? And who has no intention of becoming involved, no matter what hurt may happen. Being in love? Getting out of love is more important." Her voice was, as ever, gentle, but now it was very sad.

"And your husband, Cassa. Were you in love with him when you married him?"

"John told me that marriage was a way of life, and I

222

believed him. I have thought about that way of life a lot lately. Honour and obey, they're easy. To keep up the illusion of being in love is very difficult, the submitting to demands for which I have no response. I never had any response for John, although he is a good man and I like him. . . in a friendly way."

"And his brother, Frank?"

Dermot was not keen on playing the role of father confessor: there were things he did not want to know, but as Melia Tracey herself had told him in their phone conversations, "There's no time like the present." Mrs Tracey was very anxious to keep her sainted Frank well away from Cassa, "in that awful place full of earthquakes and heathen women. God alone knows what made Mrs Cassa fly off with Mr John to search for Father Frank. There was no occasion for her to go at all. She insisted. She insisted even though the old priest who came for them did his best to get the idea out of her head. I mean to say, after all the terrible tragic things that my dear Father Frank was after goin' through, wouldn't you think she'd leave him alone? I mean to say, I'm sure there was no harm in it, but she pestered poor Father Frank the whole summer he was home, mornin', noon and night. I said it to him, I took him aside and I said it to him. I did. I said it to him to be careful. But he only laughed at me, as if he didn't take me seriously, but I knew she was very serious, you only had to look at her face. . . I was very worried for him. But out there on the other side of the world, earthquakes and heathen women is trouble enough. Mrs Cassa doesn't know her own strength." And there was more.

Dermot repeated the question: "And Frank, the priest? You travelled a long way to find him. Were you in love with him?"

Her curved eyelashes lifted slowly and her dark brown eyes settled into a still depth, allowing the tension to surface in a gleam of tears. Perhaps Dermot was trying to help her, but he could not know, and she would never tell him, how the meeting at the grotto of Santa Rita had riven a red scar somewhere deep inside her. She could not bear to talk about Frank, and she was silently wondering if time and distance would ever heal the horrible gash.

Dermot took her into his arms and she rested against him.

"It's happening again," he said; "you have had the same effect on me since you were twelve. I give in to your innocence as if there were nothing else."

"Maybe there is nothing else, Dermot. Some kind of experience has hurt, some other kind has glanced off. I wonder at myself: I am so slow to learn the difference, but, you know, there is a certain thing you alone understand, and it is of great comfort to me – just this." And she turned around in his arms for his special kiss.

It seemed to comfort him, too. They let time pass comfortably; it had happened like that with them before in Galway, but they were thinking their own thoughts. He knew he wanted their togetherness to become their life; he wanted to ignore all the obstacles as of no account. He wanted her to pour all her confidence into him, so she could push away the thought of all the other circumstances. He found it easier now to believe that he, and only he, would become the centre of her world. He could wait, perhaps a little more time, and the moment would come. Sometimes he wondered if all men were the same: a certain woman could satisfy the infinitude of a man's need; a certain woman only, and the others were play-acting. And women? Was this damned priest Cassa's certainty? Women were not the same; their needs were transient. Could he be as certain of that with Cassa as he had been with Nicole?

Cassa was struggling with a different kind of certainty: the inevitability that tomorrow she must return to Carrick-on-Shannon and resume the life for which she, too, had cast her own solemn vows before the parish priest in the Catholic church beside the Shannon river. She had taken vows to live with a man who was now her husband until death. Her husband – the fathomless depth of the very word. She must live intimately with him in a place which had never become home despite the fact that the house was filled to the brim with her family's antique furniture. Cassa had come to hate the furniture as a prisoner hates the shackles.

"My little darling, so solemn a face! I know the very place for a drive to brush away those shadows."

"I'll bet you know dozens of such places." Cassa cheered up. "But Paris is only a stopover on the way home. I should ring Aer Lingus and book a seat to Dublin, shouldn't I?"

"I'll tell you another secret from my calls to Mrs Tracey – the very latest secret. Your husband, her dear Mr John, cannot get a seat on a plane out of Lima until Friday. And it seems to be a very, very long journey. That gives you at least two days to play with, sweet girl. Two whole days in Paris! The gift of a lifetime, darling. Now, give me that lovely smile. We'll book two seats for Dublin for the day after tomorrow, if we can get them. Saturday could be fully booked. I have to fetch the girls home from Donegal, so I'll deliver you safely to your own door in Carrick-on-Shannon. I left the Merc at the airport. How does that suit my sweet girl? Mrs Melia Tracey will be thrilled to see me – you know she is madly in love with me? I have that instant effect on talkative old ladies."

How much else had Melia told him? But he was irresistible. More than irresistible. A few days in Paris with him and his company all the way home?

225

CHAPTER THIRTY-ONE

John Gowan checked his watch with the Aer Lingus clock. It was barely possible that he had reset it wrongly on the flight, was it twice or three times? It was a quarter after midday, that was the right time. He had walked the arrivals area long enough. He had given her two hours, making more than due allowance for mishaps. She wasn't a great driver in his opinion, but two hours was enough allowance. He found a phone after a ten-minute queue. Tourists!

It was Aggie, picking up the phone after settling her pages in place.

"For God's sake, does it take ten minutes to answer a call? Put Mrs Cassa on. I presume she must be there, because she certainly isn't here."

The other two must have come out into the hall. "It's Mr John," she told them. "Melia wants to know where are you, sir? She's just drying her hands, and then she'll talk to you."

"I want to talk to my wife," he said shortly. "Put her on now."

But it was Melia who took the phone. "That's great news to hear you're back in the land of the livin', Mr John; I needn't tell you we are all very relieved. Thanks be to Almighty God and His Blessed Mother. I had them on their knees here praying for your safe passage. Aggie said we had our rosaries worn out, that's what she said. But she was as concerned as the rest of us, of course she was. We got Father Conway to include your name in the list of prayers at mass this morning – the whole congregation joined in. I read in a book . . ." Melia almost paused for breath. "We were gettin' ourselves into the whole spirit of it, don't ye know? I read in the book that earthquakes are a way of life in that place, and you never can tell when the next one will strike. I believe it's a terrible journey to come back out of it, takin' in the four corners of the earth. Where are you? Are you in London or were you stuck in Paris without a ticket to get ye home? Mrs Cassa was stuck in Paris."

"Paris!" he shouted into the phone, "Paris? What was she doing in Paris?"

"Stuck," quavered Mrs Tracey, nonplussed by his loud voice. "Are you all right, Mr John?"

"I bloody well am not all right. I rang you from a god-awful place, somewhere in Canada, and I gave you full instructions about my arrival, and I am standing in this air-port for hours. If Cassa is there, put her on. Now Melia! Now! Write down this number and ring me back immedi-ately – give the phone to Aggie. Now Melia, now!"

This took time, and a queue was forming outside the phone box. John Gowan glared at them ferociously. Bloody tourists! Baseball caps and sunhats.

Now it was Aggie on the phone and she was into the talk immediately: "I told Aunt Melia to take it easy, sir, I told her you were after a long jour. . ."

"Aggie," he shouted, "don't say another word. I want to speak to Mrs Gowan, do you understand? *Mrs Gowan!* Put my wife on the phone now!"

Aggie made three interrogation marks on the top of a new page in her book: Sir ringing for Mrs Cassa. ANS: not in.

"Mrs Cassa is out on the river, sir. It's a beautiful day."

"Feck the day! You have that bloody book in front of you. Is it written there or is it not, that I am arriving in Dublin Airport right now and my wife is to be here to drive me home? Is that in your book?"

"Yes, sir. It's all here: dates and times and Dublin Airport."

He made an effort to lower the tone: "And Mrs Gowan is out on the river? Did she take a friend on the cruiser?"

"No, sir," Aggie said, "she hadn't a friend today. She took out your skip, sir."

He took that in slowly: quite obviously Cassa was in good

health and recovered from her travels. "Why exactly did my wife not come to Dublin to drive me home?"

Aggie was in her element, with Melia and Tessie looking on. "How could she get there, sir? No bus out of Carrick-on-Shannon that early on a Sunday morning, sir."

His fury was catching hold again. "I'm not talking about the friggin' bus! There were two cars in the yard when we left home. Have they been stolen?"

Aggie was shocked. "No, sir. Certainly not. Before you went away, sir, yourself gave orders to Aunt Melia to get the hired car of Mrs Cassa's out of the yard, and yourself said you would buy a new car for Mrs Cassa, more trustworthy was what was said."

He had no recollection of that, but it was likely. No recollection of a lot of things in those frantic few days. Standing uselessly in this airport was a fitting end to an expensive and utterly annoying journey. Maybe it was just as well that Cassa wasn't standing in front of him at this minute – the effect she had had on Frank was disastrous.

"Aggie, are you still there? Could Mrs Gowan not fetch me home in the Bentley?"

"Oh, my God, sir, Aunt Melia nearly had a fit when Mrs Cassa suggested she would take the Bentley to Dublin this morning, and we had no way of knowing how to get you on the phone. Aunt Melia told Mrs Cassa that the Bentley is a sacred trust."

"Had my wife to get home to Carrick in a bus or a train or a taxi?" He spoke slowly and with an attempt at patience.

"Oh no, sir. Her brother-in-law-once-removed – he's Mr Tyson – he drove her home on his way to Donegal. He was stuck in Paris, too, as well as Mrs Cassa. He brought presents for the three of us. I got perf. . ."

"That's enough, thank you, Aggie. Expect me when you see me. I'll get a taxi." He almost knocked down the man first in the queue and didn't stop to apologise.

Dragging his heavy bag from taxi to taxi didn't improve his temper. "You should have ordered a week ago, sir." He had a hard job getting a response to a high price, no matter how he pushed it up. "There's no picking up on those roads south on a Sunday: I'd be coming back empty." Finally, he struck what the man called a bargain and they finally moved out into the traffic.

John Gowan, deprived of the security of his Bentley, was not the same man at all. Luckily for his normal peace of mind, he didn't analyse these things.

When the taxi pulled into the yard, Cassa was waiting at the conservatory, and the other members of the household were huddled at the kitchen door.

As Melia had warned the nieces, "Mrs Cassa hasn't heard the lion's roar!" And it wasn't up to them to tell her. "Watch my eyes," Melia told them. "We all play by ear in a case like this. When I close the lids, say nothing."

Tessie, the timid one, prayed silently that no dread fate would befall her heroine, and held her breath watching Mr John.

Aggie maintained a close scrutiny as Mrs Cassa advanced to her husband with a radiant smile. In the background, Melia Tracey's voice had started up her usual litany about the fatigue and the food and the weather.

John Gowan ground his heel into the cobblestones and turned for the house, his voice unnecessarily loud. "I'll see you inside."

Melia lowered her eyelids and all three disappeared into the kitchen.

Cassa was aware of playing the obedient puppy as she followed her husband up the two flights of stairs, because when she saw him getting out of the taxi, she had an immediate flash of bad conscience. The days in Paris with Dermot Tyson had been pure heaven, and they had prolonged their hours to the last moment. Instead of driving straight from Dublin Airport to Carrick-on-Shannon in the Merc, Dermot had taken her into the city to have dinner in the Shelbourne. With each course, he told her how much he loved her, and had always loved her, and how very beautiful she was. Yes, Paris had indeed rested her.

"I could take this treatment every night in the week, Dermot," she told him.

"Then, sweet girl, why don't you?"

"You know why, darling."

"Actually," he smiled at her, "I am not sure. You are married, so we shouldn't be here. I think I know the answer to that, and another thing, Cassa, a friend in Leinster House told me that divorce will be introduced here soon."

Now Cassa laughed softly. "Divorce? In Ireland? Never!"

"Might there be bigger obstacles for a suitor than a legal marriage?"

"Isn't that the biggest one?" As she watched his face, she guessed at what he was thinking.

"Forbidden love," she told him, "is never inextricable, but in Ireland a marriage is."

His face was even more handsome when he smiled. "In your own special way, my pet, you are giving me hope?"

"But don't let that run away with you," she teased.

There were no more question and answer sessions, and on the way home Cassa felt they were at peace with each other. She had realised how carefully Dermot was acting in his approach to her, and now she knew it was a strain. She had no right to be stressed about Dermot, no right at all, but care was necessary. She had greatly desired to let half-concessions become full concessions. Old-fashioned prejudice held her back, those words she had not heard since childhood when Sadora was constantly giving chapter and verse to a fifteen-year-old Nicole: wanton, reckless, debauched, unchaste. Nicole could laugh off those little

230

sermons, as Cassa well knew. However, the horrible adjectives reverberated in Cassa's mind when she surrendered herself to Dermot's sensual embrace, then drew herself away rather than give in. Her husband, John Gowan, had never seemed to expect touch or tenderness from her, and she had never known what he might have wanted her to do next. She became pregnant, and after that, there was nothing more. Their rare caresses were happily civil, almost as if marriage had freed them back into being single people. Other couples in Carrick-on-Shannon were the nicest, most at-ease couples to meet at functions and at the parties they gave for their children and for their family celebrations. If Cassa had thought about it at all, a newly married woman in Carrick would take example from those who knew, and she had.

Paris was different: she and Dermot had walked hand in hand, exchanging kisses in shop mirrors and laughingly swinging together under the trees in a park. Paris was gorgeous, but now she was back in the normal place, her bedroom at home.

"That was tough, John, having to come in a taxi. You must be tired?"

John Gowan made a big effort to be reasonable. After all, he wasn't all that perfect himself, but no need to say so. That was his own business.

"I slept in the taxi," he said. Then, abruptly, he added: "Sit down. There are some questions. What were you doing in Paris with Tyson, or maybe I should ask you, how was that arranged?"

What Cassa wanted to say, and what she said, were different: "I think you will have to ask Melia that."

"What has Melia got to do with it?"

She had never incurred his petulant anger before, and it didn't suit her concept of her husband. "John, you have forgotten that my sister Nicole, Clive Kemp and Nicole's ex-husband, Dermot Tyson, were all here on the day we got the news about Frank."

He glowered at her. "We'll come to my brother Frank later. What has Melia got to do with you being in Paris? How long were you there? You were not able to get a flight to Dublin, so you overnighted in Paris. In a hotel?" And John brushed aside his own memory of a Paris hotel.

"Not in a hotel," Cassa replied pleasantly, "in Dermot Tyson's apartment, and it was three or four days. He had the time of my arrival in Paris from Melia on the phone, as I had phoned Aggie from the airport in Singapore." Cassa thought he looked explosive, and she thought to calm him. "And you seem to have forgotten that Dermot put me up in a flat in Donnybrook, and that he took me to Connemara? Remember, John, you said how much that little holiday had improved me? We have kept in touch."

Her husband was not sure how to handle this situation. Cassa was always so obviously candid. Suddenly he remembered Father Damascene's words: "Women, by their lower nature, are devious. Your brother Frank may never be able to root out this poisoned arrow." The bare thought was unendurable: that his brother Frank might be sent home to Carrick-on-Shannon, kicked out of the priesthood, disgraced. John rounded on his wife: "Wasn't it very handy that this fellow suddenly had an apartment in Paris when Melia Tracey revealed your arrival there – all the way from South America?"

"Dermot Tyson had an apartment in Paris for years. I remember he mentioned it to me in Firenze ages ago."

"I seem to recall that he was the dreaded tyrannical Tyson! Chatting amiably in Firenze? When was that?"

"I don't remember exactly, but he took me out to lunch on another occasion. He could be quite nice when he wasn't in big trouble with the nuns in San Salvatore. And, you know, darling John, I didn't know you all that well then. That was a year before we were married."

The ghastly air flight from Peru, the let-down when he was told that Cassa had left him to face it on his own, and the revelations of the superior about Cassa's conduct with his brother Frank had induced an angry frustration. "Did you try to get a ticket at the Aer Lingus desk the same as I did? Why didn't you go to a hotel if you had to stay overnight? Going to that fellow's flat: what were you thinking of?"

Cassa recalled her delight when she had looked up at the splendid figure of Dermot Tyson and how they had laughed at his schoolboy French. "What was I thinking of?" she asked. "What should I have been thinking of?"

John shouted at her: "That you are a married woman!"

"That never occurred to me in the airport," Cassa said candidly.

"A lot of things never occur to you." His voice was coarse with anger. "Why did you insist on coming with me to Peru?"

"In the hope of seeing Frank again," she offered gently.

"You are a married woman, and he is a priest. Did that occur to you? You were not out sailing in my cruiser on Lough Key and playing around with temptation. You were in a monastery, dammit! No, you insisted on having it out with him, there, in their garden! It doesn't take much imagination to see you and him and what happened next. You got your way at last, didn't you. You were trying to give him the idea of chucking the priesthood, and then you were off fecking around in Paris!"

With the force of a fearful thump on her head, Cassa realised that Melia Tracey and her nieces were listening to every word out there on the second flight of stairs. They always listened, and until now it had never worried Cassa. The shock of what they were hearing now about her and about Frank was suddenly more than she could bear. She tried to stand up and run away, but losing her breath and losing her grip on the chair, she slid down and collapsed on the floor. Fearful of worse to come, her spirit had taken flight from the tirade of abuse.

John Gowan rushed out to the landing. "Melia, come up here! Come quickly, come quickly, my wife has fainted! Aggie, get on to Eoin, ring the doctor, get him to come immediately. Mrs Cassa has passed out. Quickly, can't you? Eoin Magner, for God's sake, hurry! Melia, here, help me, be careful, gently; I said gently. Has Aggie got the doctor? Yes, yes, the bed. And cover her, she might be cold. Melia, is my wife breathing? Are you sure?"

Slowly and painfully, Cassa opened her eyes. Who were all these people, all these eyes looking at her inquisitively? They had been listening; they always listened. She turned her head into the pillow as if she would sleep.

"Cassa, will I help you to undress?" It was John's downcast voice.

Her head still turned away, Cassa was now conscious, but her voice was broken when she tried to answer, "No. No, thank you." She had known instantly that Melia Tracey would take in John's angry words to his sinful wife as being the gospel truth, and that poor woman would be heartbroken. The sacrilegious hurt to her revered Father Frank was now out in the open.

Confusedly, John Gowan shooed Melia and her nieces out of the room. He hovered over the bed, wishing she would open her eyes and say something.

"Can I help you in any way?" he asked. "I have sent for the doctor. You'd like to see the doctor?"

Her voice refused to come above a whisper, "I suppose so." In another moment, she heard his steps going down the stairs. There was a torrent of tears choking her throat, but tears wouldn't help. There had been no one to kiss away the tears since Papa's death. That was the self-pity thing again. Get into the bathroom and wash your face and drink water and pretend to Eoin Magner that the long flight from South

234

America has had a terrible effect on you, like you want to cry all the time, and perhaps you could do with a few days in a nursing home. Would she mention this awful tendency to self-pity? No, he couldn't cure that with antibiotics. No, insist on the nursing home. . . well away from Carrick-on-Shannon. My father could always see the humour in things; I wish I could. She dried her eyes, impatient with herself.

Melia Tracey never respected anyone's wish to be left alone, but she had John down there in the dining-room, and looking after him would take priority. No doubt she was instructing him to "Get that into you, keep up your strength." Cassa was sure that whatever decision she herself took now, she would never fret for Mrs Tracey.

She sat waiting for Eoin Magner. He had wanted her to get psychiatric help; she would play on that.

He came at last, and John was with him. Cassa summoned up her wits, raising her eyebrows in surprise and forcing out a rather hoarse voice. "Eoin, what a pleasure. It must be nearly dinner-time: please stay. It's ages since you called."

"Well, thank you, Cassa, but in fact we dined earlier. We had guests – we usually do on Sunday. Today it was the in-laws." He had a nice smile, always ready.

"Good of you to call by, then," said Cassa at her most courteous.

"John seems concerned, Cassa, and your throat sounds a bit sore. Shall I have a look?"

Cassa drew herself back into the chair. "There's nothing wrong with my throat. I feel perfectly well, thank you." She threw what she hoped was a castigating glance at her husband.

"You fainted!" her husband accused her loudly.

"That was nothing." Cassa smiled at one man and then at the other. "But, as Eoin is here, may we have a few words on our own?"

"See you downstairs, then."

Cassa waited until her husband's footsteps died away. Then she stood up, closed the door and drew across the heavy doorstop. "Eoin, I am sorry you were called out. I intended to phone you tomorrow."

"What is it, Cassa?"

"I think the journey to Peru, and the journey back again, were too much for me. I seem to be close to tears all the time. I had a break of a few days in Paris, but that only made me worse – all the noisy traffic. Perhaps you would recommend a tonic?"

"All that accumulated jet lag really calls for bedrest, Cassa – plenty of sleep."

"You know, Eoin, I thought of that, too. I'm sure that would do the trick. But I dare not stay in bed here, Melia is always so concerned. That long spell I had in bed nearly killed poor Melia, up and down the stairs – two flights!"

"Yes, I know, Cassa. Her sciatica is very painful, and we have tried everything, but it has got into her bones. Wouldn't the nieces carry up the trays?"

Cassa was careful to keep her voice a little worn, and she knew she never appeared to be robust. "Oh, of course, they would, lovely girls. But would she let them? Never. Do you know of a nice nursing home where I could stay for a week or two? I think John would like to see me in good form for the wind-up of the rally!"

"He sure would. Actually, I think I know the very place: my wife's sister stayed there after a little op. she had, and she loved the place. It's not too near us here, though. It's in Skerries, overlooking the sea. Do you know Skerries?"

"I remember Skerries very well. I used to go out that direction with my father in his golfing days – a sand links called Portrane. Oh, that would be great! Would you ring them for me, Eoin?"

Eoin Magner had been taken with Cassa from the first day, and he noticed now the way her brown eyes sparkled in appreciation. "Yes, I will, Cassa. I'll make the phone call tonight as soon as I get home. With a bit of luck, they will fit you in. Would tomorrow be too soon for you?"

Cassa forebore to say, "Never too soon." On the landing, she said, "Goodbye until tomorrow," and she gave him a timid little kiss on the cheek.

In a while, John brought a sandwich and a glass of milk. War-time rations – Melia on the warpath. John had been repossessed.

"Late as it is, I have to go down to the office," he said gruffly. "Rally's on top of us. I expect to be very late coming in. I won't disturb you. Melia's got the other bed ready, the one on the first floor."

CHAPTER THIRTY-TWO

Dr Magner made the arrangements with the nursing home in Skerries, confirming the booking for Mrs Gowan, before he settled down to his weekly game of bridge with the in-laws. Trouncing his mother-in-law at her special game was always his aim Sunday after Sunday, although he seldom succeeded. She was a very crafty player, and she had her husband well versed in her strategies. She and he, now retired, played all over the county, and she was renowned in bridge circles.

"You don't usually take calls on a Sunday night," she said to him as she set out the cards on the green baize.

"Not usually, unless it is an accident. That was the Gowans. They are just returned from South America. You'll have heard about the earthquake, and his brother Frank, the missioner, being found? It was all in the local paper last week."

"I hope they didn't pick up something out there. Like a fever."

"No, no, they're fine. Go ahead, deal out my lucky cards. This is going to be my night."

"We should get that pair over for a game some night, Eoin. I've only met her once or twice, a good-looking woman."

"I mentioned that to her, Mum – Cassa is her name," said her daughter, "but unfortunately John Gowan doesn't play, and he has no interest in learning. Come on, Mum, you've shuffled the deck twice."

Her mother was dealing the cards. "They're both grand people, the Gowans, but mismatched, wouldn't you think?"

Eoin thought the same, but there was no such comment to be made. He picked up his cards, glancing quickly at his wife. A first look at her examination of her cards told him a

lot, the blink, the lift of her eyebrow. No sign of any sort
ever appeared on his mother-in-law's face, and her own man
was well trained. They each put money in the kitty and the
fun commenced.

If Cassa had been invited into the social life of playing
bridge with her neighbours in Carrick-on-Shannon (after
all, she had been accounted a useful player by Maisie Foley),
perhaps she would have found her place there. In itself,
Carrick was one of the choicest little towns on the great
Shannon River.

I thought I would be happy here, Cassa was thinking as the
Bentley speeded over the last viaduct and took the turn for
the main Dublin road. All the colourful cruiser craft were
sailing away into the distance while the drumlins were rising
to take their place on the receding horizon. I really did
think I would settle peacefully here: the place is so lovely
and John is a very nice man. He looks great this morning,
and it is very agreeable of him to drive me so far when this
is the busiest time of his year. I should make little speeches
of thanks. Since this morning when he had found her pack-
ing a few clothes, John's bearing had been most sympathetic. He was never one to have words at hand in the line of
"I'm going to miss you," and she could not find any similar
phrases. She was too guilty. Maybe it was not part of her
nature to be hypocritically pretending that she would see
him in a week. Unable to pretend, she was going to say
nothing. She remembered the last time she had said goodbye: it had been outside the Gresham Hotel, and he had
looked very sad to see her car moving off down O'Connell
Street for her holiday in Stillorgan.

That day was a very different day. Today began yesterday
when John had accused her of infidelity. He had shouted at
her the sin of infidelity for all the world to hear. Cassa's little
world had consisted of Melia and Aggie and innocent

Tessie, and for them John had tarnished the proud name of his brother Frank. Cassa could never live in that little world again. For sure, a brokenhearted Melia Tracey would never forget the heinousness of Cassa's crime, nor let Cassa forget. The sin against the sixth and the sin against the ninth. How many times had Cassa heard Melia lecturing her nieces: "Don't come running to me. The woman is always to blame." The relief of getting out and away from that condemnation was a guilty relief, yet she had to bear in mind that her marriage was meant to last until death. Solemn vows. Love honour and obey. Time on her own was needed, away from voices and listeners. There was so much to think out and resolve, and she must be fair to everyone. So much had to have been her own fault.

"By the way, Cassa, I won't be able to stay for a meal, or take you out for a meal. Tonight is the Town Council meeting, coming up to the boat rally."

"That's all right, John," she said.

"Sorry about that," John said, his eyes fixed steadily on the road.

They left the main road at the Julianstown signpost, as Eoin had instructed in the phone call.

"Have you a direction for this place from now?" John asked.

"Yes. Eoin said to keep on the road from Julianstown all the way until you see the beach in front of you: that's Skerries. Then turn right. All the houses face on to the sea. About a quarter of a mile and you'll see the name, the Strand Nursing Home, on the front gate. I'll watch out for it, John."

It was a big modern house, all red brick and white paint. There were half a dozen cars on the drive, but plenty of parking space in front. "It looks okay," John said. "But I mustn't delay. I hope this place will be comfortable for you."

"There's nowhere like home," said Cassa, thinking that

240

Melia Tracey would approve of that. "John, just for form's sake, please see me safely inside. I promise not to delay you."

They were received by a plump middle-aged lady, who introduced herself to them. She was Mrs Brady, matron and owner. She had been expecting them, she said, and would they like something after their journey? She had had several patients recommended by Dr Magner, she told them, ushering them into a bright bed-sitting room on the first floor.

"Dr Magner was of the opinion that I should see to it that Mrs Gowan took plenty of rest. Shall I have some tea or coffee sent up?"

Cassa had walked over to the bow window. "I never had a bedroom window overlooking the sea. I am so pleased. I should enjoy walking along the shore, as well as resting, of course."

"Cassa, I, er. . ." Awkwardly, her husband was holding one suitcase.

"Oh, forgive me, Mrs Brady, most unfortunately my husband cannot delay, but it is so good of you to offer refreshments. This is the busiest time of the year in Carrick-on-Shannon – the annual boat rally on the Shannon. John has a big important meeting in the town tonight."

It was there in her clear, ringing voice: she had shaken him free. It was the way one released a pigeon: she was letting John off on the homing wing. Fervently, she hoped he didn't notice that her normally gentle tone had leaped into a decisive one as she led the way out on to the stairs. "No further delay now, John. I'll see you down to the car, darling, and do get home safely. Give my love to all in Carrick. And all good luck in the rally."

He was turning his beloved Bentley out on to the Strand Road while Cassa was still waving from the steps. She watched until the big car had disappeared into the turn-off, on the road back to the Julianstown crossroads and very soon on to the main road for home. For his home. It would never be hers again. Wasn't it just as well that they had managed not to exchange a farewell kiss? She might have cried. Letting him go so coolly had not been easy after all. In the moment of parting, she knew how fond of him she had grown. If only he had not said what he had said, and now she would never know, nor want to know, what Father Damascene told John of what had been observed from the arched doorway of the monastery.

Well, at least it was good that John would be completely wrapped up in the Shannon Rally, giving her a full week to make an appointment with that wily solicitor on Stephen's Green. There would surely be a regular bus service from Skerries into Dublin, or was it a train service? The idea of being completely independent appealed to her at this moment. There was some pride in independence, and an income to match your pride wasn't bad either – and about time, she told herself. You will be thirty-six years old in September of this year of 1985. My sister Nicole will be forty in August, and she won't like that! Isn't Dermot six years older than Nicole? I guess we're all getting on.

On the dressing-table, Cassa set out her toiletries, including the same perfume she had packed for Peru. Was that what Papa would have called irony? She hung up her clothes in the wardrobe and put her underwear in the locker. There was a shelf of books and a bureau with some headed notepaper and envelopes. A timetable propped against the mirror told her that lunch was served in the dining-room at one-thirty, and dinner between seven and eight. Breakfast in the patient's room unless otherwise directed. She had no experience of nursing homes, but this notice seemed to serve the purpose. She settled into the armchair by the bow window. For today, she was going to rest. Tomorrow would be time enough to figure it all out.

CHAPTER THIRTY-THREE

Skerries is a good resort, thought Cassa, for young families with small children. The miles-long strand is exactly right for all the games the young parents can invent to pass the daylight hours. The sea ripples into view regularly, and the smallest little paddler is safe. The Skerries sand makes wonderful castles, and kids can win prizes for building little turretted fortresses. There is a seaside town with every type of shop imaginable, more varieties of shop than in Carrick-on-Shannon.

Carrick-on-Shannon and its fantastic river. . . that was a lonely part of each day for Cassa as she turned to walk back along the beach to the Strand Nursing Home. Underlying her thoughts when she saw young mothers tenderly nursing babies on the sandy hillocks, she became aware that her own life was redefining itself. She would never go cruising down the Shannon again. The beautiful river running along by the yard of the house had torn out a part of her heart and washed it away. Never again would she dream of love everlasting for a man who had pushed her aside for his own ideals. Not his fault and maybe not hers. It was all over now, and she must make the best of whatever was left. Self-esteem. A bit of character. Sadora's Rules.

By Thursday afternoon, Cassa, who had tripped quite happily around the sunlit boulevards of Paris, felt that she had admired Skerries enough. A second week might lead to boredom. She phoned the solicitor, Dick Boyce, and made an appointment with his secretary for Friday at twelve-thirty.

"No need to ring me back," Cassa told her, "as I am not at home."

Mrs Brady had given her a table of bus times, telling her solemnly, "Be in the queue at Busaras in plenty of time: all the offices in the city seem to empty out at the same time, anywhere between five and seven."

When she arrived in the solicitor's office (heart-stoppingly familiar from her father's time), Mr Boyce came forward to greet her. "It is a great pleasure to see you, Mrs Gowan," he said courteously. "I have booked a table for lunch in the Shelbourne. I trust you will join me?"

"Thank you, Mr Boyce; actually, I intended to take only a minute of your time. If you. . . that is to say. . . if you . . .?"

"Please do not deprive me of the company of so lovely a lady. Just think how my stock will soar in the Shelbourne."

Cassa would have preferred his office for what she had to say about folding up her marriage, although perhaps there were other ways to say so, without having to go into the whole story. Fold up, like the pages of a document, had felt good to her when she rehearsed it on the bus from Skerries. Seated in the Shelbourne and discussing the menu with the very attentive solicitor, Cassa realised she did not know where to begin. Or if, in fact, she should begin at all. Not here and now. No, certainly not here and now.

"So kind of you to take me to lunch," she smiled bravely at him. "So kind that I am just going to enjoy it and talk about other things some other time."

"We will go back to the office if you can spare a moment," he said. "I have a copy of a paper I would like you to keep. Your grandfather's bequests to you and to your sister were finalised at last. I lodged your money in the Bank of Ireland on Monday of last week. I am sure you noted the lodgment. Your sister took her share some weeks ago. That was the last item of her dealings with the firm. Your father would have been disappointed. Now, do please tell me what is your pref-erence in wine?"

Cassa wondered for a moment if it would be correct to tell him that Nicole had probably taken all her legal deal-ings away with her to America. But then, with Nicole, you would never know. Even a well-known Dublin solicitor would never be able to keep tabs on Nicole.

"Mr Boyce, I am sure you are a connoisseur of wine. Please choose for me."

Cassa managed to give a light-hearted portrayal of a client at lunch with her family solicitor. Dick Boyce, usually on his own, was pleased to be there with so charming a lady. He acknowledged a lot of friendly greetings from other diners with a slightly proprietorial nod in Cassa's direction. By the coffee stage, she began to feel their table had a halo around it. No wonder then that she was seen by a tall man who was actually thinking about her, someone who walked down from Harcourt Street every day to take his lunch in the Shelbourne.

"May I join you for a moment, Dick?" and there was Dermot Tyson sitting beside her.

"Be my guest," said Boyce distantly. Tyson was not his favourite person, nor was the man's wife. "Mrs Gowan, will you have a word with me in my office, as we arranged?"

"Oh, of course, Mr Boyce. I will follow you immediately. I was not expecting to meet my brother-in-law, but if you will just give me a few minutes. . . The lunch was very special, thank you very much."

Boyce was hardly out of earshot when Dermot asked, "Sweet girl, have you run away again?"

"Whatever would give you that idea?" And Cassa gave him what she hoped was a conspiratorial wink.

"Melia Tracey doesn't love me any more. I'm banned from the telephone. Aggie told me very circumspectly that Mrs Tracey never wants to hear my voice again, and all Aggie was allowed to say was that Mrs Cassa is not in residence. Dearest girl, thrown out? Or run away?"

"It's a long story: tell you some day." Cassa gathered up her handbag and her scarf.

"Have you got to go back to that fellow's office?" he pleaded, smiling.

"It would be only polite, Dermot. I arranged an interview, the lunch was his own idea, so I must. There is something I need to ask him."

"Ask me," Dermot teased. "I'll tell you anything you want to know."

"All right then," Cassa said very solemnly. "Would you let your Aylesbury apartment to me, for my own use, for me to live in on my own. Now, immediately, and for as long as is agreeable to you?" She had come up with that bright idea the minute she saw him.

"Yes," he said. "Yes! But that is not what you were going to ask Dick Boyce? Tell me, Cassa. Tell me now, please."

"I must go now, Dermot. It would not be polite to keep him waiting. Besides, I have to catch a bus at the Busaras."

"A bus?" She loved the mixture of astonishment and horror on his handsome face.

"I am staying, resting in fact, at the Strand Nursing Home, in Skerries." She took Mrs Brady's business card from her purse and handed it to Dermot. "You look slightly bewildered, darling. Lots of people travel by bus. You can see more scenery by bus."

"About Boyce, sweet girl: what question?"

"Different people take different steps to get out of a marriage, Dermot. I am going to ask Mr Boyce to set up the next step for me. That's all. Now I must go."

"Cassa, it's wonderful news, but have you thought about this? Not just running away to go back tomorrow?"

"For three whole days, dearest Dermot, I walked the strand in Skerries, and I thought and thought. . . and I decided that I have a choice. The choice is mine to make, and I have made the choice." Straight and firm, she walked in the avenue of tables in the Shelbourne dining-room, and out through the multicoloured glass doors. Too amazed to stand up, Tyson gazed after her.

CHAPTER THIRTY-FOUR

Mr Boyce was not at all sanguine that Cassa could walk out of her marriage at will.

"Your husband could have a court order taken out, obliging you to resume your presence in the family home. It might take a month or more, but a determined man would do that."

"What would a determined woman do?" Cassa asked.

"She would consult a lawyer dealing in family law, and he would advise. A judicial separation is the way to go, but a plaintiff has to have a reasonable case. A husband who is opposed to a separation can find grounds to drag on for years. . . maybe in unwilling desperation, then again perhaps in spite."

"Not loving and not trusting a husband would not be enough?"

"Reasons for the end of love and trust, cogent reasons, could be demanded." Mr Boyce wanted to help and found it easy to gaze at Cassa's face. There was, however, another point he must tell her. "Your husband knows you are a very wealthy woman: he handled all your affairs when Firenze was auctioned off, and he and I had several consultations in this office. I found him astute."

"He is not a poor man."

Dick Boyce smiled a little at a memory. "Your sister, Nicole, referred to him as the fortune hunter, never by the name of John Gowan."

"The money from the sale of Firenze is in the Bank of Ireland, scarcely touched. It has never been mentioned between us. I think John is generous and proud." Cassa's voice was insistent on that. "We have a fine house, always well provisioned, and servants."

"Is there a reason you ceased to trust this good man, Cassa?"

This was painful for her. The very act of confiding was traumatic and difficult. Just one thing in her mind was certain: she was never going back. Yet, she hesitated.

"Tell me, Cassa. Talk to me. Your father trusted me, and this firm still bears his name."

Like diamonds, tears stood in Cassa's dark brown eyes. It took an effort to wrench out the words: "In the servants' hearing, he accused me of being an unfaithful wife."

"And were you, Cassa?" the solicitor asked gently.

"Never! I was never offered the chance he thought I had taken. I have never been with any man but my husband, John Gowan. That is the truth, Mr Boyce."

"And loving him, Cassa?"

She forced herself to say strongly what had to be said before her courage evaporated. "Love ceased. Loving him stopped dead in the very moment he accused me of infidelity with his brother, who is a priest. Now all I want is a separation as far away as is possible. I never wish to see any of them ever again."

"Where are you going when you leave here, Cassa?" It was sad to witness her distress.

"My husband knows where I am – he drove me down from Carrick-on-Shannon. The doctor thought a few weeks' rest would be good for me after the long journey to Lima and back again." She held out Mrs Brady's card for the Strand Nursing Home. "This is the business card of the lady who runs the place. Even if John would like to visit me, he cannot do so this weekend, and probably not this week. The end of July and the beginning of August is the very busiest time of his year, for the Shannon Boat Rally." Cassa exhaled a long, heartfelt sigh for what had seemed a long speech. Then she added, "I'm asking my brother-in-law to let me rent a flat he has in Donnybrook."

Dick Boyce was at once conscious of the good-looking Tyson, and the possessive way he had accosted Cassa. "You know, Cassa, if you are really set on this legal separation, and in the very possible event of John Gowan putting up resistance, it would be wise to keep your name unassociated with any other man. It's considered perfectly normal for a deserted husband to presume a rival in the field. You would be very careful, I am sure."

Cassa gave him a grateful smile. "Mr Boyce, please would you take the whole matter in hand, find the lawyer for the case and have him report to you?" Boyce nodded. "I thank you with all my heart. I will rent the flat in Donnybrook, and I will take care of my good name. You trust me, don't you?"

"May I ask that you will keep in constant touch with me, in connection with the total legal aspect of the matter of separation?" He was gravely lawyer-like.

"Of course," Cassa said, relieved and a little happier.

"I may need to come and talk with you personally," Boyce told her.

"Of course," she said again. A nice little man, she thought, but in his office is the place for meetings.

As she had done when she was a little girl waiting for Papa to finish up and take her home, Cassa crossed over to the long window to look out at Stephen's Green. The trees were luxuriant in the sunshine, and the Green was full of all sorts of people in summer attire. Just for a moment, she thought of her window at home in Carrick-on-Shannon, and the brilliant greens of the flowing river through the conservatory glass. She managed to banish that vision as she went down the stairs. Better to recall much earlier times. On a day like this, Papa would have suggested an ice cream, and they would have sat on a park bench laughing at the ducks. Papa always had his handkerchief ready to wipe her hands after the ice cream.

Cassa was not too surprised to see Dermot Tyson's Merc parked outside the solicitor's office. His flashing smile would cure any heartache, she thought, as he opened the car door for her.

"Where to now, Cassa?" He seemed delighted with himself.

"Perhaps you would take me down to Busaras, to join the queue for the Skerries bus?" Cassa patted his hand. "I could walk, of course. It's not far."

He was incredulous. "You don't have to go back there. Why on earth would you want to go out to that godforsaken place on a bus? If you must go, I'll drive you there."

"Be my good friend, Dermot, and drive me down to Busaras. I will stay in Skerries until you come for me on Sunday. You will, won't you? That will give me time to reestablish my address for my husband, in care of the solicitor. And establish my address in Aylesbury Road for my own private use. I will pay Mrs Brady for two weeks and tell her that I have decided to take a little holiday somewhere before I settle back into the rest of my life."

The Merc went down Tara Street and over Butte Bridge before she had finished her little speech, and Tyson had drawn a long breath to get the words out: "We could go across to Wynn's and talk this thing out. Champagne would be good." But there was no option in the rush of evening traffic but to pull in at the bus station.

"Ring me on Sunday morning. You have the card. It's up to you, darling."

She gave him a swift kiss and waved a smiling goodbye through the windshield. In a second, she had disappeared among the throngs of commuters.

There is only one Busaras in Dublin, and at six o'clock in the evening it is packed with hundreds and hundreds of bustling people heading for the country and away from the city. Scant ceremony would be well short of a description. There was an uncertain symbolism in watching the crowded buses moving out one after the other in this very moment when she also was moving out, and away. Decisively, nothing surer. She held the thought. Another chance at happiness?

Even at contented love? No one really knows in this weird old world. . . maybe, perhaps.

Cassa, who had never travelled on a bus before today, took her place in the thrusting bus queue with the same assured calm she had found in choosing a role in her own new life. The woman-of-the-world pose did not sit too easily, for one had to cultivate a business-like bearing, stare straight ahead as if her thoughts always emerged in a single column and not in a hazy mist. All that stuff required an attitude steady enough for rolling along in a bus with total strangers. Cassa was fairly sure that an attitude must prove something.

CHAPTER THIRTY-FIVE

It took a while, perhaps a year or so, before an ordinary cliché gave Cassa a pause to catch her breath and forget the image of the old house beside the Shannon. The very ordinary fixed phrases, which people use all the time for the little turns of everyday living, were stamped on her mind by Melia Tracey's voice. Dermot hardly ever used a cliché, and she could forgive him easily if he did, but his mother had a couple of them in her soft Galway accent. One of her favourites was "How time flies", even if only a day had elapsed. She and Cassa had fallen in love with each other, and Cassa didn't want time to fly; nor did she want to be reminded suddenly of John Gowan's cruisers on the river beyond the big cobbled yard. She had steered her life safely into the harbour of the pub on Belmont Avenue. The welcome there was kindly and warm and unquestioning, carving a path for Cassa into the girls' acceptance, because Orla and Sandra adored their grandmother. Acceptance is a fine thing, and Dermot was very grateful.

Dick Boyce found a top-class family law solicitor to cope with Cassa's wish to separate from her husband. At first, there were difficulties. John seemed to hold to the impression that his wife had been unfaithful, and lots of lawyerly Latin words were involved in suggesting that if anyone was going to look for a break-up of their marriage, then surely he had the right to initiate the process. His wife's desertion of her lawful husband was no fault of his. He did not wish to be dragged into court; he was a big businessman in Carrick-on-Shannon, and he had the right to defend his name against all the derogatory rumours going around. He had never struck a woman in his entire life. It was many months before he was prepared to admit there could be equal rights, and that he had no exact or precise knowledge to give rise to the claim of his wife's infidelity, nor had his wife admitted such a claim. However, he had the advice of a very highly placed priest, and he was waiting for a letter of corroboration from this priest. More months passed before he admitted that no such letter could be produced. His lawyer had instructed John to have his brother the priest write and accuse the woman of her adultery. His brother had gone back to the mountains in Peru, and more time must pass before that dead end was finally relinquished.

Dermot Tyson was firmly of the belief that a law for divorce would soon be revealed to the Irish public. "It's in the pipeline, Cassa."

"If it were, darling, it would be all over the papers, and there would be the bishops and the cardinal speaking in all the churches, wouldn't there?"

"There are other people in the country besides the believing Catholics," he said. "The law is for everyone, Cassa."

"Yes, but would Catholics be allowed use it?" she asked.

"Hold on a minute, sweet girl. When your separation comes through, are we going to establish ourselves or are we not? Separation now and divorce later on – that's the way I see it."

"And then?" Cassa asked.

"What do you mean, my pet: and then marriage, of course, for all the world to see. Especially my relations. They're mad about wedding days."

"I don't think we could get married in a church, which is what your mother would like. I thought we could keep her happy by living the way we are, not offending anyone."

"So long as we have tied the knot legally when John Gowan caves in, my mother will be perfectly happy. We aren't going to have a fight over this, are we, sweetheart? You know I'll have my way; I always do!"

Cassa had been brought up not to argue and to understand that men know best; her mother Sadora had always said, "Your father knows best." It was safer to go into Dermot's arms, and arguing had never been her way. Most days they had a few hours together, and very occasionally, depending on the whereabouts of Orla and Sandra, Dermot stayed till morning. It seemed that all too rapidly the girls were growing into adulthood, both lovely and charming and the best of company.

Sometimes, not too often, Cassa thought a little sadly of John Gowan in Carrick-on-Shannon, and she wondered if the notion of divorce would be more difficult in his country town than she was finding it in the big city of Dublin. She was fonder of him than she had at first realised; after all, he had never done anything to hurt her. Perhaps he would find a second wife who would cherish him and make up to him for the wrongs he believed himself to have suffered. Cassa hoped good things for him.

At last a breakthrough came from the lawyers. A condition was laid down: all Cassa's antique furniture must be removed by a certain date and the insurance on it for the previous years must be paid. Mrs Tracey had packed everything that had belonged to Cassa in the trunks she had brought, and these must be removed with the furniture. No trace must remain. All expenses must be paid.

On 31 May 1990, all the problems having been finally resolved, Dermot and Cassa were married in a legal ceremony. You would think they were so used to each other that the wedding didn't mean a thing. You couldn't be more wrong.

Dermot whispered to her: "Our combined ages will soon be a hundred years. And you don't look a day older than twelve!" Cassa knew what he meant: the undoubted fact that he had saved the life of a twelve-year-old Cassa outside Donnybrook church was an essential chapter in his life story. He was developing the very slightest suggestion of a middle-age spread, but he was as handsome as ever in the photographs. The wedding was wonderful, a family affair: one Blake and dozens of Tysons. They were an exuberant lot. Not one of them had any kind recollection of the beautiful first wife, but they were very impressed with Cassa. They referred to her as "the new wife". Cassa was delighted with that title.

The long-delayed honeymoon was a month in Italy, spent in the magnificent splendour of Firenze. These weeks of bliss were Dermot Tyson's idea, to honour and immortalise his beloved Elvira, who had honeymooned in Firenze a hundred years ago.

Elvira still reigns supreme above the marble mantelpiece in his Harcourt Street Office.